Human Factors:
A Nuclear Mystery

By Randy Droll

Human Factors:
A Nuclear Mystery

ISBN: 0615828914
ISBN-13: 9780615828916

For Michele and Laren.

Table of Contents

Human Factors

Investigation of tritium worker contamination incident, May 30, 1997, at the Kankakee Advanced Production Reactor. Excerpt from interrogation of Henry McClure, Shift Technical Advisor. Principal investigators: Sheila Rowe, NRC; Howard Crowder, FBI.

Ms. Rowe: You were the one who ordered the maintainers out of the Recirculation valve room, weren't you?

Mr. McClure: Yes, for a second I didn't believe the detector, but then I remembered all the times I've been warned to always believe your instruments unless there's a very good reason not too.

Mr. Crowder: Why didn't the radiation technician give the warning?

Mr. McClure: He couldn't know anything was wrong. He had no reason to suspect tritium.

Ms. Rowe: So how could you know when the technician couldn't?

Mr. McClure: I was wearing one of the fancy tritium detectors Pete Kerwin's been trying to sell. And I had the tactile interface on.

Mr. Crowder: What in hell is a tactile interface?

Mr. McClure: Oh it's one of our toys. I wear it strapped to my wrist and whenever it has a warning it pulses so I can feel it. A tactile warning, you see. Then I can look down on its LED screen and read the warning. It had been pulsing a low order radiation warning. The fixed monitoring station in the west fueling machine bay had started to get a whiff of what was in the recirculation valve room.

Mr. Crowder: So why didn't you give the warning when it started to pulse?

Mr. McClure: Oh it wasn't enough; it's not unusual to have tritium in the fueling machine bays. I did relay the warning to the fueling machine supervisor.

Ms. Rowe: Can you prove that?

Mr. McClure: Sure. It's in my message log.

Ms. Rowe: You were the shift technical advisor that night, weren't you?

Mr. McClure: Yes.

Ms. Rowe: So your duty station was the control room, wasn't it?

Mr. McClure: Yes, but the STA doesn't have to stay there. The people who do it regular work thirty-six hours at a time, so they have to go off to sleep. They're just supposed to be on call in case an accident or technical problem comes up.

Ms. Rowe: You weren't sleeping. Why did you leave the control room to go to Recirculation valve room?

Mr. McClure: There was a message, computer mail for me on the priority channel. It was from Dennis Banks asking me to go to the Recirculation valve room to check on the work in progress.

Mr. Crowder: Why would the production manager ask a technical advisor to check up on valve work?

Mr. McClure: Oh, we go back a long way, in Canada. He knew I did field work at Darlington.

Ms. Rowe: A lot of you Canadians here at Kankakee, aren't there?

Mr. McClure: Well, it's the heavy water and tritium experience. And the control system. Kankakee works a lot like Darlington. But I'm American. I just worked in Canada for ten years, but I'm from the Midwest.

Ms. Rowe: Why can't we find a record of this computer mail message you claim you received in the priority channel log?

Mr. McClure: I don't know.

Ms. Rowe: How did you know the message was from Dennis Banks?

Mr. McClure: Well, he signed it. I mean his name was typed at the bottom. Come to think of it I don't think his name was on the standard title bar. It was just some kind of generic transmission, like from plant control, and he'd typed in his name.

Mr. Crowder: Mr. Banks says he never sent such a message.

Mr. McClure: The message even joked with me. It said he wanted to see if I remembered anything I'd learned getting the Darlington Nuclear Disaster on line. That's what we called it, Darlington Nuclear Disaster because of all the budget and schedule overruns.

Mr. Crowder: So you go to the Recirculation room because of a message that no one can find or admit to sending, and you right away detect radiation that no one, not even the radiation technician assigned to the job, can detect. And then you play the hero and give the warning.

Mr. McClure: Wait a minute. I didn't figure out there might be tritium right away. I was in the room a full minute before I got everyone out. That's why I got a dose along with the others.

Ms. Rowe: But your dose was much lower. You didn't even burn out your limit. You can still do radiation work.

Mr. McClure: Yes, maybe if I stayed in there longer, I'd have to be taken off shift work. I could do with some regular hours.

Mr. Crowder: Did you plant tritiated organic compounds in the Recirculation Valve Room?

Mr. McClure: No. Why would I? What would I get out of it?

Mr. Crowder: Maybe you had something against one of the maintainers. Maybe you're mad at your boss. Maybe you don't like nuclear power.

Mr. McClure: Then I wouldn't like what's given me a good paycheck these last fifteen years.

I

There's nothing to say you can't have two big problems at the same time, each hard enough to deal with by itself, but impossible if you have the two, or the three, or the four or more really big problems all at once.

I never liked that, even as a kid, and I tried to convince myself it wasn't so. I was sickly when I first started school, and I remember thinking strange with a fever and sitting in the bathroom feeling sick all over. And I'd keep thinking the same thoughts, desperately trying to prove that it would be impossible to have diarrhea and need to vomit at the same time.

Our bathroom wasn't equipped to handle such a contingency, so I struggled to believe it was impossible to be in such a potentially messy fix.

Later I found out different.

For a long time I didn't really have problems, not big problems anyway. Well, I did have a very big problem once on what was supposed to be a routine patrol near Phu Bai, but that was a one-morning problem, and I don't really remember what happened, and some of the things I do remember I don't tell. Mainly most everybody else was dead, and I figured I'd be next. Something happened then, and that's been following me around ever since in a little notation on my personnel records. So I have a little problem with my records, but I've always been employed and now I'm even working for the damn Department of Energy, or at least working for someone that's running things for DOE.

And then there was the way Dad left us so soon after he'd divorced my mother and remarried. But that was a family problem and everyone has those. Everyone's father dies. And I was older when he took his life. I was a grown man, fully formed with ambitions and desires of my own, so I cried and went on. It was my stepmother Darlene who had the hard job, finishing all that business Dad had left so unfinished. And she'd done most of it alone because Sheri and I moved away. She did it all alone, and then she remarried and moved to Michigan. So I didn't see her now that I'd finally come back to live halfway near where I was raised. I doubted whether I'd ever see her again. Yes, Dad had been a problem, a problem for me and a bigger one for Darlene, but we all have problems like that. All in all, life has been smooth for me. I haven't had many problems.

Of course my mother had been hit hard by the divorce and then the sudden suicide. But she'd already been separated from Dad, so the second ultimate separation of death wasn't that much worse than what had already happened. She stayed in my childhood home in southern Indiana, which wasn't that far away from my home near Moraine, Illinois, so I was now able to visit her easily.

But on that night last summer I knew I was having problems. I had the little problem of working a thirty-six hour stint as shift technical advisor or STA, and I never liked that. The DOE reactors didn't previously have STAs, but now we do. Just another add-on from the civilian power program and the NRC. Another add-on ever since congress decided that the DOE and the NRC should play by the same rules. So I had to stay at Kankakee station for thirty-six hours. Originally, after the Three Mile Island accident, STAs were to serve as a back-up source of technical expertise in case the plant got into trouble. But the control room operators aren't likely to think they need an STA for anything. For the operators, the STA is just one more expensive uselessness imposed on them by the regulator, the NRC. Today the real job of the STA is more as an on-call coordinator of all the shit which will start happening if the plant gets into trouble. Coordination of the communications and the emergency response teams and all the outsiders who will become involved. But STAs often do offer advice, even though it is rarely accepted unless the advice is what the operators are going to do anyway. Maybe it's because the STAs tend to have a better academic technical background, and they'd like to show that all that education is worth something. Maybe it's just the natural human tendency to try to appear useful.

But I had more to fret about than the inconvenience and the senselessness of my STA shift. Above all I was worried about my wife. I had to stay thirty-six hours at the plant, and I didn't know what Sheri would be doing while I was there. Something was wrong, and I didn't know what. It had been so good at first when we'd moved back to the States. I'd been so happy when we'd found our baby-sitter, Julie. Julie and my little girls, Tracy and Laurie, had hit it off right from the start and, the girls never complained when Julie was watching them. Before, when I worked the long hours, Sheri had complained she didn't have time to do her own work, that her career she'd worked so hard for was doomed, even though she was free during the equally long periods when I was off work and staying at home watching the girls.

But now we had Julie, and Sheri could work as much as she wanted. And with Julie, Sheri had even found the time and energy to entertain. And we had the room now to entertain at our big ranch house in the country. We had big backyard cookouts. And we both had more friends than we had when we were getting started in Canada. Especially after the kids came, we didn't have much time there except for childcare and work. And Sheri had complained that she couldn't work enough. With our move back to the States Sheri's work had gone well, and she had contracts all over. But then I became afraid she wasn't working. I didn't know what she was doing, but whatever it was I knew there were things she wasn't telling me. I knew she wasn't telling me everything, even though we'd been trying to talk to each other ever since we'd started the marriage counseling, ever since the time she came back from the Toronto Human Factors conference and wouldn't talk to me for two weeks.

So what was she doing while I was at the plant? That first day after she had returned from Toronto, I thought that maybe she'd just had a bad day and was mad at the world. But two weeks of the silent treatment had convinced even someone so blindly optimistic as me that something was not right. And then I'd asked her, and she said she thought something was very wrong with our marriage. And we'd talked and talked about it, but from time to time I'd think about it and not be able to think of the first reason why it was happening.

At least I was alert. I was alert with fear. Fear of losing my family. I didn't sleep. I read the books about how you could save your marriage. I read the books about what made people tick. I read the books, and I knew there had to be something more to it than Sheri was letting on.

And I ran and I lifted weights. Maybe if I looked better, maybe if I lost a few of those inches that I'd gained around the waist she would love me again, and I'd have my family back the way it was supposed to be.

So I was not an STA at peace with himself that night. I was a worried STA, a tortured STA. An STA with wild, fearful, jealous, angry and confused thoughts about why things just couldn't keep on being like they'd been.

I was alert when the STA room terminal beeped. It beeped three times for the priority channel, and I saw the message standing out stark on the screen:

> *Henry, would you go down to the recirculation valve room and check on the work in progress there? We've had a lot of problems with leaks, and there's no excuse for it; I want them to stop. With your experience on the Darlington Nuclear Disaster, I think you're the one to steady everyone out and make sure the job is done right. While you are at it, please take along one of Pete's miniature tritium detectors and put it in Slim Daniels' box at rad control. Slim's going to run some more tests and check it against some of the other instruments. If his detectors work even half as well as Pete claims, then it would be a shame if we didn't buy them.*

> *thankx, Dennis*

The message looked weird. The sender was listed as "General at Stores", but I recognized the terminal indicator at the bottom, tty-596. The message had been sent from the desk I shared at the technical section. The message was a strange one, sent from my own desk, but there was no mistaking who the Dennis was —Dennis Banks, an old Canadian friend from Darlington and now the production manager here at Kankakee. I liked to kid him about working in the US because he had been so much of a Canadian nationalist. "What Dennis? You still here? Haven't been mugged yet?" And he would look down because he knew I remembered some of the things he used to say about the States. And he knew I knew he wouldn't leave because he was making so much more money at Kankakee. Dennis must have gone to my desk in the tech section and sent the message from there. But why would he look for me in the tech section at night? Well, Dennis had been around as long as I had, and sometimes we just liked to walk. And the production manager job is never that easy, especially not here at Kankakee. We have so many choices in what to produce, and so many regulations about how to do it.

Kankakee is a real odd-ball of a station, mostly federal with just a kicker from what passes as private industry thrown in to make things interesting and to lower the cost of the tritium we do produce and the plutonium we could produce if the Department of Defense ever thought they needed it for more bombs. And we burn plutonium here, too. Plutonium from old bombs, both Russian and ours. If the government wants to make bombs, we can make the stuff to make them with. And if they want to disarm, we can burn up the stuff from the bombs. If you peer down deep into the peaceful blue water of our over-sized spent fuel bay—and I like to look into it, it looks so much like a resort swimming pool—if you peer to the bottom you will see a mixture of fuels that could not be found in any other reactor anywhere in the world. The government built Kankakee as a multipurpose machine to create and dispose of weapons material; the power we produce for Chicago is a byproduct. It's the government hand that explains why we have such niceties as Human Factors, which sometimes passes as a glorified personnel section, but also dabbles in the latest techniques for better integrating humans to machines. It was the human factors work at Kankakee and Argonne and the universities that attracted my wife, Sheri, and led us back to the states from Canada. And it's the government which explains our deluxe health physics and radiation protection facilities. The new national Health Physics center, Kensington labs, is just a mile down the road, and there's always an announcement about some new radiation experiment we can take part in.

Finally, it's not only our government, but the Europeans and Japan who are putting up the money for our glamour project, the Hydra hybrid fusion/fission development reactor. From the front gate of Kankakee station, I can see its containment dome glaring at me, a reminder that I once knew about fusion—that if I were more willful (and there had been no Vietnam) I could have been working on a glamorous, advanced technology, instead of the tired, near fifty-year old clunker-tech of churning out megawatts from splitting uranium.

But maybe it wasn't too late, even for me. They needed another shift supervisor at Hydra. I applied, but so did Laura Brault. And Laura would not be easy to beat. Even I couldn't think of any reason to give me the job rather than her unless they gave credits for experience. And what good is experience in a totally new technology where everything will be new for everyone? Nevertheless, the job announcement did ask for nuclear experience and that's something I have.

So now Dennis Banks wanted me to go to the recirculation valve room. Not an ordinary assignment for an STA. Shift technical advisors aren't supposed to do anything—they're just there, someone with a degree to point to and say "There's the expert." But don't try saying that to an operator. Say it to an outsider. The operators just laugh at STAs. Or at least some STAs. They don't laugh at me, but then they know I'm an operator too.

I looked at the message again. It was weird enough that I thought about archiving it to my hard disk, so I could look at it again later or have proof that I had indeed received such a message. But I've gotten sloppy lately about storing too many unnecessary files and then spending hours cleaning them off the disk, so I thought better of it and didn't store the message. I did cut Dennis's words and paste it into the word processing program and print them so that I could show it to someone who questioned the order. But after I had printed the words and wasted a piece of paper, I realized that anyone could have typed those words and printed them. The piece of paper I'd taken so much trouble to obtain was really no more reliable than my word.

And then there was something else that bugged me about the message. Either I must have left my tech section computer on, or Dennis Banks had known my power-on password. I'm usually very good about turning off my computer, and Dennis Banks, like me, had never been that much of a hacker. I had never messed around figuring out ways to trick people into giving up their passwords. But Dennis and I had both put in time at WorldNet simulations where there was a fairly constant contest over who could pull off the most audacious computer stunts, and I know I had been tricked into revealing my password many times. I knew ways to trick people into entering their password so I could read it; Dennis Banks would know at least as many ways as I did. The simplest was to make someone's screen look like it's asking them to log on. Then they type in their password and as they do it they're typing their password into your file. I laughed and vowed to make Dennis tell me how he had done it. Anyway, the message was strange, but it was a clear order coming from the production manager, so I had best carry it out. I pushed thoughts of the computer mystery from my mind.

I started thinking about the equipment I needed and the proper way of going about such an unusual mission. The control room would have to know, and if I was going to take Kerwin's tiny and by all accounts useless tritium monitor, then I might as well take the tactile interface from its box in the control room too. I was about the only one who ever strapped the tactile interface on. What did the control room people need touch signals for when they'd have all they could do to pay attention to the alarms going off at the panels if things ever went haywire? The tactile interface was an expensive, unnecessary toy coming from the weirdo world of human factors. But I liked toys, especially expensive ones, so I headed down the short corridor from the STA room to the control room. Even though it was a short corridor, I didn't escape the ubiquitous placards on the steel beams: "Kankakee—World Class Nuclear." And then on the next beam, more prosaically in black: "Bus 233X." Well, at least the power bus identification served a purpose. The total quality jingles didn't because we've seen too many of them and for too long.

The control room was quiet. On the sprawling panels only two alarm windows were lit, and we knew about them; they weren't a problem. I went to the shelf where the tactile interface was kept, rolled up my sleeve and strapped it on.

"Hey, STAs don't need any plant info. Or are you just putting that on to stay awake?" said Norm Bronson, the biggest and loudest operator at Kankakee.

"Well, Dennis Banks has given me a little mission. I'm supposed to go out to the recirculation valve room and check on the valve maintenance being done there."

"Don't we have mechanics to do that?" asked Norm.

"Don't ask me why, he just said do it, and with the interface I'll at least know if any of the radiation alarms are going off," I said. "Banks told me to take Kerwin's tritium detector too."

Then I caught the swing of long black hair out of the corner of my eye and I turned. Laura Brault, my rival for the Hydra fusion job, was the senior reactor operator for the shift. She turned away from where she'd been staring at the reactivity control panels and said, "They say that doesn't work, that you can't depend on it."

I fought back the urge to defend the tritium monitor because I realized I agreed with her, and yet I wanted to argue with her like I always did. I could even feel my chin starting to jut out, and I was pulling myself erect. But then I sagged.

"Well, there have been mixed reviews," I said, "but if it detects anything it sure beats hauling around a sniffer with you anytime you go near heavy water. Anyway, if you do anything too bad in the next hour or so, and you need me back here to save northern Illinois—well, you know where to find me."

"Doesn't matter whether we know," said Norm. "You've got to wear your beeper, and if we call you you'd better come, or there will be some big explaining to do."

"Yes, I'm well equipped with little gadgets—beeper, tactile interface, miniature tritium detector. Plus the regular stuff—pocket alarming dosimeter, access badge, the things we carry here in nuclear."

"It takes a lot of stuff to keep someone as flaky as you in line," said Norm. "You STAs are all alike, out of touch with the real world."

"Only reactor operators could take something like this," and I swept my arm around the panels and the MIMICs and the control computers, "and claim it had anything to do with the real world."

I turned and pushed my way through the control room doors before Norm could come up with a retort. I had to watch it with Norm; he really did think Kankakee station was the real world, and everything else was somehow false.

The recirculation valve room was two levels down near one of the two airlocks to containment. There was no way to avoid going through the first computer checkpoint at the end of the control room region clean area, but I knew I'd take the stairs because that way I could get around the ID card reader on the fifty foot level where the valve room was located. I always tried to give the computer as little information about where I was as possible, although I knew my little victories didn't mean much. So the computer wouldn't know when I was on the fifty foot level, but it would never lose me again if I entered containment. And it would only be a matter of time and a close DOE safety inspection before they put a card reader on all the stairwell doors.

Well, I liked stairs, especially the metal grated stairs you could see through in nuclear plants. And it kept me in shape—there were lots of reasons for doing the things I did besides doing them to fool the computers.

Just as I reached the door to the fifty foot level the tactile interface became excited and was tapping out a radiation warning signal on the back of my hand. It tapped the signals there because they claimed it was the most sensitive place to hit which wouldn't interfere too much with normal hand activities.

I brought the LED screen on the interface up before my eyes and pressed the buttons to scan the annunciations and warnings. It was a low order radiation warning for tritium coming from the fixed monitoring station in the west fueling machine bay. It wasn't unusual to get some tritium with anything associated with fueling, but I knew the procedures and I stopped at the next communications phone/computer station. The glaring yellow of the phone stood out from the gray reinforced concrete. Brian Maxwell turned out to be the fueling supervisor on shift. As I spoke I began typing in an e-mail message to him to give written confirmation of the readings I was getting.

"We seem to have a little tritium in the west bay, Brian," I said. "You know about it?"

"No, is it showing up in the control room?" he asked.

"No, I got the warning from the tactile interface. The alarm's coming from the fixed monitoring station," I said.

"Well, you beat the control room. They should have it too, shouldn't they?"

"They sure as hell should," I said. "They're probably trying to get through to you even as we speak. I'm sending you an e-mail with my readings. I'll check them with the control room."

"Thanks," Brian said. "I'll get right on it."

I only had to hit 1 to get the control room. Laura Brault answered.

"Looks like my tactile interface beat you to the punch on the tritium alarm," I said.

"What tritium alarm?" came Laura's reply, dry and cold and I started to not feel so happy.

"I'm getting a low level tritium warning from the west fueling machine bay."

"No such thing," said Laura.

"Well, we'll know for sure soon," I said. "Maxwell is on it. You sure you didn't forget to change a light bulb or something?"

"I'll check it out. You sure your tactile interface hasn't gone as crazy as anyone who'd wear it?"

"We'll know soon enough," I said. "See you for the post-mortem."

So we'd have to resolve why the control room and the tactile interface had a disagreement before we finished the shift. It didn't look like the next few hours would be peaceful. I could feel my mouth sinking into a frown as I approached the recirculation room.

The recirculation valve room was one of those closed-in, concrete-walled, pipework-filled, eerie, claustrophobia-invoking places that all the bright paint and banks of fluorescents in the world couldn't make cheery or even comfortable. It was hot—temperature, not radiation—and the mechanical maintainers were sweating and swearing as they were trying to re-pack one of the motorized valves. There were three mechanics in the room and a tall, thin Vietnamese who I knew well, Trung. He was another Canadian who'd signed on for Kankakee; he now worked as a health physics and radiation control technician. I don't know if Trung especially liked Illinois, but he liked to go to the gulf coast of Florida. I'd seen him sit staring at a reed-lined bay for hours. He said it reminded him of home. I'd known him at WorldNet Simulations in Toronto where he was the man who could fix any computer problem. His reputation had not suffered at Kankakee. Now he was the man who could solve any problem at all, and Pete Kerwin was after him to quit Kankakee and go to work permanently for his company, Anthem Electronics. But Trung resisted leaving his secure employment and now only worked for Pete part-time on special contracts. Trung was leaning in the doorway to escape as much of the heat as he could while still monitoring the radiation safety of the work in progress. His shoulders sagged, and he was flicking his fingernails against the Geiger counter he'd brought along. A neutron survey meter was at his feet, probably needed for another job less straightforward than the one in the recirculation valve room. The only real chance for a radiation accident in the recirculation room would be if the reactor coolant somehow leaked into the light water powering the turbine. And there was no possibility of tritium since it was a light water system. So there was no need for the plastic contamination protection suits which you had to wear when working with the heavy water systems, and which made everyone wearing one look like they'd just stepped out of Apollo and onto the moon. And there was no need to worry about being exposed to hard-to-detect radiation, like the soft betas from tritium. The usual radiation instruments were blind to tritium. Every worker in the plant wore a PAD, a pocket-alarming-dosimeter, which would shriek a quite piercing alarm whenever a high gamma field was present. And if you were warned about the gammas, then that took care of most of the normal radiation dangers except for tritium and neutrons. And the PAD could give a rough warning of neutron radiation. But to get an accurate neutron reading and any measure at all of tritium, more cumbersome detectors were required.

Trung glanced at my pocket and wrist and smiled, "Oh Henry, you have all kinds of fancy hardware. But that miniature tritium detector, I don't believe in that one. I told Pete Kerwin it was no good. He wanted me to work on the electronics, but I told him there are some things which are just impossible."

"Dennis Banks ordered me to take it to rad control for more tests. You've got to admit it would be nice if it could be made to work," I said.

Jim Hilliard, a wiry, gray-haired mechanic, looked up from where he was bent over a pipe and said, "What in hell's the control room doing down here in the real world?" He was supervising two enormous young mechanics—one a red-head and the other Chinese with big, bulging shoulders. Jim smiled at his charges to draw them into the fun of baiting control room staff. He drew breath and started in on another pleasantry, but he was cut off by a shrill, high-pitched alarm that caused me to put my hands to my ears before I realized the shriek was coming from my chest.

I grabbed Pete Kerwin's little tritium detector from where it was clipped to my shirt pocket and frantically searched for the alarm-off button. All three of the mechanics had stopped work and were laughing and holding their ears and I knew I would have a lot of explaining to do about why I'd wound up out in the plant with instruments which halted work with false alarms.

I pressed the button for the read-out on the tritium detector and was stunned to see 2.1 exp 3 millirem showing on the LED read-out. My first thought was that maybe the scale was wrong—surely there were thousands of microrems of tritium exposure in the room rather than the thousands of millirem which the readout seemed to say. Then I remembered that there was only one scale on Peter Kerwin's tritium meter and that was millirem. And thousands of millirems meant we were really talking about rems per hour. And when you have rems per hour that you haven't already known about and planned for, you get out fast.

My first reaction was fury at the instrument and at its inventor, Pete Kerwin. If it was going to show any tritium at all, it might show some whiff of what had given the low level alarm in the west fueling bay. But the damn alarm was showing a huge tritium contamination and in a room which didn't have any heavy water in it. It had to be wrong.

"Goddamn stupid meter," I said and then all the training and all the rad protection lectures came back, and all I could think of was how many times I had been told, "Always believe your instruments." I stiffened and thought of the army as I stepped into the middle of the room to do what I knew I had to do.

"Okay, we've got to get out of here, and I mean now," I said while trying to force my words out through my stomach to give my best command voice. "Let's go. Drop the tools. Let's go now!"

Trung was furious, "Hey, I'm the radiation safety officer for this job, and my instruments say everything is fine in here."

"Sorry, Trung," I said. "I've got to do it. The pocket tritium detector says this room is full of tritium." I could see his eyes bulging in disbelief, so I cut off what he was going to say before he said it. "I know it's crazy. There shouldn't be any tritium here, but when we're on radiation protection requalification training, I think you tell us to always believe our instruments, don't you?"

The mechanics rolled their eyes and smirked, but they put their tools down and started out, and I wondered where in the world I was going to take them since the damn tritium meter would probably show high level air contamination no matter where I took them. But then I thought of the rad control room, and I knew the only thing to do would be for us to go straight to rad control and dump the problem onto the experts.

But when I walked out of the recirculation valve room the readings on Kerwin's instrument began to drop, and the exponent quickly changed from a three to a two; by the time we were fifteen feet away from the valve room it had dropped to a one. The damn tritium meter was acting like there had been heavy tritium levels in the valve room which dropped off quickly outside. That would be reasonable if there could be tritium in the recirculation valve room, but there couldn't be tritium there since it was only light water pipework. So what in the hell was going on?

"If this is such an emergency, Henry", said Jim Hilliard, "Why aren't there alarms out here, and why are those chem techs sauntering toward us like there was no problem in the world?"

"I don't know what the hell's going on, but I pulled us out of the valve room because this pocket tritium detector said that there was more tritium in there than I've seen anywhere. And out here it doesn't read anything, and neither do the fixed stations. So those chem techs are sauntering because there's absolutely no sign that anything's wrong. It's out of our hands. We'll have to let the experts take it from here."

"I thought you were an expert," said Jim.

I stopped to phone the control room. Norm Bronson answered. "Norm, I've ordered everyone out of the recirculation valve room. Kerwin's pocket tritium detector went crazy in there. It was reading in the thousands of millirem per hour."

"There is no tritium in the recirculation room," said Norm. "Even STAs should know that."

"I know; I know it doesn't figure. But the detector said what it did. I thought at first I'd go to local rad control to have them go back with a bubbler and a tritium-in-air monitor, but that's not good enough. With the readings I was getting we're going to have to go to central health physics to give urine samples, and they'll probably keep us a while. So you guys are going to have to take over getting accurate readings of what's going on in the recirculation room. You'll have to keep everyone out of there until we know for sure what's happening."

"Sounds like bad trouble to me," said Norm. "You'd better talk to Laura."

And so I had to go over the same story again with Laura, and I prayed I hadn't violated any station procedures in all the confusion. Laura was not the type to cover up mistakes. But Norm was right. I had to talk to her. With a problem as big as this one might be, the senior had to be informed directly.

"You're crazy, Henry McClure, and Kerwin is crazy with his pocket tritium detector. There is no tritium in the recirculation valve room," came Laura's even voice, patiently explaining the most elementary fact to me, a guy who should know better.

"You're right, Laura, it can't be true, but you have to believe your instruments," and I knew I had become a broken record.

"Okay, go give your urine sample and take a nice break at health physics. But after I write this one up I'll be damned if that pocket tritium meter is ever allowed in this plant again," said Laura.

"Maybe you think peeing in a bottle is a nice break, but I don't," I said before I realized I was trying to squabble with her just like I always did. I put the phone down and turned to organize the inevitable. I sent Trung off to notify local rad control so they could get a reading on the tritium level in the recirculation room with a reliable instrument.

"With fool levels like what you read we'll have to go in wearing plastics," said Trung.

"Yes, you'll have to wear plastics. I'm glad you know your job," I said.

Trung was shaking his head as he left us. "And don't forget to come up to health physics to give your urine sample," I called after him, as if a radiation technician would forget that.

We were an odd bunch as the three mechanics and I headed out into the open expanse of the turbine hall. The roar of the steam and the turbines' giant whirling blades was so loud that talking was nearly impossible. Jim Hilliard, the supervising mechanic, was gray, wrinkled, and wizened; his two charges were giants—fleshy, smooth and tall like me. I stood tall and strong but marked by the years. I was somewhere in that awkward intermediate state between kids and old people called middle age. I felt young like the kids, but my birthdays told a different story.

The noise went down when the freight elevator door closed behind us, and Hilliard began playing for the crowd, "Now boys, we were all in the radiation protection requal program together. I don't remember being warned about any tritium danger in the recirculation room."

The two giant mechanics were beaming. "No, Jim. No danger of tritium in any secondary side system," the red-head said, and his smile and dancing blue eyes bore down straight on me. I had no answer.

We all fell silent on the final walk to the health physics lab. It was at the end of a long corridor just before the final full-body plant exit contamination monitors. I had my eyes firmly fixed to the concrete floor, but when I lifted them I saw people in white lab coats coming out the room and staring at us as we approached. They were turning to each other and giving quick comments back and forth. It looked like a surprise birthday party.

"So, you boys have been out overdosing on tritium so you can get out of real work for a few months," said Paul Sears, his bald top gleaming above the fair remnants of his hair. Paul was cheerful and soft, verging on pudgy. He had a masters degree in health physics and was one of the lab supervisors, so I knew something was afoot when he'd come out into the hall to meet us.

"No, it's a false alarm," I said. "Pete Kerwin's pocket tritium meter went berserk in the recirculation valve room, but that's a totally light water system, so there has to be something wrong with the meter."

Paul had no smile, but his eyes showed concern and he reached out and touched me on the shoulder as he said flatly, "There was nothing wrong with the meter, Henry. Trung just phoned in. They ran a sniffer test in the recirculation room. Fifteen hundred millirem an hour committed dose."

"But that's impossible," I said.

"Nevertheless," said Paul and he guided us into the restroom and gave us our vials for what I knew would be the first of a very long series of urine samples. And then we'd sit in the iron chair for a whole body count. And then we'd answer questions, and then we'd do it all over again until all the investigations of root cause and liability were finished.

2

Time passed slowly for me after the tritium event, even though I was interviewed the next day, and then there were more interviews on the days after that—sometimes three interviews in a day. But most of the interviews were with station people. There was one interview with the Nuclear Regulatory Commission site staff. But since there had been radiation overdoses and suspicion of sabotage in the event, I was sure that eventually I would talk with someone from the law.

I was taken off shift after my tritium exposure, even though I was still within radiation limits, and put in with the training crew.

The panels stretched on either side of me as I stood in the center of the room in the senior reactor operator's position. I stood and waited, my two panel operators seated at their respective work stations slightly in front of me. We formed a v formation with me at the vertex. And then it happened. It seemed all the annunciation windows lit up at once, and paper began shooting out of the monitoring computer's printer—we still had a monitoring computer even though Kankakee was under direct computer control. Monitoring computers just provide information to the operators, but at Kankakee computers normally provide direct digital control of the plant, and the operators are more monitors of the computer than they are controllers of the plant. This is one more respect in which Kankakee station is so unusual for the USA; at the other stations there is no central control computer, rather separate control systems for the key plant systems. The human operators are still responsible for the overall control.

My neutronics/primary energy panel operator was a trainee, and a new trainee at that. He had jerked when the panels lit up and he was erect and was scanning the panels intently, as if he could memorize the hundreds of warnings and off-normal indicators.

"Relax, Jerry," I said. "It's an easy one. Just a big LOCA. I'd say a total break of the outlet header in loop two. Nothing for us to do except watch and verify safety system action. Call up incident procedure three and let's go through it by the book."

In the old days we would have all pulled out a big binder containing the emergency procedure, but now we all just keyed in the procedure code and the procedure appeared taking up half the screen on our over-sized monitors. The critical safety parameters appeared on the other half, except when we clicked the mouse on one of the procedure steps. Then any parameters important for that step in the procedure appeared in a red-bordered window overwriting the safety parameter display.

"Wait for computer verification of the procedure choice," I ordered.

"What's to verify," said Ned Banthien, an old-time SRO. "Can't be anything else. I don't know how many times I've trained on big LOCA, and this is one of them for sure. Only thing that makes the panels light up like that. I can tell it by the glare."

"Now gentlemen," I said. "Remember the gravity of the situation. I don't think we'd be taking it so easy if this were real."

And of course it wasn't real. There has never been a big LOCA, loss-of-coolant accident, anywhere, but every nuclear plant in the U.S. has a simulator to train the operators to handle the things that aren't supposed to happen and probably never will. Simulators were where I'd gotten my start in nuclear, and I still had a love for them; I think I liked simulator time more than time in the plant. Of course that wasn't uncommon—things were always happening in the simulator, unlike the plant where everything was boredom except for the classic event at three a.m. when boredom becomes terror. But, except in simulators, no one has as yet seen the panels light up for a total coolant break.

The simulator was fancy, a new one running on the newest and fastest RISC computer. The thermalhydraulic code used six equations and could do in real time what the most advanced safety codes couldn't do with unlimited time just two short decades ago. When I had started out we struggled to make a one equation model stable and fast enough to run in real time. Real time means that the computer makes the simulated panels react exactly as they would in real life. Events happen at the same pace in the simulator as in the real plant.

I had once been a simulator programmer. I knew how to write the computer codes to simulate how the reactor coolant would change temperature and pressure and flow rate. And I wrote codes to show the reaction of the plant instrumentation to the change in coolant properties. And others wrote codes to cause the pointers and indicators on the simulator panels to change in response to the instrument signals.

Now I work in the real plant, and have done so for the three years that Kankakee station has been operational. I don't have to write programs to cause temperatures to change, instruments to fail, alarms to sound. The world does it by itself. God does it. I just have to react.

With the programming experience, I know I look at some things differently from the other operators. I've stared at curves on computer screens so long that I know what sets of equations do. I not only think about the huge reactor coolant pumps which I can see during shutdowns or when we have to go in for high radiation work, but I have a feel for the equations which model what the pump does to the coolant. Equations are a model, a model of how things work, an abstraction. The pump doesn't really have the equations inside it. You can have a feel for a pump by seeing it start up, by looking at how the instrumentation reacts, by feeling the pipes. But I have a feel for how plots of variables react when the pump model equations are changed. In some ways the equations are friendlier. They are what they are. If they're complicated you may not know exactly what they'll do when you change something, just like you don't know exactly what the plant's going to do from one moment to the next, but at least you wrote the equations. There's nothing there that you didn't code, although the code will most certainly have properties that you didn't expect.

And now we have a big sign saying "This is the simulator." And we've made the carpet different and some of the paint a little different from the real control room so we don't have a repeat of the accidental shutdown when an operator thought he was in the simulator and pressed the scram button as a joke.

They'd put me on the week of simulator training right after the tritium exposure event, but it was done more to give me a break from the discipline and atmosphere of the plant than because of the tritium dose I had taken. I had only been in the recirc room for three and a half to four minutes so I wasn't in there long enough to take a big dose like the three mechanical maintainers. But even so, the tritium concentration in the room had been high and the urine samples said I'd taken eight hundred millirem, almost half the dose I'd be allowed in a year under the new rules. The three maintainers were all burned out; they'd all taken at least four times the yearly limit and they'd been reassigned to fossil stations. But I had no problem. I was control room staff and we normally didn't get much dose. I could have been in the control room right away. It was highly unlikely that in the next year I'd pick up even a tenth of what I'd taken in those few minutes in the recirc room.

And the treatment for tritium exposure had been pleasant. Take plenty of fluids to flush your system. And beer works as well as water, probably better.

The LOCA went smoothly, as LOCAs tend to do until the simulator instructor installs some additional malfunctions. High and low pressure emergency coolant had both engaged properly and at the right time. Fuel temperatures had gone low, and I was wondering when the bad news was going to come. Capparelli, our simulator instructor, was known for throwing in malfunction after malfunction until finally no operator could deal with them all. Capparelli's "crash and burn" scenarios we called them. And you came out of a simulator session with Capparelli sweating and hollow inside. But tonight the panels suddenly froze and Capparelli called out "Fine fellows, now we'll reset."

All the lights on the panels went dark. We heard a click, and then the panels lit back up in the one hundred percent full-power configuration. We had really done nothing during the big LOCA except watch the panels and verify automatic safety system operation.

Capparelli walked up to me and handed me a note. "They want you in the station manager's meeting room Henry. Another investigation of the tritium event."

"Well, it must have been at least three hours since I've answered any questions about that," I said. "I was afraid they'd forgotten about it."

"They haven't forgotten, Henry," said Capparelli. "And Henry, I think it's the law this time. Dennis said something about the FBI."

"It had to come," I said. "Doesn't take a rocket scientist to figure that someone must have put that tritium there. It didn't get there on its own."

"Especially with them talking about organics," said Capparelli.

"Especially," I said. "Maybe a meteorite brought it down. Looks like you'll be short for training."

"We'll do minimum complement exercises. Don't worry about us, Henry. Just be careful what you say."

"In nuclear the best policy is just to say the truth," I said.

"Tritiated organics aren't nuclear," said Capparelli.

"I wouldn't know a tritiated organic if it stepped up and bit me," I said. "Catch you next shift for some more easy exercises."

I had to leave the cool of the training center and go out into the mugginess of an Illinois day turning hot after a rain. The rain still contributed some coolness, but you could sense it getting hotter and building toward an unbearably hot and humid afternoon and evening. I could see the abandoned weathered-wood and concrete structures of the old ammunition plant on one side, and the modern steel and glass of the Kankakee administration building on the other. And looming behind, the reinforced concrete of the reactor containment soared above the metal sheathed turbine, service, and auxiliaries buildings. An existing military ammunition plant had been a natural place to put a weapons material production reactor— and the large pre-existing base of commercial nuclear reactors ringing Chicago had also made the question of adding one more reactor less an issue in this industrial region crowded with refineries, chemical plants, and electrical generating stations, both nuclear and fossil-fuel fired. And it was in such a heavy industrial region that the absence of smoke and smells from nuclear plants was noticed and appreciated.

Of course we still had demonstrations outside the gates, and people always asked whether I glowed in the dark when they learned where I worked. I had never really chosen to be a nuclear worker—it had just happened—and now I was typecast. I was a nuke, an engineer, a workaholic, a polluter, a destroyer and radioactive. But there continued to be people like me in most of Europe, North America, and industrialized Asia because, much as people disliked radiation, the dislike was never quite enough to shut off the thousands of megawatts that poured out of the plants as if generated from nothing—no piles of coal for fuel, no smoke, no smells.

Frank Marzak, the station manager, had a meeting room directly adjoining his office on the top floor of the administration building. It was there he held meetings concerning longer-term projects and concerns that did not have to be dealt with in the next few shifts. He had another, larger meeting room in the common services area of the plant. It was there he held large weekday morning meetings with his workgroup supervisors and other invited parties to discuss and plan the actions to be taken in the short term.

Of course the office in the administration building was a lot nicer and more comfortable. The center table was of rich, dark hardwood and the chairs were high-backed leather. But the daily meeting in the plant was where exciting meetings took place, where the debates on how best to keep the plant operating were thrashed out.

Marzak was a big-chested bear of a man and his gray hair was bristly and short-cropped; I tensed in anticipation of an exchange with him as I opened the door to the conference room. But Marzak was not there. Instead I was faced with the supervisor of the Human Factors Section, Blair McKenna, and a man and a woman who I didn't know, but who looked intently and unsmilingly at me as I approached.

Blair shook my hand and said there were more questions about the tritium overexposure incident. I said I already knew that. The woman was Sheila Rowe from the Nuclear Regulatory Commission, the NRC. The man was a slightly smaller scale but less friendly version of Frank Marzak. He wore a blue suit with pencils in the pocket, he was named Howard Crowder, and he was from the FBI. I had never heard of the FBI visiting any place where I had worked before. I had certainly never been interrogated by the FBI. As far as I knew I had never known anyone in the FBI, unless it had been some undercover operative when I had been first student, then soldier, and then student again in the sixties and seventies.

Blair motioned me to a seat on the other side of the table in front of them; then he excused himself and backed out the door I'd just come in. Mr. Crowder gave me some kind of warning that there was indication of sabotage, of violation of federal law, and that the interview was part of an official investigation. I said I understood that and had expected the police to become involved.

Crowder said, "We'll be recording this interview, and we'll want you to sign the transcript after it's over. Do you understand?"

I said I understood, but said that as many times as I've been interviewed about plant events, I had never been recorded nor had there ever been a transcript.

Ms. Rowe was a thin, intense young woman with a long face, long legs, and curly brown hair. Like Crowder, she had a blue suit and her upper body was leaning stiffly forward as she asked the first question: "I understand you ordered the mechanical maintainers out of the recirculation valve room the night of the event."

"Yes," I said. "The tritium detector I was wearing alarmed. We're taught in nuclear to always believe your instruments, so I ordered everyone out."

"I understand the radiation safety technician assigned to the job did not detect the tritium," said Crowder.

"He couldn't have," I said. "Tritium is very hard to detect, its radiation is so low energy. Since there's not supposed to be any tritium in the valve room, he hadn't brought a tritium detector. So there's no way he could have known that anything was wrong. If I hadn't come in they would have finished the job, and we wouldn't have known about the overexposure until they contributed their weekly urine sample."

"Are you a radiation technician?" asked Crowder.

"No, but I've always taken an interest in the subject. I've had radiation protection training both in Canada and here. And I've........"

"The point is, Mr. McClure, how could you know about the tritium when the radiation technician didn't?" asked Ms. Rowe, and I realized I had been about to launch into a lecture on radiation protection. Well, I do like my work.

I then saw how intent Ms. Rowe and Mr. Crowder were about my answer, and I began to worry about something other than the mother of my kids not speaking to me. Ms. Rowe and Crowder were staring at me like I was the answer to how they were going to get their next promotion in the nuclear investigation hierarchy. The tritium in the recirculation valve room had not been natural; someone had put it there, and I seemed to be the one acting suspiciously that night, going places outside of my duty area, warning of tritium when the radiation technician couldn't detect it. If I had been in Rowe and Crowder's place, I would suspect me too.

The questions continued. Rowe and Crowder took turns coming at that night's events from all the angles. I kept thinking I should have a strategy; I should be careful; I should have a method for answering their questions. But the questions came too fast and I just responded. I heard them and my answer came out, an honest answer because I knew better than to lie without having worked out all the details carefully, because I knew that Rowe and Crowder would check out every last lead looking for a contradiction. And I kept worrying about what was in my message log.

Finally they stopped asking questions and Crowder said the official interview was over. I got up to leave but Crowder said, "No, please stay seated, Mr. McClure. You have to sign the transcript."

"Won't someone have to type it up from the tape?" I asked.

"Someone will, but they've been doing it even as you speak," said Crowder. "Real time transcripts, that's how you nukes call it, isn't it?"

"Yes, real time simulation. That's why the simulator can act like the control room. The programs run in real time," I said.

I had heard of the programs that take keyboard shorthand input and produce English output, but I hadn't suspected that my interview would have merited such care. I was wrong. I spent only a few minutes in my chair trying to think soothing thoughts before a woman came out of Frank Marzak's office. Her expression was blank and she didn't look at me. She handed a stack of white paper to Crowder and immediately turned and went back into Marzak's office, closing the door behind her.

"Please check the transcript over for accuracy and whether there's anything you wish to add," said Crowder as he held the papers out to me.

I took the papers from Crowder and began to read what I'd just been through. There was the business about why I'd gone to the recirculation valve room in the first place, and my only excuse for that one was that I'd received the message from Dennis Banks ordering me there. Dennis's denying he'd ever sent such a message coupled with my being unable to produce electronic proof did not put me in the best light.

Then there was the part about Laura:

Ms. Rowe: The mechanical technicians who were doing the work said they were surprised that, on the day before, Ms. Brault checked on their work, and then the next day you showed up. Why did Ms. Brault go there the day before?

Mr. McClure: I didn't know she had. I admit it's unusual. You'll have to ask her.

Page after page of what and why I'd done things, and whether I could prove it. Twice they asked me straight out whether I'd planted the tritiated organics. And there was a fairly long section about whether I had any anti-nuclear proclivities. I kept saying I didn't want to bite the hand that fed me.

Then I came to the section that I'd liked the least about the interview, not that I had enjoyed any of it. I had done unusual things that night and a very unusual thing had happened, and it looked that I might have had advance knowledge that there was tritium in that room. But why would I have done such a thing? Sabotage is a very willful act, but I knew that Rowe and Crowder would not have to look too far to come up with proof that I could be very willful indeed at times. I could pit my will against all sorts of superior powers. I read on into the bad part:

Ms. Rowe: You have children, Mr. McClure?
Mr. McClure: Yes, two little girls.
Ms. Rowe: That's nice. So things are okay at home.
Mr. McClure: Well, my wife Sheri and I have our problems. Like everyone.

So I had lied after all. I had lied because it was something I wanted to hide. I had lied, but I knew that the station instructions would not allow me to lie for long. I had no desire to read further. I turned the papers over and signed the signature line.

"You have nothing you wish to correct or add?" asked Crowder.

"Not right now," I said. "I realize there are things in here that I'll have to back up. See the network manager, Lucy Watkins. She probably has some way of finding more about the message I received from Banks. She's a regular wizard at finding out who's doing what on the network. And I did notify Brian Maxwell, just like I said."

"We never said you were lying," said Ms. Rowe.

"No, you didn't," I said and realized that I should just stop talking. They said I could leave and so I did.

3

It's hard to make a minivan feel like a hot rod, but that was what I was trying to do when I left the plant after my first official interview with the FBI. Maybe I'd talked with the FBI before back in my university days after Vietnam, but they would have been undercover, and I never knew for sure. And then they'd been so obvious and stupid. The people I talked to might have been local police or even concerned citizens—not real G-men.

The simulator training had already ended when I'd gone back to the training building, so I spent the rest of the shift doing self-study of the emergency procedures for small loss-of-coolant accidents and ATWS, anticipated transient without scram. I'd studied the same stuff many times before, but there were always things that seemed a little different from what I'd remembered. "Repetition is the key to all true learning," is one of the phrases that go through my head to keep me doing something I've done before.

But repetition of my grilling by the NRC and the FBI was not something I wanted. I dreaded what I knew was going to happen. There had been sabotage at Kankakee, radioactive sabotage, and there would be no limit to the measures taken to discover the saboteur. And right now I knew I looked like the likely candidate. I would be dealing with Ms. Rowe and Mr. Crowder and many others until the mystery was solved.

I took the small road by the creek with its twists and turns and the trees growing close to the road. The road made it seem like there was nature, nice hiking country, and not the mile upon mile of flat corn and soybean fields interrupted and laced by power— the lines of silver towers, arms drooping wide and connected by the cabled catenary curves of the high-voltage trunk lines. And besides the power lines, there were only the gray concrete silos interrupting the green flatness. And some of the power lines ended in giant versions of those silos, the equally gray concrete of the nuclear containments.

I turned right onto the state highway with its line of Pfister Hybrid signs and then immediately left onto the small road that led to Sheri's house, the house I had learned to love. When we decided to move back to the Midwest, I thought we'd find a big old white frame house, the kind I had grown up in. But Sheri found a long, low brown ranch house on a shaded gravel road. The house was shaded, too, with hickories and basswood, maples and oaks, and there was a wooded rise in back. It had a big yard, and there was a sunny part near the fence where the girls set up their croquet wickets.

The driveway sloped down to a basement level garage. I didn't like that—water and snow go down. But we weren't in Canada any longer, and I had been conditioned to deal with snow problems a lot worse than we'd found in Illinois. Sometimes I missed the challenge of going out early before work to move mountains of snow. Once it had been moved off the driveway, you could point to the piles of white and say, "There, I did that." It wasn't always so apparent what you had done in the old nuclear game.

I left the van in the drive. We rarely went to the trouble of putting it into the garage, and now the garage was accumulating debris that might be used again sometime. Now it was hard enough to put one car in the garage; two cars didn't go in unless I had just done one of my very occasional rampages of cleaning, organizing, and mostly throwing out.

The sweet smell of the wildflowers and the tiger lilies hung in the humid, stagnant, shaded air as I went up the steps to our front door. I loved the tiger lilies. They reminded me of trips to relatives I had now forgotten, relatives who lived on farms in the hilly south with flowers everywhere around the house, and there were so many people it seemed I was related to all the world.

It was different now. We'd spent so many years in Canada where we knew no one, and I had never taken the time to seek out the relatives I knew I still must have. Anyway, the ones who used to throw the big get-togethers were now old. The young lived in towns and were too busy with their jobs and children to think about holding together the idea of a larger family. Or maybe they still were having parties, but I had been away so long that they had forgotten about me.

The front door opened and there was Tracy, her straight black hair beatle-cut, her arms open wide and a big gap in her smile where two of her front teeth were out. I scooped her up and swung her around. She was our youngest at seven and a hug from her could make a lot of electrical generation problems seem small.

Tracy didn't want to let go and she was saying, "Daddy, you know what?"

And I didn't know what and she said, "Mommy and I made a cake and I got to lick all the icing 'cause Laurie didn't help."

I set Tracy down at the top of the short flight of stairs that led to the main level. Sheri was in the kitchen, her back to me; she was cutting something on a cutting board with a paring knife.

"Hey, so you made a cake, and Tracy helped!" I said.

Sheri didn't turn to me, her shoulders drooped and everything seemed to sag as if she were being sucked into a big hole in her stomach. I could make out a soft "Yeah," and then she pulled herself back upright and erect and continued cutting the carrot.

So there it was. I had been irradiated with tritium in a sabotage incident; I had been interviewed three times by Operational Experience, twice by the special multi-division investigation committee, once by two NRC people from operations, and now by the NRC and the FBI together. I was a suspect of having planted the stuff that I'd been contaminated with, but none of this had sparked the least interest in my wife of thirteen years. She still wasn't talking to me.

There had been a lot of stress with our moves and the two careers and the children, and I realized that maybe I had stopped trying to have fun and had begun viewing life as one day of work and hassles after another. But I had caught myself at that, and had looked at my wife and children, and realized that a woman as talented as Sheri and who looked as good as she did deserved more. And I had tried to show her how I felt, and I thought it was working, but then the trouble started after she returned from Toronto. She had come back; she had finished her contract there and was expecting to get the final payment, and she had quit talking to me.

I went up behind her. She kept her back to me. I reached across to her hip and turned her; she was looking down and I tried to find her lips but she turned her cheek to me. She didn't talk to me, and she didn't like to have me kiss her.

I had thought it would pass, I thought maybe she was sad to have the Toronto contract behind her since it was our last real connection to Canada. I thought maybe she was sick, not feeling well, in a bad mood. But a month of silence is more than a bad mood, and

I constantly thought about what might be going wrong and what I could do to fix it.

Our family was perfect. Everything was going fine for us. Sheri's business as a human factors consultant had never been better. She had to turn away work, and she had so much business that two free-lance contractors now essentially worked full-time for her. That, combined with my secure job at Kankakee and before that at WorldNet Simulations, made us comfortable financially. We had the additional pride of knowing that we had done it all ourselves. There had been no inheritances or gifts to make our path easier. Sheri had made a success in the highly competitive world of human factors consulting by hard work and ability, and I had always been able to become accepted as competent and capable by my various employers. And we had Laurie and Tracy, as bright and pretty a pair of little girls as a proud father and mother could possibly want.

"I guess I'll go find Laurie," I said and turned to go.

"Henry," Sheri spoke my name.

Her voice was soft and yet firm and commanding. I turned, half-afraid of what she would say.

"Laurie and Tracy have been invited over to the Lewark's this evening. Can you take them, or shall I?"

"Oh, that's fine," I said. "I can take them and you can check your e-mail." The key to Sheri's business was her modem and fax machine; she spent more time with computers now than I did, even though I was supposed to be the computer expert of the family having done little else but sit at a keyboard and type in simulation code for three years.

"Good," she said, and I thought she was going to say something else, but then the look in her gray eyes changed, and they faded into some faraway place and she turned back to her cutting board.

I don't like to confront problems. I like to think that time will pass and things will get better. But the silence was extreme; it was like the time she had come back from Toronto. I had to speak. "Sheri, what is wrong?"

She thought before she spoke, her head nodded down and did not come back up and she spoke slowly, "Why do you say something's wrong?"

"You don't talk to me, I speak to you and half the time you don't reply. And you don't like me to kiss you."

"I'm surprised you noticed," she said. "I didn't think anything was that much different from usual."

"Not different from usual!" I said. "You think not talking to someone is usual?"

Her gray eyes had their fierceness back as she looked at me full-face. "When Tracy and Laurie are gone, we'll talk then," she said.

I knew I had been about to yell and I wanted to make things good. I wanted to catch Sheri's eye, but she had turned away, turned back to her cutting. I touched her upper arm just below the shoulder and squeezed it. I hung my head and left the kitchen and called out "Where's my big girl Laurie?"

I didn't get an answer, but I didn't really expect one from my ten-year old. Laurie liked to watch TV and draw and read, and she tended to lose herself in all of these pursuits, so a greeting from Daddy would pass unnoticed. I like to watch TV too, and with Laurie I had someone to watch it with, and an excuse to watch it.

I found Laurie in the lower playroom. She was surrounded by toys—little cars with little children to ride in them. She lay on her stomach, her eyes glued to the television. It was an educational channel on the cable, a show about Minoan civilization. Laurie would watch anything. In front of her was a big square of white Bristol board with scores of colored pencils and markers scattered on top of the board and to either side. I could see that Laurie had been drawing palaces with towers and domes. Towers and domes and colonnades, more ornate than anything I had ever attempted when I was a boy and full of King Arthur and Robin Hood.

"Laurie, you want to do something real instead of watch TV?" I said. "I'll show you how to countersink a screw so it doesn't stick out."

Trying to teach my girls the little I knew about woodworking was my feeble attempt to combat the sexist division of labor and to give my girls a chance to decide they didn't need a man to hang pictures or to put together unassembled furniture.

"Maybe later, Daddy, I like the show." Her eyes, unwavering from their focus on the TV, were almost lost beneath her light brown, once blonde hair. She had the lightest hair in the family, and it always made me happy when she tossed her hair, even when she was mad or about to hit her little sister.

"Okay, but right after it's over turn it off and I'll take you and Tracy over to the Lewarks."

Laurie didn't look up, and she didn't say anything.

I stood between her and the TV. "Listen young lady, I don't have to take you over to see Susie Lewark. You can stay here and do your homework or help me with the grass if you'd rather."

"Oh no Daddy. I want to play with Susie, but I do like this show, so could you not stand in front of the TV."

I stooped down and patted the top of her head. "Okay, my little ancient history specialist. You can finish your show, but you have to promise to get in the car right away after that."

"I will Daddy. I'll go jump right into the car; you won't believe how fast I'll be."

If she was fast at all I wouldn't believe it, but that was one of the little prices of parenthood. Some children are easy, most are not.

I went to the cold cellar for my first beer. The rules against drinking at a nuclear plant are strict, and I follow them. But I would not be on duty for twelve hours, and I needed the preparation for what Sheri would say later.

The kids dashed straight into the Lewarks' house as soon as the door opened. The mother, Veronica Lewark, had children the same age as my children, but I knew she was at least fifteen years younger than me. My children were as beautiful as hers, but I knew that I'd be keeping us from winning in any "best-looking-family" contest. Veronica and her husband Bill were so young, so strong, so full of cheer.

We said the usual parents-exchanging-kids things, and then I drove slowly back to the house Sheri had chosen for our first American, first Illinois home. I hadn't felt sure about the house when we first moved in, but now I loved it as much as any house I had ever lived in. The house, my children, my wife, our family, the cars, the cat and dog, the grass, trees and fences—they formed a magic right-ness in the world. This was the way things were meant to be.

Sheri stood before me in the kitchen. She at first looked down, but not for long. She looked straight at me and there was firm cold-ness in what she said. "As you know, I have been unhappy for many years. I have tried and tried but nothing works. I want a separation. I'll move out with the girls if you want, but I don't want to live with you any more."

Of course I should have known. It had been what we had been talking around in our talks with the counselors. But I thought it was a problem that could be worked out, that could be pointed to and she'd say "Fix that" and I would and then it would be okay. I did not know it would be like this, that she would say something so final.

"But Sheri, I love you. You and the kids are all I have. We've been happy. I know things have been rough with the kids and our two jobs, but we can be happy again, I'm sure of it."

And I said this "But Sheri" and that "But Sheri" and I quit sleeping and I thought constantly about what could make her love me again, but I accomplished nothing except to have her agree to stay in the house and not leave provided I slept in the downstairs bedroom. And so I slid into a life of surface normality, going to work each day and exchanging gossip about who had been interviewed and what the FBI was going to do next. And I'd go home at the end of the day and deal with the kids and mow the lawn and do the other things that fathers do. And when I woke up in the morning for a day shift, my kids were there in the house with me.

4

Work life at Kankakee was almost back to normal with only the unresolved tritium sabotage dampening the free-wheeling, easy camaraderie typical of work in Kankakee operations. The technicians and operators followed the rules more closely, and they watched each other. There was a nervous tension, a tension coming both from the official investigations and the workers' fear of further radiation overexposures. The tension lurked in the background ready to pounce on the saboteur. There had to be a saboteur, and I knew that I was very much a suspect.

At home my girls were beautiful. Tracy and Laurie did not notice a thing; they thought it perfectly natural that their Daddy was sleeping in the basement. And they played and squabbled like all little girls. Only Laurie sensed something of the change. She noticed how I sat in the evening, and she twice asked, "Daddy, you look sad. What's wrong?"

And I would smile and say, "I'm sorry Laurie. I'm not sad. I was just thinking."

"You look sad, Daddy."

"I'm not sad. Come give me a hug."

And she would. And Tracy would see us and then she would want to give me a hug too.

They put me back on shift right after the week of simulator training. I was on graveyards and ready to go in for my second shift since the recirc room event, but I had to report in early because I had a memo calling me in to Human Factors.

There were pickets at the plant gate. They had signs about tritium polluting the water and tritium spreading throughout the human body and "We don't want our children to Glow in the Dark!"

I slowed much more than the other cars going in, but the pickets were not aggressive. If I had been on the picket line things would have been different. We would have stopped the cars and forced a delay in the shift-change, or the police would have had to come and clear us out. But it had been a long time since I'd picketed anything, and it had been some time since I had decided that nuclear power would be with us for a very long time.

And then, out of the corner of my eye to my left, was a tall, erect man with chest thrust out who I hadn't seen since the days when I did picket quite regularly. I had seen Ken Seagraves on the television news reports. He was with the Chicago Energy Coalition, and I suspect the reporters liked to put him on the air because he was stunningly handsome. His body was powerful, lean, and athletic and his face shone crisp and clear with blue eyes, and there was even a cleft in his square chin.

It made me feel better to think that he and I were about the same age.

I wanted to stop and talk with him for old time's sake, but it wouldn't have looked right for a shift supervisor to fraternize with the antinuclear pickets, and there was a car behind me wanting to come in. So I drove ahead without Seagraves seeing me.

The memo calling me in to Human Factors had Judy Peterson's signature on it. That didn't make me sad, even though it meant I had to report an hour early for my graveyard shift, because Judy's definitely not a bad looking woman, and we've always hit it off well when we talked. I was starting to look at women again then, and Judy was one of the first I started looking at and thinking about. And I looked at women more and more as the problems between Sheri and me went on. I'd think of the kids and that would make me sad. I'd stop feeling sad when I thought about another woman. It was like there were two tracks in my head, a sad track when I thought about my family, and the other woman track when I didn't.

As I made my way through the tangled jumble of partitions in the administration building, I wondered whether it was the time to report my family problem. This wasn't a one-morning problem like in Vietnam, and at first I hadn't been sure how big a problem it was since it had been building up on me slowly, growing and growing. Until the tritium incident, it was all I thought about. Kankakee personnel reliability procedure CNK-5 required all operations personnel to report any family problems involving violence or having the possibility of leading to separation or divorce. Central Nuclear had adopted the policy to show compliance with the federal fitness-for-duty regulations. But since we handle weapons material, Central Nuclear often goes way beyond the Code of Federal

Regulations in its own policies, and CNK-5 was one of these occasions. Procedure CNK-5 was worded so broadly that it was impossible to enforce but was easy to use against you after-the-fact. I moved down a long corridor, at the beginning lined with physical plant design engineers in closed offices, and at the end occupied by the six-person human factors section. Judy Peterson was sitting erect and alert behind the first desk in the section. Her straight red hair hung almost shoulder length with just a trace of curl up and out at the ends. I didn't want to tell her anything unpleasant. I especially didn't want to tell her on nights; it would be better on a sunny day. I always had some excuse for not reporting that my last thirteen years had been a total waste.

"Must be important for you to be staying this late. It must be a record for someone on days," I said.

Judy told me to sit down. I tried to smile at her but she wasn't having any of it.

"Henry, we'd like you to take one of our tests again," she said.

"Gee, it's been a long time since I took one of those. What's the deal, you check up every now and then to see if anyone's gone crazy?"

She looked me in the eye, and then she finally smiled. "No, Henry...well, kind of. You know I'm human factors and that's what we do."

"Well, okay. We do lots of crazy things in the good old nuke game. What kind of test is it?"

"Oh, you've taken it before, Henry. It's one of our standard personality tests, the short version. I'll show you the test room and you bring it out when you're done. Then I want to talk to you a while."

Judy was acting stiff and so strange that I was really trying to figure what could be going on. Did she already know Sheri and I were seeing a counselor? Sheri was in human factors too as a private consultant. Maybe Sheri had been talking even though I'd told her not to say anything before I'd reported it. Judy rose and I followed her toward the last room in the human factors corridor. On the walls were pictures of the new German control panel displays as well as some of the Kankakee station operators using the latest in US and Canadian tactile interfaces, the same type that I'd taken with me the night of the tritiated organics event. And then came a picture with me in it. I was scowling at the newest know-it-all from the tech section who was demonstrating the latest method for rendering human operators obsolete.

Judy showed me into a little pastel-painted room with two rows of school-type writing seats lined up. "Just follow the printed instructions," she said.

"Ain't you takin' a lot for granted?" I said. "You know that tritium dose I took last week might've scrambled my brain."

"Henry, it could only have helped," and she wheeled primly and left, closing the door behind her.

She was right. I had seen the test before, all about what I'd think if I saw my mother crying, or a baby on top of a car, or what would I do if my best friends were holding me tight and wouldn't let me go. And then there'd be the same questions again, only with a little different angle.

Why in hell had they called me in for this? We had a plant to run after all, and Kankakee still had enough enemies in Congress who'd be watching every step we made.

I took the test out to Judy after forty-five minutes. She smiled and said, "How about some coffee."

"Sure, I'm still going to have to work this graveyard, aren't I?"

"Yes, Henry, unless this test shows you really are crazy, and not just pretending." Then she did one of those government lab high-tech things. She fed my answer sheet into a scanner and immediately bar and pie charts started coming out of a color printer on her desk.

"You got a map of my brain now?" I asked.

"Oh, it's very crude, Henry," she said lightly. But she wasn't looking lightly at the charts; her eyes weren't missing anything on that printout. I always knew Judy was smart. She knew it too, but I don't mind arrogance so much if there's something behind it to give it some justification.

"Henry, do you like your job?" she asked as if she were just curious.

"Sure, I like it okay. Well, it's just a job, but for a job it's okay."

"You were in Vietnam, weren't you?"

"It's on my personnel record," I said coldly. I knew that the rest of my talk with Judy would not be pleasant.

"You were hospitalized there, weren't you?" she asked, her voice level as if she were just passing the time.

It was that again. I thought maybe I'd put it behind me, but there it was again, and this time it was a red-haired woman I liked who was putting me through the torture.

"Yes, I was hospitalized, and to cut this game short it wasn't for battle injuries. I was wacko, plain and simple, so wacko that even the lifers noticed."

"What did you do that was so crazy?" she said, just like that, no emotion, looking at my chart, not at me.

I could feel myself losing it, going somewhere I hadn't been for quite a while. I tried to stop, but I couldn't. "I spit on a major. Yeah, and I cried a lot. Crying all the time I was."

"You spit on a major. Why did you do that?"

"He was an officer and he was there. Could have been anybody, could have been you if I was supposed to salute."

"So you have these feelings of aggression now, Henry?" she asked.

"Well now that you mention it, I am feeling some aggression. Matter of fact I don't think I've been this mad in quite some time."

"I mean, in general. Have you been feeling mad at someone at work? Someone other than me," she said, and I stopped feeling mad at anyone and started to think and wonder where this was all going.

"I'm sorry, Judy. I don't like to talk about Vietnam, that's all. I've been feeling very well, there's no one special I'm mad at. What in hell is going on, anyway?"

I could see the tips of her teeth tugging at her lower lip. "We're going to want to talk to you again, Henry. Brian will want to talk to you. And someone from the NRC too."

"Not the NRC again. I'm not that crazy."

"Did you write this letter, Henry?"

The letter looked sick, red and blue lines of crayon and tidbits of newspaper clipping pasted on, and in big black letters, "I do Beta Burn."

"I've never seen that letter before," I said, trying to keep my voice level.

"I didn't think you did, Henry," she said. "We'll have to call you in again about this letter and, you know, about other things. Oh, there's one more thing. I should have covered this first."

"Okay, so let's cover it now," I said.

"It says in your file that your father committed suicide."

"Yes," I said with the sinking feeling that came whenever I had to tell someone how my father had died.

"Did he have a serious illness?"

"No. No physical illness. But he had suffered occasional deep bouts of depression for many years."

Her face was turned away from mine and her eyes were to the floor when she said, "I have to ask whether you yourself ever think about suicide."

"Not very often. Not very often at all, and I never think about it for very long," I said.

"Did you think about it after you had your breakdown in Vietnam?"

The wound to my soul was as searing as it had been that day in Vietnam when I realized I was the only one in my squad left alive. I wanted to hit her. I wanted to wreck the office. I wanted to smash the whole Human Factors section and probably the rest of the building. I said, "Yes."

She waited but I just stood there glaring at her. Then I managed to say, "Any chance you could tell me what the test and all these questions are about?"

She met my eyes for a second and shook her head stiffly and looked away. There was nothing for me to do but go to my shift and try to pretend things were normal.

5

I was steaming at Judy but I still had to do my shift. I pushed out into the dark to cross over to the plant. As she said, it was her job; she had to do it. But why did she have to do it so well? Human Factors. With all the people who could give me trouble, why did it have to come from them?

It was one of those overcast breathless nights, still stifling-hot at ten, one of those nights good for corn and tomatoes, but not for people. The heat made me madder, and then I thought of what I hadn't told Judy, but would have to tell her or someone like her. And I'd have to tell them soon or I'd have another problem. Then I thought there couldn't be any sorrier jackass than me.

I've been through the plant entry rigmarole too many times for the delay to bother me, plus it was cooler inside. I didn't have anything to put on the conveyor that ran through the x-ray, so I stepped right into the arched portal of the weapons scanner and stood still a full ten seconds. I counted one-and-a-thousand, two, so I'd be sure they wouldn't send me back. Then I stepped up to the second in-line monitor, this time for bombs. I never knew whether it sniffed the explosives or what, but you only had to stand in it a second, so I had the rhythm down perfect and rolled in time off the ball of my right foot and stepped smartly up to the only open window in the glassed-off security cage. There was only one guard inside and I didn't know him. It wouldn't have made much difference if I had.

I bent forward to the mike, "Five-fifty-nine."

The guard went to the rack and pulled out my key card and my photo I.D. He came back unsmiling, holding my photo card to his chest so I couldn't see it and said, "What's your name?"

I don't usually smart-off, but that night I did, "Henry."

"Your full name."

"Henry McClure."

The guard put the two cards in a tray on his side of the wall and pushed it out through what looked to be an earthquake-proof flap in the security window.

I picked up my two cards, and it was good I was fast about it because the tray went back through the flap with a mean jerk. I pinned my photo up high on my chest as per regulation and stepped up to the bank of floor-to-ceiling high turnstiles. I started to feel better. I always liked pushing against the big silver metal spokes and making the big wheel turn. I put my key card into the slot and waited a half second for the green light. Then I stepped between the teeth of the first turnstile and pressed my way through. Now I was in my world, a loud humming, whining, grinding world of concrete and steel through which flowed torrents of steam and high voltage. A world of procedures and rules and experts and layer on layer of bureaucracy. A world I hadn't chosen but had somehow drifted into and now it was mine, the place where people knew who I was.

I turned and went up the stairs to the work-control area. Outside, I picked up my hardhat from the rack, and then I stepped into the big room which was bright with the sick glare of the fluorescents. There were three control techs inside, and one of them was the only big surprise I'd had when I'd followed Sheri back to the States and found the job at Kankakee. Jim Haskel had known my wild side after Vietnam.

I pulled my dosimeter out of the wall rack and walked to the nearest automated calibration unit. Again, I used my key card and pushed the dosimeter cylinder into the receiving tube. Now the computer knew I'd moved from the turnstiles to the work control area. Warning messages started flashing on the CRT that I couldn't take any more dose this quarter. The tritium event had done that to me; then I realized there'd be lots more questions about that, too, and I started to lose the good feeling I'd got coming in.

"They still let you go into the control room, Henry," said Jim, a big grin showing through his reddish excuse for a beard.

"Sure, no danger of real work there," I said. I'd been a control tech in Canada, and I missed it at times. And with stations like the Candus or Kankakee, the automated control was so advanced that the control tech could be the real human key to whether the megawatts went out or not.

Jim and the two others were heading out into the plant, but at the door Jim turned and gave me the clenched fist, "Sharp struggle, brothers and sisters"

He liked to do things like that, he liked to remind me. I surprised him and gave him the clenched fist back.

Jim knew a lot about me. But then I knew a lot about him. If we went down, we'd go down together. Besides, we still liked each other well enough. Of course I'd always thought that deep down inside, at his very core, he was crazy. But then people said that about me too.

There was one more primitive thing I had to do before going in. I had to sign the dose control ledger. I had to certify that I knew my dose limits for the shift. Unthinking, I pulled out my ballpoint and started to sign. It was blue. That wouldn't work, it had to be black. I cursed and fished out one of the pens beneath the ledger. Why they had to have signatures and all in black was something I failed to understand.

I used my key card again, but this time the door looked like a door. I stepped through and walked fast straight down the corridor which led to the control room. I still thought like a control tech, and I took note that the computer had updated its location mark on me. It knew where I was, but at least it didn't know what I was thinking, not yet anyway.

I stopped at the glass outside the control room. The room was busier than usual because it was shift turnover time. The day shift staff were formally informing the graveyard shift of the plant state and work in progress. And before the day shift people could leave, I would have to sign specifying that I had been sufficiently briefed, and that the plant state was acceptable as turned over to me.

I could see Laura Brault leaning over the lead control station. She wore her hair loose in the control room and part of its silky straight blackness was draped over the left CRT display. Laura was my technical advisor for the shift. It flashed on me to wonder whether I would actually ever take any of her advice, and then I rejected the general idea as too unlikely to be considered. And then I realized that the same thought must have crossed Laura's mind, because she was no fool, especially when it came to nuclear operator politics.

Laura and I seemed to always want the same things, except she wanted them more. She'd been put through for Shift Supervisor qualification training before me, but then I'd come through in the next group, and I'd never held it against her that she'd scrambled so hard to get on the first list. But now we'd both put in for the control room job at the Hydra experimental fusion/plutonium breeder station, and I'd noticed Laura trying hard again. My university had been a long time ago, and even though I'd specialized in fusion and had a better background in the field than Laura, I'd heard her drop the line that her studies were more recent and not out-of-date.

Laura was talking to Jim Higgins, the RO at the lead station. Ned Banthien, the control room supervisor for the shift, was at the panels. Normally he should have been sitting with Jim at lead control, but Ned was of the old school and loved the panels. I don't know what he would have done if they'd built Kankakee like the new European and Asian stations, just computer screens for control, no panels with their banks of switches and alarm windows. Just desks with computer screens, and maybe a MIMIC display, that was where real control was now.

The operators liked to badmouth the Kankakee control room. Either they were computer jocks and mocked the panels, or they were old-line operators who thought a needle on a gage had to be more reliable than a flashing number on a computer screen. Me, I loved the Kankakee control room. I knew the reactor cooling panels were on my left, the reactivity control on my right. I sat at the computer terminals where the menus for bringing up information were fast, convenient, and capable of unbelievable detail. And I could check whether the arcane info I could bring up on the screen was consistent at all with the physical feel of the lights on the panels. The computer was my brain, the panels my body.

Above the center panels was the biggest and prettiest display MIMIC I'd ever seen. All the important systems and a lot of unimportant ones could be seen there, colored lines tracing the circulation paths for the different system flows, flashing pump symbols for pumps that were on and dead blackness for those that were off. And clear digital readouts in red for forty key parameters. The MIMIC was my heart, or was it my guts?

I always tried to remember that the MIMIC was a translation, an interpretation of the measurements that I could find if I worked hard enough to find them on the computer screens. The panels with the lights were elemental, the old way of doing things. The MIMIC was stylized, a picture translation of the panels, a translation that was supposed to get at the essentials. But it was a translation, and I tried to always remember that no one could be totally sure what was essential and what was not. The computer screens had it all—all the measurements, essential or not. But it was a skill to know how to work with them, a skill I had from my years at the keyboard, but a skill that a lot of operators like Ned Banthien either didn't have or didn't care to use because they preferred the old way with the panels.

I knew that Laura and Ned and Jim Haskel had been interviewed by the NRC/FBI investigators about the tritium incident. And I knew from what Judy Peterson had showed me that we'd likely all be interviewed again. That incident wasn't going to be put behind us easily. I knew the investigation would make us jumpy sooner or later, and I wished I could turn around and go back home. But then I remembered that my home wasn't that much of a home since Sheri had shut me out, and so I pulled open the heavy door and stepped into the control room.

The change in atmosphere hit me almost like a blow. The lights were brighter, there were more people, and the people were a team—they talked to each other. Especially with the two shifts in there together it was almost like a family.

Shift turnover went smoothly. Rex Shields, the day shift supervisor, was, as always, very meticulous about the turnover, but Kankakee was running smoothly and it only took us fifteen minutes to go over all the current work plans and for me to sign the shift turnover forms.

The day shift had not been gone five minutes before phones started to ring, and I watched my crew speaking intently into the phones and then rushing to check the panels. It had all the signs of trouble, and I didn't really want trouble on a graveyard. For that matter, I never like trouble at a nuclear plant. I'd much rather be bored.

I walked to the lead station and said to Laura and Jim Higgins, "Tell me it's going to be another nice easy shift"

"Sorry, Henry, we're leaking and the operators say it's raining at eighty-seven point five inside containment"

"Heavy or light?" I asked.

"Heavy," said Laura and her mouth curled up in an ironic smile; she enjoyed the fix we were in. Light water doesn't cost anything and it doesn't directly cool the fuel at Kankakee. With a heavy water leak we were leaking money, and we might likely be leaking primary coolant, and there's not that much expensive heavy water cooling the fuel at Kankakee. People think small when designing heavy water systems.

I looked at Jim Higgins, "Any reports of where it's coming from?"

Jim punched some keys and pulled up another data set on his screen as he replied: "We know for sure there are two leaky motorized valves in purification. The field operators on days got a visual on it in the sight ports"

"How much we losing," I asked, hoping they wouldn't tell me what I figured they would.

"Two or three," said Laura.

"Two or three what?"

"Two or three gallons per minute of course"

I had to pause then because I keep the station's primary heavy water coolant inventory in my head as kilograms. I like to have a very good idea of the basics, like how much water I have to work with. But then Station Procedure one nineteen says you shut down within two hours if you're leaking four gallons of heavy water a minute. I've got that converted to kilograms per second in my copy of the procedure.

"If it gets worse we'll have to shutdown," said Laura.

Ned Banthien was close enough to hear what Laura had said. He shrugged his shoulders. I looked long and hard at the main MIMIC above the panels and then said, "Where are we right now, Laura? How would you describe the current plant state?"

"We're at one hundred percent power and we've got a heavy water leak, a reactor coolant leak since, if it's coming from RCS purification, it's coolant"

"And how long have we been at one hundred percent power?"

"A hundred seventy-four days. You can read the production board as well as I can," she said.

"Well, reactors don't like to change. When they're doing something you'd best just let them keep on doing it. So I'm not going to move this reactor which is happily turning out one hundred percent power; I'm not going to move it down to zero percent power unless I've got one damn pressing reason"

"I'd call a heavy water leak a pressing reason," said Laura.

"We don't have to shut down unless it gets up to four. Moreover I'm going to assign the field operators to track down every last bit of this leak so that we know exactly where it's coming from, because if we can do that it won't be an unknown leak, it'll be one we know every bit about. And once we know the leak source, any probabilistic safety study in the world will tell you it's safer to stay at power than to start monkeying with a machine that's working right"

"That leak gets much bigger and you'll have to shut down. And if you don't, I won't shed one tear if the NRC fines you good," Laura said and then walked over to the shift technical advisor table in back of the operator control stations.

I told Ned to assign all the field operators to finding and stopping the leak, and then I took the chance of the momentary lull to escape into the shift supervisor's office. I closed the door. With the door closed it was almost like I was on a planet beyond. The office was strangely quiet, noise got swallowed up in the walls, and the lighting was almost as bright as at the panels. I had the safety reports, the station design documents, and nearly as much plant info available on the PC as at the actual computer control stations. I could look busy and hide inside the shift supervisor's office.

A damn leak and a borderline one at that. The kind that drove the field workers batty. They didn't like getting splashed on when they were in accessible areas. They knew it was reactor coolant, and they didn't take comfort in how clean Kankakee has always been. We've never had a big fuel leak at Kankakee, and we can quickly pinpoint even little leaks with the channel detectors and quickly pull the fuel. That's the beauty of the channel reactors like the weapons material production reactors and the Canadian Candus. They could do that at Chernobyl too, but then once someone says that anything has any resemblance to Chernobyl people get nervous. Might as well say don't build boats because they have similarities with the Titanic.

Laura pulled me away from my paperwork at 2:15 a.m. She handed me a strip chart of the D_2O reactor cooling water storage tank level. It had fallen six-tenths of a meter during our shift.

"We're pushing the limits, and that leak's not going to go away," she said.

Two field operators in anti-contamination clothing tried to enter the control room. The alarms went off; they were contaminated. One of them was big George Barrett. I could see him curse and step back. He yelled, "Are we running a reactor or some kind of exotic shower spa? You go into eighty-seven five and you'd best take your swim suit"

The other field operator, Omer Ridenour, said nothing. He knew the next step was to go to decontamination, and he didn't make it into anything dramatic. It was part of the job.

People don't like the unusual in a nuclear plant. They especially don't like unusual things they can touch, taste, see, or smell. The radiation's different. They know it's there; it's part of their job, but they never feel it. But if you can smell something it might be radioactive, and you know it's going into your lungs.

I took a scan of the control room. People were looking at Laura and me, and the looks weren't kind ones. They were all wondering what we were going to do, and I figured the majority thought we should shut down.

I turned to a man I knew wouldn't get excited, "Ned, what's the report from the field on that leak? Any chance of stopping it?"

"That's what I hoped George and Omer were going to tell me before they set off all those alarms"

"You tell me what they've got as soon as they're clean," I turned to Laura. "We keep running, auto-pilot, just stay on course"

"You going to let storage go down more?" she asked.

"No, we'll start pumping makeup water into it"

"Then how will we know the leak rate?"

"We'll correct for what we pump in. Could you handle the calculations, Laura?" I said and felt pleased as hell with myself. I was sure the flow meter on the makeup line indicated low. I needed every bit of leeway I could get to keep Laura from making me shutdown. And then I did my nuclear rationality check. Maybe the leak was bigger than it looked. Could we be losing more coolant than I thought? Was I just being stubborn because it was Laura telling me to shutdown?

I looked at the panels and then up to the MIMIC. On top and on the bottom were the critical safety parameter displays. They were all perfect. Subcooling margin fine. Zone controllers fine. Radiation levels fine even with the leak. One hundred percent power. Safety parameters all exactly where they should be. Nothing wrong except a few field operators and maintainers getting excited about sprinkles inside containment. It would take more than that to make me shutdown.

I could see Laura talking to Jim Higgins. I could have made her sit at the technical advisor's station since she was doing a lot more than giving advice. More like organizing a revolt. But I figured Ned would see that Laura and I both had some points in our favor. And I knew that he was still proud of the production record he'd set at Bradley station in eighty-six. Ned didn't like to shut reactors down any more than I did, maybe even less. I looked around the control room and counted four people not part of my official control room complement. The word was out that we were in trouble, and people were coming in to watch. There was nothing I could do to shut off the argument about whether we should shut down. I just had to hope that they found a way to bypass the leaks. I returned to the refuge of my office and the calming task of checking work plans.

At 3:30 am I started searching the station procedures database for everything regarding unknown leaks and requirements to shut-down. There was a time limit involved. You couldn't run for more than two hours with a reactor coolant leak greater than four gallons a minute. I had a strong case that we hadn't got to four a minute, so I hadn't chewed up any time yet. I leaned back, smiled in relief, and looked out at the control room. My smile disappeared because Laura had her head down and was coming with her longest, lankiest strides toward my office.

"We're losing four and a half gallons a minute," she said from the doorway. She didn't step inside.

"How did you measure it," I asked.

"Storage tank level. Corrected for that damn makeup water we're pumping in"

"What's the time?" I asked.

"Three-forty-three," she said. "Plenty of time to have it down to zero power hot for the day crew"

"We've got two hours before we have to shutdown," I said. "I want the field reports." I stepped to the door and she stepped back to give me room to pass. I called out, "Ned, come give me the bad news"

Ned turned and came toward me with the operator's walk—unhurried. He came right up to me and smiled through his grey mustache. "Seems we're in a bit of a pickle, Henry"

"Any way to get the leak down?"

"Omer and George think most of it's coming from one of the purification control valves, CV-122. Trouble is, as you might suspect, it's pretty hot down there with the gammas coming off the purification columns and the other assorted crud that winds up in purification piping. I've got a crew down there now thinking about how to set up shielding to go in and repack the valve"

"Can't we shut down that line and use CV-124?"

"Sure, but then we'd have to violate the station instruction on staying in the high purification regime"

"That's not a safety instruction," I said. "We can violate it if safety's involved, and I'd say putting this machine through a shutdown transient is a safety concern, wouldn't you Ned?"

He shook his head and said, "You get no argument from me there, Henry. All that thermal stress and general confusion. Best to always take things real slow. Of course running with a four gallon leak is a safety concern, too"

So there it was, two sides to the question, and I could make the decision. "Bypass CV-122, Ned. Open CV-124 to maximum on manual, and get them working on getting CV-122 back into service ASAP. And get me a new reading on the leak rate"

"Right-oh," said Ned and half-turned. He faced me again with a twinkle in his eye and said, "You'd best watch yourself real close, Henry. They'll be going over this one with a fine-toothed comb"

"Nothing new," I said. "I've never got stung too bad before"

"What about the tritium incident in recirculation"

"Hey, that wasn't me, I just happened to be there," I said.

"People think it was a strange thing to happen, you being there. You weren't part of the job at all"

"Like I keep saying, I had a message on my screen telling me to go to recirculation. I wasn't just touring exotic plant areas"

"Okay, Henry. But people wonder who would send you such a screwy instruction," Ned said and then turned and walked toward the charging/purification panel with the same, near-obligatory, unhurried walk. He called panel operator Higgins over as he walked.

Ned's words put a new light on some of the looks I'd been getting. Yes, people would wonder why I had been in the recirc room. And my story about the message on my screen from the production manager was starting to seem strange even to me. It didn't show up in Dennis Banks' message log. It didn't show up in mine, but I'd disabled receipts to save disk space. It was an unlikely story, and yet I had read that message. I had read the message and dutifully donned a hardhat and walked the considerable distance to recirculation. But the only thing that made it real was my memory.

I sat at my desk and started filling in the paperwork for rush work. My heart wasn't in it. I would have rather been wrestling with that valve or drumming heavy water or anything real and not administrative. But there it was. To do the real job you had to have the paperwork, and the paperwork passed through me.

Ned came into my office. "Rad control and the mechanics are in place to go in. Jim isolated the line five minutes ago. Can't see any change in the leak yet"

"It's such a little leak it would be hard to see the change in tank level, especially with us pumping in makeup," I said.

Ned said, "Well, we'll have to stop the make-up soon. We're near the high-level mark in storage now. We might get a better measure then"

"Okay, stop the make-up and try to get a reading. And the paperwork for the valve re-pack is ready. I want the whole team up here in my office for the job briefing now"

"Right-oh," said Ned, and he wasn't so slow in leaving my office, and his head was shifting fast as he scanned the panels.

I checked the control room clock. Four-ten. It was a bad sign I hadn't heard more from Ned. I hadn't been sleeping enough, and I kept thinking back to my exchange with Judy Peterson about Nam and then what Ned said people were thinking about the tritium incident. Christ, I knew there had been a message on my screen. Addressed to me so I had to have my password to read it. It had been there and that was why I had gone to recirculation. But at four-ten in the morning it's hard to believe that anything is for sure, especially when all the operators know we're losing water fast enough to force a shutdown.

The valve re-pack crew came into the control room at four-fourteen. Their eyes had a late-at-night, early-in-the-morning wild look, but they were cheerful and exuded the confidence of a crew that works together well and knows they can fix whatever's broken. They were all in brown anti-Cs, a grimy, earthy contrast to the control room operators in their street clothes. Anti-Cs for anti-contamination, but they looked like clothes you'd see on an auto mechanic. Anti-Cs, but then they were allowed to be more contaminated and still be used than anything except the plastic suits. The laundry took care of most of the contamination on the anti-Cs, but it left some of the fixed stuff, the stuff that stays stuck to something and doesn't spread all over the station and cause us problems. The fixed stuff was almost a friendly reminder that we were special, we worked with radiation.

The crew looked good, like they were ready to do the job, and do it fast. That was always the way to do jobs in purification. The contaminated heavy water came in contaminated and went out clean, at least if you ignored the tritium. But that meant the contamination stayed in purification, in the filters and resin columns and screens. It plated out on the pipes and valves, and now there was a purification leak which meant lots of tritium in the air. But this crew looked like they would do the job right, and then I might not have to shut down. I prayed Ned would tell me the leak was under four. Then we could fix the valve fast and bring the purification back into the high regime on the day shift.

I went up to the re-pack crew and asked, "Where's your rad control tech?"

"Oh, he's right behind us, he just stopped for ear protection," said a kid who looked too young to work at Kankakee. "There he is."

I turned to the door and was surprised to see Trung and a younger rad control tech, Marty O'leary, come through it. I hadn't seen Trung since the overexposures in the recirc room. Somehow, by staying in the doorway and by going to check another work group during the time the mechanics were in the recirc room, Trung had managed to not be burned out. He had taken more dose than I had, but not anywhere near what the three mechanics had absorbed.

"Trung, you're not planning to go into purification after all that dose you took in the recirc room?" I asked.

"No, Marty's going in. I'm just making the plan." Trung was frowning, he didn't look at me, and his movements were stiff and sharp. He started filling in the protection measures and exposure prevention boxes on my forms while simultaneously briefing the crew on how they would do the work. Right away I stopped him: "You're going in without plastics?"

Trung stopped his writing, at first avoided my eyes, but then raised them slowly to meet mine full force. "Yes, for the first part of the job the mechanics will go in with just respirators. They will have to do some rough work at first, so we may dislodge some loose contamination. That's why we're using the respirators. But plastics would slow us down too much on the work we have to do in there. So we're going to take a higher dose but just stay in there a short time. Once the grunt and hack work is over, we're going to all back out, clean ourselves up, and go back in wearing full plastics, and I'm going to check everyone close to make sure the plastics are on right. No use to go to all that trouble if we're going to make them useless by not wearing them right. No holes, everything tight, and plenty of air"

"What's the dose rate in there?" I asked.

Trung continued meeting my eyes with a flat glare. "Bad, but not that bad. Just under a hundred millirem an hour. We've jacked up the ventilation to max. It might be less now"

"And how long are you going to stay in there with just a respirator"

Trung spoke calmly but with tense conviction: "The guys say they can have the valve open in half an hour. Let's figure an hour. So we have at worst two men each getting a hundred millirem of tritium. There are gammas in there too. We're going to try to shield, but the plastics won't help against them. So if we can do the job faster without plastics, then that's the way to go"

Trung's argument was flawless. Using less protection in the interests of getting the job done faster was good radiation protection practice. Just like keeping a reactor at steady power was less risky than shutting it down. It was all explained in books, but someone always complained whenever you started to put the philosophy into practice. But not this crew. They knew Trung knew his stuff and wouldn't let them catch more dose than absolutely necessary. And at five in the morning people started to think less about radiation than just getting the job done and going home.

But I was bothered by the way Trung was acting. I went up to him and said, "Trung, you seem bothered by something. Is something wrong?"

The whole control room could hear Trung's reply: "Yes, Henry, something is wrong. I'm wondering how you knew to adjust the pocket tritium detector so it would work on just the level that happened to be in the recirc room. I know what a piece of shit that detector is. No way it would work unless you had adjusted it beforehand."

My heart began to race as I remembered the stares of the Vietnamese who saw me as the enemy. I felt almost as if in combat, but I managed to say evenly, "Trung, I swear I didn't touch the detector. I just picked it up to take to rad control for tests. Just like I was ordered."

"A funny order Dennis Banks says he never gave!"

"Yes, a funny order. But that's the way it happened. And I was in there with you. I took dose too. Why would I have done that if I knew what was in the room?"

"It makes a good alibi for you to take a little dose. You take a little dose while the rest of us take a lot. Then everyone thinks it was an accident for you like for the rest of us. But that detector working good like it did couldn't be an accident. Someone had to have rigged it."

"Just like someone had to have put the tritium there, Trung," I said. "But it wasn't me."

Trung looked at me a full five seconds without saying anything. Then he said, "Okay, Henry, maybe I will believe you—for now. So here's the work plan and you be sure we don't take any more dose than we have to."

The paperwork was in order. I had seen the work briefing and it was by-the-book. The time was four-thirty-five. "Okay, guys," I said. "We've still got a chance to keep from having to shut this baby down. Get out there to the entry door, but don't go in till I give the word. All bets are off if the leak is still bigger than four because there's only eight minutes before we have to shut it down. If we shutdown we can take our time on the valve re-pack, let things cool off awhile down there, blow out the tritium and mop up the water. But if it's under four, I want you in there, and I want you to get that line back in service just as fast as you can"

Trung pulled himself erect, almost as if at attention. He pivoted and walked away quickly with long strides. The rest of the crew filed out slowly. It was just another job to them. That's what it should have been to me, too, but somehow I'd been caught up in wanting to keep the reactor at full blast. It had become something personal with me, something I wanted to show I could do. I forced myself to sit down at my desk and stare at the papers. But I only could stand it for two minutes. I tried to keep my movements slow, but not very successfully, and I went straight up to Ned Banthien and said, "You got a number on that leak, Ned?"

Ned looked at me and smiled: "Well, we need to keep watching it. You know how tricky it is judging from storage tank level, but it seems to be about three point five, maybe a little less"

"That's great, Ned. Pipe the word to Trung's crew to go on in and start the valve work"

"Right-oh," Ned said and he was unhurried as he strolled to the transmitter. It was a good sign that Ned was moving slowly. It was more than I could do.

"That leak goes up, even a little bit I want to know about it," I said and Ned nodded. Then he caught himself and said, "Yes, I'll let you know right away." Then he smiled and said, "Almost forgot the communication protocols in all this excitement"

Nods are frowned on in the control room, and Ned had caught himself relaxing into non-nuclear communications. But he had caught himself, which is better than I do a lot of times. We've all been taught to say what we're going to do and to say it loud and clearly. That can work well in real life too, but sometimes it may make you look a trifle too earnest, perhaps a little slow, and maybe too boring for the fun crowd.

I was tired, but happy. My shift was almost over, but I was going to have a reactor at full power for the shift turnover. And although the next shift would likely be struggling to track down and fix or bypass all the leaks, the chances were that they'd be able to keep the reactor running while they did it, and Kankakee would continue to send its six hundred megawatts out into the Chicago grid. And with the Dresden and Byron stations shut down, the Chicago grid was happy for the power.

I thought how good my bed was going to look when I got back to the house. My troubles with Sheri didn't even seem so important compared with the pleasure I would get from just flopping down to sleep. I hadn't felt that way for quite awhile, but when you have worries you have a tendency to keep driving and abusing yourself hard until finally exhaustion gives you no desire except to sleep.

I was preparing the shift turnover papers when it started. I glanced at my watch—five twenty-five, not that much time before my shift would be over. But I felt it, something was happening to radiation levels in the primary reactor cooling system. I felt it in the code being tapped out on the back of my hand and wrist by the tactile interface.

I glanced out into the control room. No one looked worried. Laura was smiling contentedly behind her display terminal. Ned was chatting unconcernedly to Jim Higgins. I looked at the panels and there was no reason for them to be concerned. No annunciator panels had lit, and the MIMIC hadn't picked up anything yet.

Probably if you looked close at a strip-chart recorder you could see what I was feeling. The tactile code for primary circuit radiation kept up. It wouldn't keep up for long before all hell broke lose in the control room.

I shouted to Ned and Jim from the door. "I think we've got radiation problems in RCS. Check out all the monitors. Check whether it's failed fuel"

Ned called back, "The valve repair crew is in there at valve C-122. Should I pull them out?"

"No, check it out first. I got it from the tactile interface. Maybe it's gone haywire or needs a new battery or something." As I returned to my desk I hoped desperately that that was it, that the interface was playing tricks on me.

But calling up even the first radiation monitoring page on my screen showed it wasn't the interface that was screwy. I keep a close tab on radiation levels in primary—it's gotten to be a habit with me—and I could see at a glance that something had changed, and it wasn't a change I liked. One of the channels was close to alarm levels and the whole circuit was already higher. I wondered if the radiation technicians with the valve repair crew had picked it up yet.

I went out to Ned in front of the reactor cooling panel. "You see it?" I asked.

Ned shook his head. "Doesn't look very comforting. Maybe we can get CV-122 back before it gets too bad. With full purification we can keep going with failed fuel and let the day shift call in the experts to decide what to do about it"

"We won't need the experts, Ned," I said. "Get the crew out of purification. And start us on a slow and gentle power runback. Real slow. We'll shut it down, but nice and gentle"

"How slow?" Ned asked.

"Real slow. How about half a percent a minute?"

"That'll only put us at ninety percent for the shift changeover," Ned said.

"Then we'll have to stay over until the day crew is comfortable with things. Maybe they'll see something I don't and want to bring it back up again. That is unless things get worse and we have to trip or shut it down fast"

"Right-oh," Ned said. "Sorry it didn't work out Henry"

"I'm sorry, too. I was starting to feel good about keeping the plant up. First thing I've done right in quite a while"

"Don't start feeling down on yourself, Henry. You know your machine and you don't always play it by the book. Half the shifties I know would have shut down right away just because they'd be afraid of being charged and fined for operating with the leak. And that would be crazy because the safest thing was to do exactly what we did"

"Yeah, we did everything right but it didn't get us anywhere, did it?" I said. That was the story of my life, doing everything right and not getting much to show for it. I wondered if that showed up on the personality test Judy Peterson had given me.

And then from the general rule that nothing in real life is clear, Laura was with me saying, "Henry, I see we've got some contamination in primary, but it's not that bad. Maybe it's just a crud burst. I think we can stay with this thing and keep the reactor up"

"Well, I've already pulled the valve team out"

"You can send them back in, Ned told them to stand-by," she said quickly and intently.

"The paperwork will have to be re-done. The work protection plan was based on one hundred millirem per hour gamma in there. I'll bet it's already doubled and it'll probably go higher"

Laura looked like she could have stamped her foot if she wasn't in the control room. Finally she sighed and said, "You're right of course, that's the way to do it by the book. But we could have fudged things a little there. You pulled them out so quick. They'll probably have to do the job anyway and then the fields will be higher"

"Not if we shutdown and give purification some time to cool-down. And that's my guess about what will happen. We're going to zero percent power hot," I said, and I wondered why I felt so happy saying it.

Laura said, "It was your call. Maybe if we'd shutdown sooner the fuel wouldn't have failed"

"Then it would have failed when we tried to bring power back up. Or it would have failed a week later. Those things don't disappear. They're going to get you sooner or later"

Laura shrugged and left. I was feeling groggy and light-headed from the night shift and I called after her, "Hey Laura, you think you and I will ever agree on anything?"

She turned, smiled, and kept on walking, "They say anything's possible if you wait long enough"

I said, "Well, I'm good at waiting"

"I'm not," she said and walked out my door and back behind the control consoles to the technical advisor's desk. I wanted to look at her longer but thought better of it.

I was surprised when my replacement, Maarten Vandervelen, walked through the control room doors at five-forty-five. I was at my desk and was pleased that the paperwork was in order. I'd been keeping up with it as we went along through the incredible night, and I could foresee that it wouldn't take more than fifteen minutes to turn the plant over to him. My screen showed reactor power at ninety-seven percent. Like I'd told Laura, if the day shift could figure some way to avoid it, they'd have their chance to bring the unit back up. And they'd probably get a medal for keeping the megawatts flowing.

Maarten was a big man, broad-shouldered and fair haired, square in the shoulders and square in the head. He had an engaging grin, and I figured he could get by on charm most anywhere. But he'd needed more than charm to hold the job he held now, and he was one of the best. Most people liked working on Maarten's shift; there was something about his solid stance and go-slow approach that inspired confidence.

"So they tell me you're taking the power the wrong way," said Maarten, the big grin showing not the slightest trace of worry or pressure.

"I tried to keep it up, Maarten. We had a RCS leak over four, but the guys managed to get it back to about three and a half so we didn't have to take it down because of the leak. And I had a crew out there repacking valve CV-122 which was the one they'd bypassed to get the leak rate down. We figured we could get high-purification flow back in plenty of time. But then we got fuel failure in channel thirty-six and I ordered the valve crew out of there rather than take the extra dose. None of the work protection plans had considered what to do if there was failed fuel or if the gamma dose went up. So I guess that's going to be one of your first chores, Maarten, figuring out how to get that valve work done"

Maarten asked, "How fast you bringing it down?"

"Half a percent a minute," I said.

"That seems a mite slow to me, Henry. I think I'll bring that up to three-quarters a minute"

"That might be best," I said. "I didn't want to close out your options. You might have thought you could keep the unit up"

"Multiple leaks pressing the limit and now failed fuel. No way, young man. This unit is going down to get all fixed up. When things get too bad it's no use trying to just throw on patch upon patch until the whole crazy pile of patches breaks down, and then you've got real problems" He looked down, taking his eyes away from mine, pawed the floor in front of him with the toe of his safety shoe, and then raised his head to look me full in the face: "Speaking of problems, Henry, the reason I'm in a little early is that the FBI is out here bright and bushy-tailed wanting to talk to you as soon as you get off shift. My favorite human factors guru, Blair McKenna, is with them"

Even though facing another grilling on the recirculation valve room tritium incident was the last thing I wanted to do, since what I really craved was sleep, and even though I should have cursed the FBI and Human Factors clear to hell, I still had to smile remembering the little love lost between Maarten and Blair McKenna ever since the root cause analysis report on a loss of backup heat sink incident we'd had two years ago. Maarten had led the investigation, but Blair had done a major rewrite on it, and it was Blair's version that had gone to the Nuclear Regulatory Commission as the mandatory Licensing Event Report. Blair was as soft, unctuous, and conniving as Maarten was big, broad, and straightforward.

I spoke with my duty voice, "I guess we'd better go through the paperwork for the turnover. I'll try to give you the quick tour, but since we have been having rather a lot of activity this fine summer night, I'd better not give you too short a briefing"

Maarten nodded, so I took him through the events of the entire night, the argument over whether to shut down earlier when everyone had been forced to wear plastics to go into elevation eighty-seven point five, and then how the leak had gone back under three point five after CV-122 had been bypassed. How we'd tried to fix it quick so we could have high purification back. And how everything had seemed like it would work, but then the failed fuel had showed up and that would change all the radiation exposure calculations for the men trying to fix the valve in purification. Maarten just nodded from time to time as I took him through it. Nothing ever happens exactly the same way twice in nuclear, but Maarten had worked enough shifts in different kinds of plants—PWRs, BWRs, and now this crazy Kankakee cross between a Candu and a high flux weapons production reactor—that this new situation fit comfortably into his memory of various small leaks early in the morning at the other stations. And since he intended to bring the unit down, that simplified his choices enormously. He could patch the unit up by the book, send out crews to find every last leak, and let the radiation die down some in purification before sending in the crew to do the valve repair.

Maarten signed the turnover sheet and Kankakee was his. I went into the control room, shook hands with Ned and Laura and told the entire control room crew that we'd done a good job that night, even though we hadn't been able to keep the unit up. Then I said goodbye, saying I'd been called away for a special mission, and when they tried to find out what it was, I wouldn't tell them. But the smiles weren't there like they usually were. Jim Higgins' look was almost a glare, and I knew that I wasn't trusted in the control room anymore. The Kankakee crew wasn't any more afraid of radiation than any other nuclear crew, but they only wanted to take what came with the job. They didn't want anyone playing games or settling grudges by giving them more.

Strangely, I didn't sense any additional hostility from Laura; it was just our old rivalry, the jockeying for better position in the hierarchy. And I was glad that Maarten and Ned were treating me as they'd always done, as an essential member of the reactor crew, no better and no worse than anyone else. Yet there had been sabotage; everyone knew it as there was no other explanation. There had been sabotage, and I had been there for a reason which I could not prove. Maarten and Ned were old-timers. They would know enough to hide their suspicions. And they had to be suspicious because I would have been if I were in their place.

I shivered from fatigue as I walked to the showers. I didn't have to take one since I'd only been in the control room and other "clean" areas. But I did have to give a urine sample and that was done in the "clean" side of the radiation clothing change room. I would have to give a urine sample every day until the health physics people were convinced that the tritium had been flushed from my system.

Any kind of liquid helped flush the tritium out, and I looked forward to the beer flush I'd give it after I'd talked to the FBI.

I walked through the swinging door into the "clean" side of the men's shower room. Three mechanical maintainers from the valve repack crew were crowded around George Barrett. I could hear "tritium maniac" ring out loud, but then I saw George give the men a caution signal by turning up the side of his mouth, pulling his head back, and then tilting it forward in my direction. The men still had their towels and were just starting to put on their street clothes. It was exuberant locker-room talk, but it turned into silence when the men knew I was there. I just nodded to them and walked into the big restroom where a box of urine sample vials was kept at the end of the bank of sinks. I felt tense, so I knew the only way I'd be able to pee would be to go into one of the stalls. I picked the third from the last one and entered.

I felt exhausted and it was awkward holding the sample vial in between my legs. I looked up at the usually blank door and read "Don't trust Henry." Someone had carved it in with a knife, so even our zealous janitor staff which usually obliterates any graffiti immediately would have to spend some time and money to remove the traces of this anonymous warning about my character.

As I placed my warm vial in a circular slot in the sample box, I knew that the friendly men in the change room, men with whom I'd worked for nearly three years—I knew that these men thought I was capable of exposing them to a radiation overdose. And these were men who I'd ordered out of the purification room rather than expose them to the rising radiation from the failed fuel. And Laura Brault, after her speeches about safety, had wanted to keep the reactor up and keep them in the purification room.

Well, I'd known for a long time that the world is not fair, not fair at all.

6

I made my way back to the Human Factors area and I was disappointed when I saw Judy Peterson's desk was empty, although I knew she wouldn't be there since human factors specialists don't do shift work. It had been unusual for her to have been there the previous night to give me that screwy test. Behind her desk and to the right was the HF supervisor Blair McKenna's office. The slip Maarten had given me said that the FBI wanted to talk to me there.

Blair's door was open, and I could see it was the same crew who'd interviewed me in the initial investigation: Howard Crowder, the short, square, blond bulldog of a FBI man and Sheila Rowe from the NRC's Enforcement division. Crowder announced that this time Blair, who had a nice smile on his soft smooth face, was going to sit in on the interview.

I recognized the papers in Blair McKenna's hand. It was the output from the test Judy Peterson had given me nine hours earlier. It seemed a long time ago in a different world, and I wondered that anyone could take it seriously. All I took seriously at that moment was the chance to get some sleep.

I knew I was in trouble so I acted confident, "Gee Blair, I'm spending more time here than I am over at the plant where I think they still need operators."

Blair just said, "We're sorry for the inconvenience, but you know this is important. You remember Mr. Crowder of the FBI. He wants to ask you some more questions."

I nodded at Crowder and took the one seat on the other side of the table from the three others. Then I said, "You know, I just came off shift and it was one of the toughest ones I remember. We had a leak and then some guys got some dose from a fuel failure. And I had to take one of your human factors tests before going on shift. They may say you're applying duress to me by not letting me sleep."

Crowder said, "Okay, we'll keep that in mind and we won't be so formal this time." He looked down and then snapped back up, a stern look in his eyes, "Mr. McClure, we understand that you served in Vietnam."

I nodded. He already knew that.

"What did you do after your discharge?"

I wanted to get to the point: "As you can see from my personnel record, I went back to school at the University of Wisconsin."

"I see," said Crowder. "Did you draw the GI bill?"

"Of course," I said.

"That's really a good deal, getting paid to go to school. That wasn't bad, was it?"

"No, no. It was fine. Anything that gives me money I like."

"Were you involved with any anti-nuclear groups when you were at Wisconsin?" he asked.

Crowder was close, but he was still a little off target. "No, I suppose I had some questions about nuclear power then, but I was never in a group or anything."

Crowder was dramatic about drawing a piece of paper out of his briefcase and spreading it before him. There was a picture stapled to the bottom. "And I suppose you never participated in a May Day march?"

There was no use denying it. I always knew there had to be a file on it somewhere. "As you probably already know, Mr. Crowder, I actually helped organize a May Day march. Matter of fact something happened to me before the march which was one of my defining moments, one of those flashes that change your life."

"Really," said Crowder. "Well, we can come back to that later." He pulled a big glossy black and white photograph out of his briefcase and put it before me. "Can you tell me who this is?"

I had seen the photo before. It had appeared in the street papers "Free for All" and "Takeover" in Madison. There were lots of people I knew in the photo. Some of the most important people in my life were there. But it wasn't them that Crowder was pointing to. Crowder had tapped his index figure on the tall, gloriously handsome figure standing right beside me. I made a point of looking Crowder in the eyes and said, "Yes, I know him. His name is Ken Seagraves. He was in the history department."

"That's the lawyer Ken Seagraves who's always in the news with the Chicago Energy Alliance, isn't it?" asked Crowder.

"Yes, Ken has apparently stayed radical through all these years," I said.

Sheila Rowe entered in, "And you, Mr. McClure, have you stayed radical through all these years?"

"No," I said. "I have enough trouble just making it through each day."

"But you were a leader, you were very committed," she said.

"Commitments change. Commitments disappear. I can't imagine doing the kinds of things I used to do," I said.

"When is the last time you met Mr. Seagraves?" asked Crowder.

"Now this is a coincidence. It seems like a long time ago now, but I happen to have seen Ken Seagraves standing in the picket line when I came in for this shift about fourteen hours ago. Other than that, I haven't seen Ken Seagraves since I left university," I said.

Crowder made me say that I hadn't been in contact with Ken Seagraves a few times more. Seagraves was in the news, and Kankakee station was in the center of that news with headlines about an untested defense production reactor and the DOE's poor record in avoiding contamination at its sites. Seagraves always had been good at getting in the news. I kept saying that I hadn't seen Seagraves and I hadn't known him that well even back in Madison. But I kept staring at Crowder's photo. Corinne was appropriately at the left, her face uplifted and laughing. The Chairman, Ransom Rulko, was beside her. Sheri was beside the Chairman, her angular body held erect and her eyes fixed sharply askance. Directly behind me, toward the center, was Jim Haskel. He had a red beard even then, but no one seemed to have noticed that there was another Kankakee worker besides me in the photo. And if they didn't notice it, I didn't see any reason why I should either.

"At the last interview you said you weren't anti-nuclear," said Crowder.

"I'm not."

"So why are you in this anti-nuclear demonstration with Seagraves?"

"It wasn't an anti-nuclear demonstration," I said.

"There were anti-nuclear groups in it, weren't there?" asked Ms. Rowe, holding up a sheet of paper as she said it.

I didn't like the way things were going at all. "I really don't remember. It was a long time ago. There probably were some anti-nuclear people in the coalition. We had all sorts of groups in that parade. Sure, the American sixties left had an anti-nuclear flavor to it, and what's left of it still does. I don't. Ken Seagraves and I disagreed about a lot back then, and we probably disagree about even more now. I make my living in nuclear, and I don't feel guilty about it."

"Are you in communication with the Chicago Energy Coalition?" asked Ms.Rowe.

"No. I haven't said or written a word to them."

Then they asked me about other organizations and there were a lot of them. They got into politics so I had to deny being a Socialist Worker or an International Socialist. Then I denied belonging to a variety of other brigades and factions.

"I don't belong to any political party of any kind, if that will shorten things," I finally said. "I never have."

"Well this incident could be the work of a disgruntled individual," said Ms.Rowe.

"Probably," I said.

"Why do you think that?" asked Crowder.

I started to realize how little I had actually thought about the incident. My personal problems were so intense that I hadn't really thought much at all about how tritiated organic compounds had made their way into the recirculation valve room. "Organizations can't just walk into a nuclear plant and plant radioisotopes. Only a person with a plant access badge could have planted the tritium."

"And what would have made them do that? It has to be someone who's anti-nuclear, doesn't it?" asked Crowder impatiently.

"I'm sorry; I haven't really thought much about why someone would do that. It could be anti-nuclear, overexpose some workers and get a big press play about tritium and about how it's just the Kankakee station which has so much tritium in it. Maybe someone thinks tritium's especially bad."

"It is especially bad, isn't it, especially the tritiated organics?" asked Ms. Rowe.

"Maybe. They say it stays in your system longer. The stuff we took in is real exotic. The health physicists are having a picnic studying us and plotting out how long it takes the tritium to clear our systems."

"It would have to be someone who knows a lot about radiation to plant something like that, wouldn't it?" asked Crowder.

I didn't much like Crowder, but he had a point. "You don't get tritiated organics at the corner store. No, someone would have to know a lot to purposely use tritiated organics. Of course, someone might have just taken something at random."

"You know a lot about radioisotopes don't you?" asked Crowder.

"I know something, of course. I'm not a health physicist. It's not my specialty."

"When we interviewed Pete Kerwin, he said you have a very extensive knowledge of radiation effects, radioisotopes and all that. He went on and on about how you know so much more than the usual reactor operator," said Crowder.

"I suppose I do. I studied some of it formally in college, and I try to keep up on what's significant in my working life."

"Haven't you participated in some of the experiments at Kensington labs as an advisor to the researchers?" asked Crowder, warming to the ease of putting me in a corner.

"Yes, I have. Experiments on plutonium use, they wanted me for that. And other experiments with tritium for the fusion reactor project. I volunteered for those. Canadians have a lot of experience with tritium, and I started out wanting to work with fusion."

"In other words, you're quite an expert in plutonium and tritium and probably a lot of other radioisotopes, aren't you?" Crowder concluded his case.

"It would be ridiculous for me to try to say no," I said. "But it's not my specialty."

"What do you know about tritiated organics?" asked Ms. Rowe.

"Just that they don't leave the body as fast as the normal tritium, so if there were a lot of tritiated organics formed, they might have to lower the allowed emission limits," I said.

"Did you ever work with tritiated organics at the Kensington labs?" asked Ms. Rowe.

"No."

"Mr. Kerwin said samples of tritiated organics were stored in the labs where you worked at Kensington," said Crowder.

"He should know. I didn't make it my business to check out what was in all the cabinets," I said.

"Did you move to Canada because you didn't like the United States?" asked Crowder.

"No, it was a purely personal matter. My wife had some good opportunities to pursue human factors research in Toronto. I'm glad to be back in the States."

"You didn't seem to be glad when this picture was taken." Crowder's thumb came down sharply on my face in the photo.

"That was a long time ago. But, this patriotism thing you're on is bullshit. Did you serve in Vietnam Crowder?"

"No, but I'll ask the questions."

"Well I did, so I have every right to go to any damn demonstration for any damn reason that I damn well feel like." And after I said it I could feel my pulse, and I knew that the shift had been too long, that I'd gone too long without sleep, and that this interview could be dangerous indeed for me.

"You had psychological problems in Vietnam, didn't you?" asked Ms. Rowe.

I began to wonder why it was always women talking about my mental problems. "Yes, I cracked up. You've read my record and I suppose that's why Judy Peterson gave me that stupid test before I went on this god-awful shift."

"Do you and your wife know Pete Kerwin well?" asked Ms. Rowe.

"Yes, I've probably known Pete as long as anyone at Kankakee. We knew him in Canada and I worked with him when he joined WorldNet Simulations. My wife, Sheri, probably knows him better than I do because she's been working with him on some of his latest projects."

"Kerwin was the one who invented the miniature tritium detector you were wearing, the one that let you give the alarm when no one else knew anything was wrong, wasn't he?" asked Crowder.

"Well, I think he had a lot of help from Trung, one of his associates here. Trung did most of the electronics, but Trung has given up on the detector. So it's just Pete who's promoting and trying to sell it," I said.

"Mr. Trung was the health physics technician assigned to the recirculation valve room work, wasn't he?" asked Crowder.

"Yes."

"And Trung helped develop the tritium detector you were using?"

"Yes."

"You've known Trung a long time, haven't you?"

"Yes. He's one of the smartest engineers I've ever met."

"Do you confide in Trung?"

"No. He's a good friend. A great guy. But no, I don't confide in him."

"And how about Pete Kerwin, the man Trung worked for. Do you confide in Mr. Kerwin?" asked Ms. Rowe.

"Well, Pete and I get along well. I like his sense of humor. But I don't think I've done much confiding in anyone lately. I've not had any great need to confide," I said, and then I realized I was a liar. I had a very great reason to confide but just hadn't done it.

"So would you say Mr. Kerwin is one of your best friends?" asked Ms. Rowe.

"Well, that may be going a little far. We've worked together, you see, and that may have introduced some little tensions between us."

"Why is that?" asked Ms. Rowe.

"Oh, when we met at WorldNet Simulations we were both doing thermalhydraulic modeling, and there was some rivalry between us. And I've been on the other side of some other little disputes he's been involved in since," I said, and I could have said a lot more about the feelings I had for Pete Kerwin, but those feelings are hard to put into words, especially in an FBI interview. I felt so tired, and I started to feel a tingling in the nerves of my fingers and hands. I said, "Look, I think I've been quite cooperative, and I would be happy to answer some more of your questions which make me look so good, but I've really come off a very tough shift, and I'm starting to feel very strange and exhausted. Couldn't we do this later?"

Crowder was a changed man, smiling, almost chivalrous. "Of course, Mr. McClure, we realize we're giving you a grilling under very trying circumstances. We've covered most of the areas we wanted to haven't we, Ms. Rowe?"

Ms. Rowe said, "Well, there were some technical questions I wanted to ask to verify exactly what happened the night of the tritium contamination, but I can easily put those off to a more convenient time."

"So, Mr. McClure, thank you for your cooperation. And we will be wanting to talk to you again, but please, right now, why don't you go home and get some rest."

I fought down the urge I had to shake their hands, and finally just nodded "Okay" and walked around the table to the door.

I pulled myself erect and squared my shoulders as I walked out of Blair's office. I had nothing to be ashamed of; in fact I knew I had handled the shift damn well, even though it hadn't turned out the way I wanted. It could have turned out right; it should have turned out right; it was only luck and the failed fuel which would make people second-guess my decisions. Luck and the FBI and the general suspicion about me.

But people have to fight against bad luck, and I felt I was ready to fight, even though I was tired as hell, or maybe because I was so tired. And my day was already looking up. Judy Peterson was back, picking up a stack of binders from her desk and moving them to the bookshelves. She looked fresh and clean, slim and rested. Seeing her made me happy, but then I thought about Sheri, and I thought about how scared I was that the FBI would ask me about my family life again as they had the first time. And I thought about personnel reliability procedure CNK-5 requiring the reporting of family problems, so that the psychological good health of operating crews could be assured. And I knew I had to report my problem; I should have reported it before, especially with all the controversy about the tritium contamination. But I didn't want to have to report it to Judy, even though I knew I had to.

"Anything more you folks will be wanting me for this shift, Judy?" I said.

"Oh Henry, you look like you've just come out of a prisoner of war camp."

"Yeah, and I don't think they've been playing it too strict with the Geneva conventions, neither," I said and hung my head before choking out the next words. "Actually the shift work is the least of my problems. Could you give me one of the forms for reporting personal problems—you know the ones, the procedure CNK-5 forms."

I could see her straighten and then stifle any reaction. I suppose it's part of the professionalism of personnel sections. "Certainly Henry, it's fairly self-explanatory, but feel free to call me if you have any questions about the form."

"Thanks, I'm real tired now, but I'll try to get this in to you as soon as I can."

Judy's eyes were fairly brimming with sympathy as she said, "You know, Henry, I had to give you that test last night. It's part of my job. I just want you to know that I hope everything turns out all right for you."

"Thanks a lot Judy," I said. And then I remembered that Sheri was going ahead with our barbecue. As far as I could tell Sheri hadn't altered her social whirl a bit during our marriage breakdown. Sheri usually invited Judy because they shared the same profession. And I realized I would like it if Judy was at the party, so I said, "Will you be coming to our barbecue?"

"Oh sure. I wouldn't miss one of your parties. I suppose it must be hard for you giving a party when you're having problems. And I really respect you, Henry, for coming forward and asking for the CNK-5."

I was going soft fast, and I might have started crying, she was so beautiful, so I reverted to standard operator relations, "Sure, I know, everyone really respects the shift crews. Everyone's behind us one-hundred-percent." And I walked off with the operator walk, a mannerism, a swagger of "I don't care." And as I walked I felt relieved that I'd finally worked up the courage to take the first step toward reporting the problem between Sheri and me. It was something that had to be done if I wanted to keep my job, and I wanted to keep it. But at the same time I felt sad because reporting the problem was one more step towards acknowledging the problem's reality. It was one more step taking me away from Sheri.

I knew I wanted to write a special report on the events of last night's shift. It didn't matter whether I wanted to or not, I knew I would be asked to do it, so I walked up the stairs towards the cabinets in the tech section where the forms were kept. And as I reached the landing before the paired green-framed glass doors, I realized I was heading toward someone else I had to see. Someone who could help me, I hoped. Lucy Watkins, the network administrator.

I went through the doors and turned left going past nuclear systems engineers' work cubicles and then veered right down a walled corridor which entered into a big bright room, smack in the middle of which was Lucy Watkins' desk like a sentry post guarding the new power, information.

There are some computer people who have neat desks, who sit erect, who wear neat clothes and look sharp like a brand-new computer. And then there are people like me with chaotic desks, who slump till their heads approach keyboard level, and look like they're on the verge of breaking out screaming under the myriads of details needed to keep the system running.

Lucy Watkins was of my ilk, although she wasn't slumping backwards like I did, but rather forward so she was looking down at the keyboard and then rolling her eyes up to glimpse the monitor. With her years spent on the network, her curly muddy blonde hair had become more and more unruly, and it sprayed out in wild abandon. She was tall and big-boned and her face was round with pudgy cheeks and sparkling eyes. And she was busy, always busy. I walked up right in front of her and she didn't look up.

"You're working too hard, Lucy," I said.

She looked up but her fingers didn't stop typing, "Oh hi, Henry. What's up, can't you stay away from the computers?"

Her fingers were still moving, but she was looking at me with full attention, so I said, "Maybe I wouldn't be having so many problems if I'd stayed with the computers, Lucy, but it can't be helped. I was hoping you could find some proof that I'd received a message ordering me to the recirculation valve room the night of the tritium overexposure incident. I'd also appreciate it if you could show me who was in the plant that night and the two days before."

"FBI beat you to it, Henry, but I don't see why I can't give you what I gave them. It's all open network information."

"Do you have anything about the message Dennis Banks sent me?"

"Sorry Henry. We do have a record of you receiving a message, but it's a message from you to yourself. It came from your PC in the tech section and you read it in the STA room."

"I was afraid you'd say that. I saved the message to a word processing file and even printed it out, but it's not really proof since I could have done that myself too."

"And it's worse, Henry. Whoever sent you the message knew the power-on password for your PC. Then they used the generals Stores password to get on the network. We've added a field to the network logon data that tells when the PC which is logging on to the network was turned on. Your tech section PC had been turned on just seventy minutes before the message was sent. You received and read the message within thirty seconds of its transmission."

"I couldn't have moved from the tech section to the STA room that fast," I said.

"The message was sent by timer. We have a record of that, too. The command file in your computer told the e-mail system to send it twelve minutes later. And if that were the end of it, you could have done it. You did go through the turnstiles during that time, Henry."

"What do you mean 'if that were the end of it?' Is there more?"

"Yes, there is more—much, much more." She cocked her head and smiled a sympathetic smile. Little crinkles formed at the edges of her eyes, and I knew that Lucy at least thought I was innocent.

"I hope it's not the final proof I'm guilty."

"No, but it doesn't help that much since it points to someone equally unlikely to have done such a thing."

"Thank you so much, Lucy, for the confidence. But since no one at Kankakee would be likely to do such a thing, then my being an unlikely culprit doesn't mean that much. So what do you have?"

The famous timed message that you claim ordered you to the recirculation valve room might have originated from another point on the network."

"What do you mean?"

"Someone sent a command message to your computer to go into e-mail. Maybe the command caused your computer to send you that message."

"That's a little tricky, isn't it?"

"Tricky, yes, but not impossible with our e-mail system. Of course routines to take over another machine remotely are commonplace," she said with just a trace of the computer expert's haughtiness.

"Okay, so which machine took over mine?"

"Your machine was sent a message from Trung's workstation on the floor above yours in the tech section," she said.

"So Trung sent my computer a message that caused it to send me a message twelve minutes after the command message executed?" I asked.

"Let's say we know Trung's computer sent you a message. We don't really know what the message did. I have a hard time believing Trung would do such a thing," Lucy said.

"When was the message sent from Trung's machine," I asked.

"Just at the start of the shift," Lucy said. "But just because it was sent then doesn't mean that the person who sent it entered it then. It could have been another time-delay message."

"Can't you search Trung's hard disk and find out?" I asked.

Lucy smiled. "We could, Henry. But unfortunately Trung's machine has suffered major hardware problems. His hard disk is completely corrupted and unreadable."

"Does Trung know?" I asked.

"About his computer. Sure. He reported it as soon as he discovered it," she said.

"No. Does Trung know his machine ordered my machine to send a message to me? The message I claim was signed by Dennis Banks."

"I assume the FBI told him when they questioned him this afternoon," she said.

"The FBI knows?"

"Of course. I told them as soon as I figured it out."

"Well, if anyone would know how to make my machine send a message to me, Trung would," I said. "But Trung was irradiated too and, you're right, he would never do such a thing."

"No one in their right mind would," she said. "So I suppose it must have been you."

"Thanks a lot, Lucy. And you say whoever did it knew my power-on password?"

"That's right. For your computer to have done anything it would have to be turned on and the power-on password entered. Have you given your password to someone or left it lying around on a piece of paper?"

"No, but I use a really simple algorithm for changing it, so I never forget what it is. If someone learned it last year, they could probably figure out what it is today."

"If I were you, Henry, I'd try to figure out who that person might be," she said.

"Lots of people knew it at WorldNet simulations," I said. "I made no secret of it there; we worked with each other so closely. But I've worked with so many people on computers that it could be anybody."

"Will you take security more seriously now?" she asked.

"Yes, I suppose I will. It wasn't just a prank; people were irradiated on this one."

"No, it was no prank. Everyone is very upset about it, but I guess you know that," she said.

"Yes, I know that. You said you could give me what you gave the FBI," I said.

"That's right Henry." She reached into her top right desk drawer and pulled out a three and a half inch diskette. "As a matter of fact I already have it all on this floppy. And I have the plant access records for the day of and the day before the incident on hardcopy."

I took the thick stack of computer printouts that she held out to me and quickly went through them. I checked the access records for the sector in which the recirculation valve room is located first. Laura Brault had been there the day before. So had Jim Haskel. Even my wife and Pete Kerwin had been there the day before. I was at first puzzled by that, but then I remembered the control room revamp project they were working on. Trung had been there both days. Dennis Banks had been in the plant the night of the event. And, of course, if he had been in the plant he couldn't have been sitting at my tech section desk composing a message to be sent out by timer twelve minutes later.

"What's on the floppy?" I asked.

"Oh, the same stuff only more of it. And there's radiation dose data, so they can figure out if anyone else was exposed to the tritium. The FBI also asked for personnel files, but I can't give you those, except for your own."

Is there any data on who might have been in the tech section area at the time I received the mystery message?"

"Well, we don't really keep very good records of who enters the tech section from the administration area. We do have work rosters and some sign-in and sign-out data. We have the visitor's roster. And of course anyone who enters the tech section from the plant goes through the key-card door, so you can't go into a radiation zone and then into the tech section directly."

"Can you give me those?" I asked.

"I don't see why not," she said. "It will make mighty dull reading, though." Her fingers were flying on the keyboard and I went around the desk to stand in back of her. "There it is," she said. "Give me the floppy."

I handed it to her. She slipped it into an external drive and her fingers typed in a complicated Unix copy command. The disk drive began whirring as file after file was copied onto it.

"How about my message to the fueling machine supervisor."

"On that you're in the clear, Henry. We keep a log of all messages sent from the in-plant computer stations, and you definitely did inform Brian Maxwell about tritium in the fueling machine bay. Brian and the control room people remember it all very well, since no one could figure out why the control room panels didn't show the warning."

"That was the first thing that went wrong that night," I said. I looked at the piles of printouts in my hand. And I knew that those piles were dwarfed by the information on the floppy. "They ought to invent an expert computer-cop system to automatically go through the plant data and figure out who could have done what when," I said.

"You mean who besides you?" Lucy asked.

"Yeah. This has been a long hard shift Lucy. Thanks for all the data. I need all the help I can get," I said. I glanced around at the computers spread out along the walls and then into the special computer rooms behind. The computers could control anything. This time it happened to be a nuclear plant. "You've got some great equipment, Lucy," I said.

"I know Henry, but too much of it."

I made my way back down the corridor and then retraced my steps by the system engineers' cubicles. I was thinking about Trung, going over everything he and I had gone through together, trying to remember any sign that he might stage a radiation accident. I couldn't think of anything unless he was hiding hatred of Americans or of Americans who had served in Vietnam. By some miracle I remembered to go to the forms cabinet and pull out a CNK-20 form for filing a personal statement of what occurred during an unusual plant event. Then I made my way downstairs. Coming up from my left a man was walking briskly, evidently in more of a hurry to reach the exit post than I was. I recognized the mop of curly reddish hair immediately. There were big swatches of gray in the hair now, but Pete Kerwin's lean, angular frame and—as he turned toward the door—his triangular, sharp face were little changed by the years.

"Hello, Pete," I said.

He looked surprised, almost shocked or worried, and he actually turned away from me for a second before recovering and smiling his usual twisted, clever smile. "Well, Henry, how nice to see you again." Then he looked down and stepped close to me. "The FBI and the NRC asked me a lot of questions about you. And I'm sure they didn't trust me because I'm Canadian."

"Yeah, they told me. You know I was carrying your tritium detector with me. That's what gave the alarm, and the FBI has a hard time understanding why I could know there was tritium there when the radiation technician didn't."

"Yes, they asked me about the detector, and I assured them that it is a wonderful instrument in spite of the bad reviews some of the Central Nuclear people have given it."

"Trung did a lot of work on that detector, didn't he?" I asked.

"I think Trung did some work on it. But he wanted to shift to my plutonium work," Kerwin said.

"Trung was actually in the recirc room during the event. He doesn't think much of your detector, even though it's what gave the alarm that kept him from getting more dose."

"Trung has been rather moody lately," said Kerwin. "I'm actually somewhat worried about him. You know he's very bitter about the war and what happened to his family, don't you?"

"It would be hard for him not to be," I said, "but I don't think that would affect his technical opinions."

"I suppose not," Kerwin said. "But Trung has always been too much of a perfectionist. The marketplace doesn't want perfection; it wants improvement, and my miniature tritium detector is definitely an improvement over the competition, the bulky sniffers and such. Actually we've received some orders for the detectors since the accident. Word of what happened gets around fast in the nuclear grapevine."

"Yes, word gets around fast. Only problem for me is, I think the word that's going around is that I'm some kind of crazy who gets his kicks by planting radioisotopes and burning out people's dose limits."

"This is terrible. I'm sure it's so hard on Sheri and you. She's been so happy with our computer-based training project, and now she has this to worry about. She was really upset the other night."

"I'm rather upset myself. And the worst thing is that I know the person who did it is trying to pin it on me," I said.

"I don't know who it could be, Henry. You don't have any enemies. There are the usual workplace jealousies, like with you and Laura, but I don't see her doing anything like this. Couldn't be anything in your past, could it Henry?"

"No, I can't think of anything," I said. "But I do have more information on the e-mail message that ordered me to the recirc room and started off this whole nightmare."

"I thought Dennis Banks denied giving you that order."

"He did. But now Lucy has figured out that another computer sent my computer an order to send the fake message to me."

"Whose computer was that," he asked.

I wasn't sure I should tell him, but in spite of the little disagreements we'd had at work over the years, I still liked Pete and couldn't hold back on him. "Trung's computer sent my computer a message."

"And can they prove that Trung sent it," Pete said.

"Well, it was his computer."

"Yes, but someone might know his password, or maybe his computer was sent an order from yet another computer," he said.

"Oh my God," I said. "If this keeps up we'll get the computers going in a loop giving orders to each other and we'll never know who gave the first order. But Trung doesn't strike me as the type who would be too loose with his password. He's had network management responsibilities before. Once you've done that you never forget about computer security."

"Yes, he would be careful," Pete said. "But there are always exceptions. Laura Brault knew his password."

"Laura? How do you know that?" I asked.

"Oh, I suspect Trung and Laura are especially good friends. I know they did some joint work at Kensington, and it was heavy on the computation. They used to use one of the Kensington computers, and at the same time offload tasks onto their Kankakee tech section computers remotely."

"I didn't know Laura did that kind of thing," I said.

"Oh, I'm sure that it was Trung who set up the computer links, but Laura is a quick learner, and I'm sure I've seen her run the three computers all by herself."

"That is interesting, Pete. But I can't believe either Trung or Laura would do anything like that. Laura and I have had our differences at work, sure, but nothing to cause anything like this."

"And you've had no differences with Trung?"

"No. Trung and I have always worked well together. He fixes everything for me just like he does for everyone. I can't think of anything. Maybe the whole thing never happened."

"Well, keep thinking about it. But something did happen, and we can't escape that. Someone is responsible. If there's anything I can do, just say it. I've told Sheri that already. You know we go back a long time."

"Yes, we started not being able to do any more harm than crashing the computers with a divide-by-zero overflow, and now we're in the real world with real radiation and pipes that leak. Well, at least I am. You've been getting a little abstract and theoretical again, or maybe entrepreneurial I should say."

Kerwin smiled almost abashedly, and then he reached up and patted me on the back. "Well, we can't all be shift-grunges, you know Henry. I've had all of the shift-work that I need, but now I'm busier than ever. As a matter of fact, I'd like to stay and talk, but I have to get to Urbana for a technical review."

"Sure, Pete, you'd better get on the road. Don't let the long-hairs intimidate you."

"I never do. Say hello to Sheri and the kids for me. And I'll see you at the barbecue."

So Pete would be at the barbecue, too. He usually was because of his projects with Sheri. Of course lots of Kankakee technical people did work with Pete's company, Anthem Electronics. I watched Pete hurry down the stairs. He went everywhere in a hurry, he had so many projects and promotions. I began to feel jealous. I could have been like him. Back at WorldNet Simulations I had always felt just a little quicker, just a little smarter than Pete Kerwin. Just like Trung was smarter and quicker than Pete, quicker than me, too, but I didn't like admitting it. But now Pete was a man in demand, an expert, a man who had products for sale, while Trung and I were still working for salary. Of course Pete didn't have kids, and I did. And he didn't have Sheri; he didn't have beautiful and brilliant Sheri who was easily as successful as Pete Kerwin. But Pete had Marie-Anne, and Marie-Anne was beautiful and French. And then I remembered that I didn't really have Sheri any longer, so I sighed the sigh that came so often with each new day of my troubles. Pete was prosperous and successful and had a beautiful wife, and I wasn't sure what I had. I remembered the barbecue, and I hoped that Marie-Anne would come too. Marie-Anne and Judy Peterson and Laura Brault. I wanted lots of pretty women to be at my party. I went through the doors and got my forms and headed as directly as I could toward the parking lot.

There were still pickets at the plant gate. Pickets from the Chicago Energy Coalition. They could be seen from Interstate 55. It would make a good newspaper photo background with the towers of the refineries and chemical works stretching along Arsenal Road and the new gleaming structures of Kankakee and Hydra looking like new and tougher, more beautiful weeds growing in an ancient weed lot. Seagraves had always had a knack for playing the media, and I suppose he had refined his skills in the intervening years. Funny how things come on you all at once. I had hardly thought about Seagraves and organizing and demonstrations until the FBI had asked me about him. And now, on leaving the interview, I could see the pickets which showed what the FBI was talking about was real.

And Seagraves had been part of sabotage before. Seagraves and Jim Haskel and me. Me most of all. But Seagraves couldn't have entered a command to have a message sent to me at a later time from my own PC. That smacked of WoldNet simulations, someone who knew networks and operating systems in depth, not just the usual commands. Someone like Trung, the man who could fix any computer problem. But he had been irradiated too. Someone like Trung, but there wasn't anyone as expert as Trung.

I would have liked to have smiled and acted friendly with the pickets. But I was too tired and who knows who might have been watching, filming, recording, taping? I drove slowly past the pickets and took the small roads home. I didn't want to get mixed up with any fast traffic.

7

The alarm blared much too soon and I had that groggy, dead feeling that comes from sleeping in close-shaded rooms on summer days. I had to make the appointment with the marriage counselor; meetings with shrinks were the proof that I'd made it through another week.

I have to admit that Kankakee treated me fairly. The report on my shift with the heavy water leak concluded that I had acted properly in trying to keep the unit up. Nothing changed in my work. The only problem was the undercurrent of suspicion about the tritium incident; that incident had never been satisfactorily explained in spite of the extensive investigations conducted by multiple agencies and governments. The State of Illinois had even set up its own special group to study the event. Nearly everyone in operations had been interviewed about the events of that night.

But work was not my main problem. The problem with Sheri made everything else small. I had become so alive, so awake, so desperate with the problem. I wasn't sleeping; I was reading save-your-marriage books and how-to-talk-books and trimming my eyebrows and every bizarre thing that I could think of to make her look at me again.

We'd had two marriage counselors. Neither of them had done me any good since I'd never imagined leaving Sheri. The shrinks made me imagine it, and when I said it would be terrible they said maybe it wouldn't be so bad. The first one had worked me over, insisting I was nervous, and wondering why I didn't yell at Sheri for the terrible things she was saying about me. "Why don't you tell her?" he kept saying.

So I tried to think of all the things I didn't like about her and tell her about them. I tried real hard, and I tried to go beyond the basics like "How can you say you can't remember why you married me?" That had bugged me about Sheri—memory. There's not much you can do when a person claims she can't remember.

"You remember our kids?"

I didn't have to say bad things about her very long before she was mad as hell and slammed the door behind her. I wasn't surprised. I guess that's why I'd never before tried to think of all the things I could complain about and then tell her about them. It makes me mad to hear why I'm no good too. I'd normally have to be upset to complain to her. But the counselor said I had to open up so that's what I did.

Next time the shrink chewed me out for using sarcasm. He hadn't told me about that the other time. I should have told her I didn't like her memory without being sarcastic. I wondered what else the shrink had left out.

So we'd gotten another counselor, Dr. Juliet Chambers. She'd first called us in individually before meeting us together. So I'd told her about how Sheri wouldn't speak to me after coming back from her Toronto trip, and how I'd do anything to make Sheri change her mind, but she just kept saying that she had been unhappy for a long time and she wanted a chance to be happy in her life. And I just couldn't understand because I thought we'd always been happy. Dr. Chambers had listened and sympathized with my story, and she didn't say I should tell Sheri what made me mad about her. Instead, when we came in for our first session together, she'd announced, "Well, I think you should split up." This was like an augury from the goddess, a goddess who was our counselor, who sat so erect and angular in her chair with such penetrating eyes. And you could almost see the snakes growing out of her hair. And I could feel my stomach pulling me to the floor in my despair. And I'd said, "Well, maybe I won't be here for our next session. Maybe I'll just be gone."

"What do you mean, gone?" asked Dr. Chambers.

"I don't know, be somewhere else, just disappear where I won't have anything to remind me of what I've lost."

I was outraged but thought I couldn't fight it. Dr. Chambers was our counselor, the one we'd chosen to advise us, our intimate advisor, and when your intimate advisor tells you to do something, you have to do it. Otherwise it looks like you told all your stories and said all your feelings in bad faith.

And now Sheri was repeating Dr. Chambers' line, only more forcefully. She wanted a separation. She wanted out of a marriage that had only made her unhappy. And each statement, each added dismissal of our life together was a fiery torch incinerating anything I ever thought I'd been.

I picked out blue jeans and a shirt that I hoped would make me look good and piled into our minivan for the drive to the counselor. Sheri and I had always arrived in separate cars for our counseling sessions since she seemed to be always working. It was like we were two ancient enemies arriving for near-hopeless peace negotiations.

Sheri was already in the room with Dr. Chambers when I arrived. I couldn't help myself from thinking how good Sheri looked. I did that a lot when I had a chance to see her. Her profile was to me and I tried to freeze it, her long, thin arcing nose accenting her ash-blonde hair, her posture erect and energetic, the jutting of her breasts, high and alive like a young girl's. Then she turned to me, and I took the pressure of her grey, unforgiving eyes. Her energy and ambition were reflected in them and coupled perfectly the sharp angularity of her face. I remembered the time fifteen years before when I'd first taken a close look at those eyes in a bar in Ann Arbor, I think it was when I looked at her then that I knew I wanted to stay with her forever, and I felt the shock of the last two months coming back over me.

I took my chair next to Sheri; we always were in the same chairs. I wanted to switch chairs some time to see if that would make things go better, but somehow I'd never quite managed to pull it off in Dr. Chambers' office.

Dr. Chambers looked at me. "Sheri's told me that you've discussed separating, but that you still don't want to do it."

"And I'm very afraid that this will lead to my becoming very, very depressed if we keep going on this way," Sheri broke in.

"Yes, Sheri, depression would be a possibility in your case, but right now I'm more concerned about Henry. I sense despair in the way he talks, especially at our last meeting. I sense desperation. You said your father suffered from depression, Henry?"

"Yes, he had infrequent, severe attacks of depression."

"And this depression is what finally caused his death?"

"Yes, I told you that before. He killed himself, but I was twenty-eight when that happened. It made me sad, of course, but it wasn't as bad as if I'd lost my father when I was a kid," I said, trying to avoid any hint of despair.

"Had he tried to kill himself before, Henry?"

"Yes."

"And have any of your brothers or sisters suffered from depression?"

"Not that I know of. Everyone gets sad, of course."

"Of course. But Henry, it's important to be able to see the positive sides of even the saddest situations. Can't you see anything positive in the idea of separating?"

I couldn't say yes, so I didn't say anything. I sat there silent looking first at Dr. Chambers and then at Sheri. I looked them both in the eyes.

"I'm asking about your family and your father Henry because there is evidence that depression is more prevalent in some families than others, either because of genetic factors or because of something about how the family functions," said Dr. Chambers. "Have you ever been depressed or worried about doing what your father did?"

"It's only natural that someone gets sad sometimes. And I have wondered; I've thought that since my father did it, maybe I'll do it too. But I've always come back to knowing that much as I loved my father—and I did love him—I'm not like my father. There are many reactions to things that he had that I just don't have. He got excited about things that I don't get excited about. I do things that he would have never done. I am not my father."

"Of course not Henry," said Dr. Chambers. "It's just something that I think we should be careful about."

The office was air-conditioned. It was a beautiful day with sun streaming in the window and irises in bloom just outside the window. I didn't feel like speaking, and I thought maybe the world could just freeze that way, and that if the world froze then I wouldn't ever really lose my family.

Dr. Chambers said, "One of the reasons Sheri has for wanting to separate is so she can find someone she can feel closer too, someone who she can talk to and communicate better than she thinks she will ever be able to do with you. Maybe you'd like to talk to someone else too. Maybe there's someone else who's attractive to you. Someone at work perhaps?"

I could barely speak, "Oh, no, no."

Dr. Chambers looked down and spoke quietly, "Oh, you don't want to."

"No."

"Well, I'm very worried about you, Henry. I think I can help you see that it won't just be bad that will come out of a separation. I would like to have a session with you alone to talk about your feelings and how you think about a separation. Would that be alright, Henry?"

She was our counselor. She was the one we had picked to advise us. I couldn't say no, even though none of the advice we had yet received had been anything I wanted to hear. I wanted to hear how I could get my marriage back. I wanted to keep my family.

"I suppose, but I don't think you'll be able to make me feel cheery about a separation."

"No, and I'm sorry, I don't usually go so far as to recommend that people separate."

And then there was more. Sheri wanted to know the best way to tell the kids. And among the admonitions to tell them over and over again that it's not their fault, I said, "How can there be any good way to tell kids that the mother and father that they've grown up with and that they've been happy with are going to move apart and that they'll have to shuttle from house to house to see them?"

"There are a lot of homes that are not very good homes. A separation can stop that kind of bad atmosphere between the parents, and the children can develop separate, good relationships with their parents individually," said Dr. Chambers.

It was her job to have the answers. I had no answers. The talk turned to advice on lawyers and mediators. I sat there thinking about my father. He had been so strong, and I had been so happy with my family. I'd thought my father was the strongest man in the world, that nothing could hurt him. I had been sure my family was the best family in the entire world. And I knew my two little girls had to think that way about their family, and they were right, we did have a great family. We had everything going for us.

And my Dad had killed himself. He had suffered fits of depression since early manhood, and he had one when I was a kid. I didn't understand. I just remember him staying in the bedroom all day and my mother talking to him. But I was a grown man with my own family before he did it. I couldn't imagine what I would have felt if he had done it when I was still a kid.

"I'm sorry," I said, "I know I'm off the subject. But I still don't understand. I don't understand why this is happening to me. I won't know what to say if someone asks me why we split-up."

"How many times do I have to tell you, Henry? It just doesn't work between us anymore. I want a chance to be happy."

"But how can you not be happy? We have a great house, two great little girls. You're a success at your career; you can pick and choose the work you want. You have so many opportunities that most people don't have."

"We didn't get married to go after those material things Henry. I want more. I want to feel alive, that I have some kind of connection with where I live and with someone I love. You go off to that nuclear plant everyday. I'm sorry; I just can't connect with that kind of life. You talk about radiation and science. I just think about people. We aren't alike; we're not alike at all."

"Well, no two people are exactly alike. But we've done so well together for so long. We must have been enough alike to go through all the moves and juggled schedules that we have."

Dr. Chambers leaned forward. "Henry, you're trying to change Sheri's emotions by arguing, by reasoning. Do you think that will really work?"

"Oh, I suppose not. But show me what will work. I will do anything," I said.

"Henry, nothing you can do will work. Sheri feels about this very deeply. Any effort you make to try to get her to change her mind will be a wasted effort. There is nothing you can do to change things. In a way that's very bad news, but in another way it's important that you know this so that you won't blame yourself for not doing something to make her stay with you."

And so the oracle from the gods again. We had to separate and there was absolutely nothing I could do to change Sheri's mind. The counselor had said it. We had chosen the counselor, we had presented our problem in good faith, and the counselor had resolved it. And it was a resolution. We must separate. I must quit trying to think of things that might change the way Sheri felt. We must get on with our lives, put the past behind us, find someone new.

How I cursed that resolution. How I felt defiance well up and tighten my neck and chin. If my marriage was to end, it would damn well end with a struggle.

We left together. Sheri's car was farther out in the lot, and she stopped as we came to the van. We hadn't said a word.

"You seem really upset," she said.

"Upset! I'm a hell of a lot more than upset."

"But why, you're a man, you'll be able to find someone younger, someone not as crazy as me."

"Oh, so now you're doing me favors! You and Dr. Chambers and everyone who sits calmly and makes pronouncements to destroy my life. Just like that. One minute everything's all right and the next minute you tear everything up and smash it all to bits and pretend it's a reasonable thing to do," I said.

"I think you should try to calm down. This happens to lots of people. Think of all the people we know who've been divorced. Some of them will be at our party. You haven't forgotten the barbecue, have you?"

"Oh my god. The goddamn barbecue. I have to cook hamburgers and smile and talk and pretend the world makes sense."

"You're going to be there, aren't you? Because I'll have to get someone else to cook the hamburgers if you aren't."

I didn't want to answer her. But I knew she wouldn't have any trouble finding some other man to cook hamburgers for her, and I didn't want that to happen. "Yeah, I'll be there," I said.

"Are you going to be all right?" she asked. "Do you want me to drive you?"

"No, I'm not going to be all right, and you've driven me quite enough already!" I don't usually slam doors, but I did this time and I drove unseeing, miles going by unnoticed, another part of me doing the driving, not my racing consciousness. And I kept wondering how I would tell my kids. How I would say goodbye.

And I became aware of a hole there. Something deeper than sadness. A pit that I dare not look into. A pit of saying goodbye to my girls and living apart.

Then I remembered Judy Peterson's red hair and thought of ways to ask her out. And I kept driving. Judy would be at the party. I couldn't ask her out at the party with Sheri there. I couldn't see myself ever having the guts to ask her out.

It had gotten hot in late afternoon, and the fields were green with surging growth. The air was so humid and thick that I imagined plants could take root right in the air. And I thought of Vietnam and the rain and the green and the jungle and I thought about Trung staring out at the Gulf. And I wanted to live like I had then. I wished I had some marijuana; I wished I had drugs, but I couldn't use those, not and work at a nuclear plant. They would catch me using drugs in no time under the fitness-for-duty program and the mandatory testing. But if I couldn't have drugs, I could drink whiskey.

I don't know why they called it the Highlander with all the flat land around, but that was its name. It was a sort of cheap camp and trailer park with a pond and some rental boats. And they had a bar there too that was always dark and it had a window air conditioner which kept it cool. They served greasy, tasteless food, but I hadn't stopped to eat.

The bottles behind the bar looked as good as bottles anywhere. A young, overweight girl who looked like she should still be in high school was behind the bar and moved with even more deliberation than a nuclear operator over to my stool. "What would you like?" she asked.

I asked if they sold liquor by the bottle. They didn't so I ordered Miller beer and two shots of Old Granddad one-hundred. "I guess you think you're a hard drinker," the girl said.

"I guess I do," I said. "And I'm in a hurry."

I thought the beer would never come, she dawdled so with getting the glass and turning the spigot to let the beer in. And her return walk to my stool was as slow as the first time she'd come over.

I grabbed the beer and drank half of it before she had even turned to get me my whiskey. She looked like she was going to say something to me, but I glared at her and I was relieved that she resumed getting me my whiskey without my having to listen to whatever it was she might say.

I had to think about the barbecue. I liked to do it with real charcoal, not the easy way with propane, although we were so damn prosperous we had both kinds of barbecue. We had both kinds of barbecue and a nice house and two good jobs and two beautiful little girls and Sheri was going to smash it all.

It would be Sheri's friends at the barbecue. She always said I should invite more of my friends, people I knew in nuclear operations or wherever. Judy Peterson would be there because Sheri had invited her. And Pete Kerwin would be there, but it would be Sheri who had asked him. And I thought about trying to look up Ken Seagraves and having him at my barbecue for old time's sake. That would shake up Kankakee management, having me entertain the Chicago Energy Coalition leader. Howard Crowder and Sheila Rowe would take notice, too.

But if I couldn't invite Ken Seagraves, I could invite someone else who had been in that picture of Ken and Sheri and me and the rest of the May Day organizing committee.

The Highlander was such a sleepy bar that most of the phone books by the pay phone were intact. I looked through the Moraine book and had the luck of finding only one J. Haskel listed, and it was an apartment so it had to be him.

I got Jim's machine and thought Jim had one of the most upbeat, inviting greeting messages I'd ever heard. It wasn't anything special that he said, it was the way he said it, and it made me want to leave my message and made me think I'd be doing something good by doing it.

After I'd left the invite on Jim's machine, I wondered why Sheri and I hadn't had him over before. We had been comrades, after all. We had all wanted to change the world. But I suppose Sheri and he had been in different factions, and Jim's winding up as a control technician put him in the nitty-gritty of nuclear operations, and Sheri wasn't really happy with the day-by-day work that made nuclear reactors go. She found it exciting to work on the design, to try to match human and machine skills in a theoretical way, but she didn't like the idea of adjusting knobs and opening valves in a radiation zone.

I forced myself to wait for the waitress to bring me another whiskey. I drank it down straight without setting down the glass. I felt the buzz almost immediately and that helped me tolerate the lengthy process of paying my bill. The waitress kept punching the numbers back into the calculator. I even gave her more tip than I wanted to because I didn't want to wait for her to make change.

The Walgreen's on the outskirts of Moraine had charcoal and liquor. I chose the cheapest pint of vodka and waited till I was on the county road before pulling over and drinking a quarter of it down. The idea of the barbecue was starting to not seem so bad. Long ago Sheri had said I was wild. She seemed to like me being that way at the time. I might be that way again.

Pete Kerwin had already arrived for the party when I came into the house to greet my Laurie and Tracy. His wife Marie-Anne came up to me immediately, and we kissed on both cheeks the French way. I thought she should be a Viking, her hair was so blonde and her cheekbones so high, but she was French from France. Pete and she had met when WorldNet Simulation assigned him temporary duty in Montréal. She was probably the reason that his assignment, which was to be six months maximum, stretched out to a year and a half.

I grabbed a beer from the refrigerator on my way out to the back deck with my charcoal. There were more guests out there, and I noted approvingly that Judy Peterson appeared to be alone.

Then I was surprised to see Laura Brault walking toward me, not quite as fast as she did when she was mad about something I had done in the control room, but fast enough to make me think there was something definite she wanted to talk to me about.

"Henry, the FBI is about to drive me crazy. I've been called in three times and it's all because I happened to go to the recirculation valve room the day before the accident. No, I've said that wrong, it couldn't have been an accident. I mean the day before the tritium sabotage. Have they asked you questions about me?"

I looked her in the eyes, and went about my business of starting the charcoal while reflecting on her question. I didn't want to tell her I hadn't told anybody anything if I had. "Laura. I'm trying to remember everything that went on in all the interviews I've had. I can't remember a single question about you. They did tell me you had been in the recirc room, though. That was a surprise to me, but it makes me look a little better since it shows I'm not the only control room worker who winds up out in the plant. By the way, why in the world did you go there?"

"Oh, I was bored. I was STA and I'd finished most of the standard paperwork and done most of the tests, and you know how frustrating it is being an advisor when there's nothing to give advice about. And you know that if something big happened, you'd just be busy setting up the emergency routines and wouldn't have any time to think about advice. So I was bored and when I'm bored I like to walk. So I looked at the work schedules and decided to take a walk to check on what was going on in the recirc room."

"So you told the FBI that you were there because you were bored?"

"More or less. I may not have used those exact words."

"Gee thanks, Laura. It makes my excuse look much better. Of course it would help if Lucy Watkins could dig up the actual text of the e-mail which ordered me there. Which reminds me, how expert are you at taking over other people's computers remotely and making them transmit e-mail messages?"

"Not good at all. I can route processing through other computers, of course, but I wouldn't have an idea how to trick the mail program into sending out a message."

"Well, if you can take over other people's computers remotely, you're most of the way there. I wouldn't put it past you. You're obviously even quicker than I thought."

"What's this all about anyway?" she asked.

"Lucy has proved that my computer received a command file from another computer on the network. The theory is that this command caused my computer to send out a message addressed to me."

"I didn't have anything to do with that," she said. "I didn't even turn on my computer that shift."

"It might have been a time-delay command. You might have sent it to me days before and it just sat there waiting," I said.

"Well, if it's like that, anyone could have done it."

"Not just anyone. Someone who's fairly clever with computers. Someone who understands command files and network protocols," I said, and as I said it I was thinking that there are a lot of people like that in nuclear plants.

"That's not me she said. I'm just a simpleton with computers."

"That's not what I heard. I heard Trung had taught you a lot and that you were a very apt pupil," I said.

Laura's face reddened and her voice became clipped. "Trung and I have worked together, and he did teach me something about accessing other computers, but only for computation and off-loading tasks. We certainly didn't do anything to interfere with other people's e-mail. I don't think Trung even knows how to do that."

"Yes he does," I said.

"Can you prove that?" she asked.

"No. But I know he does. Trung can do anything."

"It's too bad he doesn't receive more reward for his knowledge," she said. "Does this have anything to do with what the FBI were questioning him about yesterday?" she asked.

"Probably," I said.

"And you told them that I might have sent that command file to you?"

"No."

"What did you tell them about me?"

"I told you before, Laura. I didn't tell them anything about you. They didn't ask me anything about you."

"You're sure you haven't said anything to the FBI about me?" she asked, and her eyes were absolutely imploring.

I finished my beer. "I'm sure," I said. "But now that I think of it, I guess there was plenty I could have told the FBI about you."

"Like what?"

The first hamburgers were going well, and I judged I had some time before they had to be turned. "Just a minute, Laura, I have a powerful thirst tonight." I walked over to a cooler jammed packed with iced beer. The new beers were merging nicely with the earlier whiskey and vodka and I felt there could be nothing better than cooking hamburgers on my deck with people drinking and laughing. I remembered back to the years before Sheri and I got together. I liked to throw parties then. I liked to do anything that came to mind, be crazier and more fun than anybody. And I realized there really was a lot I could tell the FBI about Laura, a lot more than just saying that she knew Trung's password. I wondered if I could make up for Laura's crack that my education was "dated" and all the second-guessing she did on any decision I made on my shift.

"I could tell them, for example, that it's not just me who did work at Kensington labs. That I'm not the only control room operator with a good science background. I'd tell them that Laura Brault also has done radiation experiments at Kensington labs. And I just remembered. Are you still trying for your PhD Laura?"

"Yes. And I'm very close to it. All I need is the thesis."

"The topic wouldn't be tritiated organics, would it?"

"No. I'm doing neutron shielding calculations, and I'm using Kensington's neutron sources as an experimental check."

"That sounds very interesting. But you would have had as much access to Kensington's tritiated organics as I did."

"That's ridiculous. I didn't even remember what tritiated organics were when that NRC woman told me that was what had contaminated the recirc room."

"Well you see. That's where my 'dated' education gives me an advantage because I did remember something about tritiated organics when they brought it up. Kind of a double whammy. Tritium which wants to spread itself evenly throughout your body with the water and the organics which want to be part of your body. Just a super delivery system for beta radiation."

"It gives me the creeps thinking someone could plant something like that on purpose," she said. "It was just luck that you discovered it when you did. We might have only found out we had a problem when people's urine samples started coming back full of tritium."

"You can thank Pete Kerwin's detector for that," I said. "You've worked with Pete before, haven't you?"

"Oh yes. I met him right after I started work at Kankakee. Lately I've been working on an efficient advanced neutronics code for him. You know he's thinking about bidding on simulators?"

"I didn't know that. But Pete seems to have a knack for gathering expertise into a team and rolling out with a product."

"Pete Kerwin has the broadest range of technical and business knowledge of anyone I've ever met," said Laura.

"Oh thank you for thinking so much of my husband," said Marie-Anne who had come up behind Laura. "Although I am sometimes concerned that he has too many young female admirers."

Laura was looking blankly at Marie-Anne, so I said, "You've met Marie-Anne, Pete's wife, haven't you Laura?"

It turned out they hadn't met, so I corrected that and they exchanged the briefest of handshakes.

"Are you the Laura who asked my husband for a recommendation for a control room job at the Hydra fusion station?" asked Marie-Anne.

"Yes, and I need to thank Pete for writing it," said Laura.

"And why didn't you ask Pete for a recommendation, Henry?" asked Marie-Anne. She peered over her drink and I could see her cheeks dimpled from the smile hid by the glass.

"Oh, I don't know. I guess I didn't think of it," I said and hoped she would drop the subject.

"Oh, and there is my brilliant husband now. And with your wife, Henry," she said while touching my arm. "Well at least she is married. I hope that is better."

"Then I shall fix that," said Laura and she walked over to Pete and Sheri, but stopped for a beer on the way.

"And will you now dance with me Henry McClure?" asked Marie-Anne.

I don't remember ever not dancing with a woman who looked as good as Marie-Anne, but on my back deck with my kids in the house and with me as lonely as I was, I gave the excuse that I had to watch the hamburgers. Then I thought why shouldn't I dance with a blonde French woman, but when I tried to speak to her she was away. She had found another man, Dennis Banks, to dance with. Dennis stood six foot four and was ruggedly handsome. And blonde Marie-Anne with her high cheekbones and almost extravagant breasts stood out like a movie star dancing in the dusk. And I remembered that I had once liked to dance. Sheri and I had not danced since before Laurie was born. Maybe if I took Sheri dancing, maybe she would look at me again if I did that.

And why shouldn't I dance with my wife in my own back yard? I walked across to Sheri and Laura and Pete, touched Sheri on the shoulder, and said "Shall we dance?"

"Oh no Henry. Pete has Laura and I excited with how much money we're going to make working on his contracts."

"You should dance to purge yourself of nefarious materialistic desires," I said.

"It's materialistic desires that raise us above the animal level," said Pete. "And speaking of materialist desires, do you have any Canadian beer? I don't like this watery American stuff."

"Yes. We even have Moosehead, which is something we didn't have in Ontario," I said, referring to trade restrictions between the Canadian provinces.

"Why is it, Henry, that the Americans can't make a decent beer," Pete kept on.

"I suppose it's the same reason there's never been any Canadians on the mother-fucking moon," I said feeling absolutely inspired by drink. I would avenge myself for every anti-American slur I'd kept quiet about when I'd worked in Canada.

"Maybe we should dance," said Sheri and she fairly shoved me toward Dennis and Marie-Anne.

"I've been waiting to use that line for a long time," I said.

"Shut up, you buffoon. Pete is my business partner and I have lots of Canadian associates, and you should remember that you have a lot of Canadian friends, too, so don't insult them."

"I didn't do anything except what he'd already started," I said. "But let's dance."

"I have no intention of dancing with you. You go back to your hamburgers or offer our guests another drink or some of the snacks. Just stay away from me."

I watched her walk back to Pete and Laura. I went back to the hamburger grill and indeed there was more work to do there. But then my Laurie came out the back door leading Trung, Jim Haskel and Lucy Watkins. Seeing Laurie definitely made me feel better, and I also knew that Trung and I would have to talk. I put two regular hamburgers on a plate and then added one of my Trung specials, an oregano burger, and walked over to them before they could disappear into the party.

"So you've discovered my daughter, Laurie," I said.

"Yes, Henry," said Jim. "She's been giving us the tour of your house, and a rather complete tour it was, I should add."

"Yes," Lucy said. "We know your laundry room, your workshop, and all the details of the bathrooms."

"Laurie always does a good job," I said. I offered the hamburgers. Jim and Lucy each took one, but Trung said he had already eaten.

"It's one of my oregano burgers, Trung. I've never known you to turn one down."

A thin smile appeared on Trung's face, seemingly in spite of himself. "Okay," he said and reached slowly for the burger.

I looked at Trung. "It's been rather dull at work the last two days. I understand my FBI friends have been entertaining you rather than spending all their time with me."

"They did talk to me," Trung said.

"Yes, I understand there was a command file sent from your machine to mine, but it cannot be recovered because your hard disk has been corrupted."

"That is a gentle name for it," Trung said, and looked fixedly in my eyes. "The hard disk was erased and then someone dowsed the entire computer with water. Someone trashed my machine."

"Oh my," I said. "Did you have back-ups?"

"Yes, I have back-ups. But I don't like wasting time reloading stuff that should be there. And I don't like all these radiation tests I have to take."

"You don't have a backup from the days around the recirc room event, do you?"

"No, the last time I did backup was the week before the recirc room disaster," Trung said.

"Trung does much better than most people with backups," Lucy said.

"Backups, what are backups?" asked Haskel and rolled his eyes.

And then Laura was there beside Trung. She put her hand on his shoulder and turned to face me. "Henry is having trouble deciding whether it was you or me that sent his computer a command file," she said.

"These command files and fake messages are all a smoke screen," Trung said. "No one will prove anything chasing these things. Too many people know each other's passwords. Too many people know too many tricks. Including you, Henry McClure."

"Come on, Trung. I never do tricks. I wouldn't know how to order another computer to send a message."

"You could know," said Trung. "If you wanted to do something, you could do it. You would read the manual and then you would do it."

There was an embarrassing silence with Trung and I meeting each other's eyes.

And then there was a hand on my shoulder. Pete Kerwin's. "Ah, Henry and Trung. The perfect candidates for my next detector. I'm afraid I don't have one which will do internal dosimetry yet."

Trung fairly glared at Pete. His mouth moved, but he said nothing, and I realized he was restraining his urge to speak with his stronger urge not to break decorum. He had more than once infuriated me with his manners.

Laura said something to Trung. She led him into the midst of the dancers and they were jiving. I had never seen Trung dance before. He had yet another talent.

Lucy came close to me. "Trung is disturbed, I would say furious."

"I'm fairly furious myself," I said.

Pete said, "Did you see how Trung acted. He is very moody. I have seen him much worse than this. I can understand part of it, but there is more there."

Then Marie-Anne pulled Pete into the dance. Jim asked Lucy, and I was left alone.

I could ask people if they wanted cheeseburgers. I could offer them beer and I could drink more myself. But the drinking didn't help. The evening had lost its charm. I wished I could take Jim Haskel over to Sheri to talk about old times, to show her a friend we'd both had before we'd moved to Canada. I would have liked to have talked with Ken Seagraves, but he was probably in some cramped meeting room planning the next demonstration, and I couldn't invite him to one of our parties anyway. I felt alone, but then I remembered Tracy and Laurie. I went into the house. Tracy was already in her bed, sleeping through all the noise. But Laurie, having found no more takers for her house tour, was downstairs watching television. I sat down and watched with her and was happy to be home.

8

Kankakee came up peacefully after the purification leaks had been fixed and the failed channel refueled. We settled into a long production run, just churning out electricity, no experiments with special fuels and no tritium or plutonium to produce for bombs.

We couldn't have brought a Canadian Candu reactor back up so quickly. We would have had to wait for the xenon to disappear. But our all-purpose mission means we have enriched, zippy fuel available. And our computers and neutronics codes are so advanced, so complicated, so sophisticated, and there is so much faith in them that they just jammed enriched fuel into some of the channels, adjusted the initial calibration to match what they thought the special fuel was like, and the computers and the self-correcting reactor control algorithms brought the reactor back up, forced it through the xenon-poisoning barrier. It's scary to me what the Kankakee computers do. Humans would have been biting their nails and sweating it out and moving slowly with self-checking to the maximum if they tried something like that with a hodgepodge of fuels. The computer does the same thing; it checks itself, or at least that's what they keep saying, and everything in reactor control seems to work flawlessly. I have to admit that I sometimes wonder what they need operators here for. What would we do if the computers went wrong, and how would we know that they were wrong in the first place?

Work was not really a problem; the plant was working so smoothly, although there were still the after-effects of the unsolved tritium contamination. But no other sabotage had happened, and it was a beautiful summer so discontent and the pickets at the plant gate disappeared.

It was anything but peaceful for me, of course. I had never felt so full of desperate striving. Striving for something that would shake Sheri, halt her in her tracks and make her begin to think about me in a new way.

There was exercise. Central Nuclear had its own worker's exercise room and I went there for lunch instead of eating. I even got a key so I could go there either going into or coming off shift. I felt my body changing fast from the exercise and not eating and staying up half the night worrying. I had to buy pants with a thirty-four waist, the same size I wore coming out of high school.

And coming out of exercise I did not feel depressed. I felt great and the aerobics class music went round and round in my head and I walked fast; I felt I had spring in my calves, and people told me to slow down. They asked why I was in such a hurry. Even work was going well. I identified a deficiency in the chemistry parameter reporting system, and barrel-chested Frank Marzak , the station manager, devoted nearly all of the daily ongoing-conditions meeting to determining how best to correct it. That was what we were supposed to do, identify deficiencies and have them corrected.

I could look better, maybe that would change her. And I could be alert to what she said. I could try to understand. I could ask questions. The books had lots of advice about how to talk.

But she did not seem that interested in talking to me, and I felt strained and phony when I tried to use the techniques. That's the way with techniques.

There were flowers, of course. I brought some home. But I had always bought her flowers; these were just unusual for there being no special reason. But she already knew I loved her and did not want to lose her. She knew that, and she did not care. Thirteen years, five moves, two children, and she did not really care.

I took my form CNK-5 in to Judy Peterson. I had to force myself to walk up to her because I had been thinking about her all night.

Judy Peterson had a smile for me. Her face was not freckled even though her hair was red. Her clothes were neat and crisp; she was thin and pert, like the tips of her up-curling hair. And I looked to see the rise of her breasts, just below the third button from the top, the last one she had buttoned. There were fine lines in her forehead, she was younger than me but how much younger?

When I thought I had a marriage, when Sheri was my wife and we were a couple, I had never thought about other women. I didn't think about whether they were married, whether they had boyfriends, whether they were lonely. I had enough to do keeping my own family running without thinking about others. Maybe I have a selfish nature; maybe I'm self-centered, unaware, dead. Withdrawn from the life which surrounds me. But of course Dr. Chambers had said "Perhaps someone at work," and of course I now did think about the women at work. And I noticed where the rings were on fingers. And I noticed whether they looked happy.

Judy Peterson looked happy. But she also looked beautiful, and her sharing the same human factors profession as my wife drew my thoughts to her all the more.

"I'm very sorry Henry," she said. "I'll pass this on to Blair, and you know there may have to be some measures taken."

"Yeah, you may have to take me off shift for a while. That will be a real penalty."

"Yes Henry, you may have to work regular hours like a human being for a while. And it's good that you have so many skills, that you can work in the tech unit and who knows where else. I'll pass the form to Blair, and we may ask you to talk to a psychologist."

And without knowing I was going to do it I said, "That would be nice if I could talk to you, you're a psychologist aren't you?"

Her left shoulder rose slightly, stiffly, her head tilted slightly to the right, she looked down and her mouth pursed just a second. I was sorry I had said what I had said and she said, "No, Henry, I don't do psychological assessments. You will talk to a psychologist and they'll give us a report and I'm sure you'll be back at your regular job in no time."

"You don't really have to hurry," I said. "I could use some peace and quiet. I could take vacation."

"That might be a very good idea. And Henry, I really am sorry about you and Sheri, and I hope you can work things out. You know sometimes there's quite a gap between the way engineers think and the way people who aren't so technical think."

"You think I think like an engineer?"

"Oh, no. I'm sorry Henry. I just don't want you to blame yourself too much. Sometimes these things just happen."

"Sure. Thanks." I turned and walked away wondering how anyone could be as beautiful as she was. And I knew that she had to be married or living with someone or have a boyfriend at least. And also wondering how I would find out and what I was going to do about it?

And then I thought, don't mess things up, you old fool. You get along perfectly well with Judy Peterson, so why spoil it? I could see how she stiffened and looked flustered at the least hint of flirting.

And I felt guilty because I was supposed to be doing everything to win Sheri back.

I suppose I should be ashamed of some of the things I did, some of the tricks I tried in hopes of making Sheri want me again. The books said the sexually attractive scent was in your sweat, especially the sweat from near the breasts and groin. And so I would get up early and exercise and take my sweaty tee-shirt and wring it in the orange juice. Sheri loved orange juice, she drank it every morning and with it she drank my sweat.

I suppose I should be ashamed, but I'm not ashamed. Sometimes it's a shame not to be desperate. Sometimes a shame not to be stupid. To always be in control, to always act sensibly—that is a shame. And my desperation is the greatest compliment I could ever pay to Sheri.

I was assigned work assisting in planning an upgrade to the second shutdown system trip logic. The second shutdown system was a Canadian import; the traditional American pressurized and boiling water reactors have just one rod-based shutdown system and consequently a large amount of accident analysis is concerned with cases in which the shutdown system does not activate. Kankakee is such a complicated reactor, and the fuel configurations used are so varied and so potentially conducive to a runaway power pulse, a nuclear power excursion, that a second independent shutdown system using different power sources, different controllers, and a different physical mechanism for stopping the chain reaction was included in the design. As in the Canadian Candus, the second shutdown system is supposed to remove the possibility of the ATWS event—anticipated transient without scram.

The progress in instrumentation and controls, like the progress in computers, is so rapid that it's not unusual for stations to be developing upgrades to control systems which were first developed only a short time ago. Station pride becomes involved; most nuclear workers like to think that their station has the most modern equipment in the world. In the case of Kankakee, this was usually true because nothing was too good for a station that could burn disarmed weapons material, produce new weapons material, and produce power from natural uranium if it had to. For nuclear engineers Kankakee is a dream station, a station which can do everything, a station with which all kinds of experiments on exotic reactor fuels can be run, a station which can provide data to confirm or disprove the latest computer codes in regimes that could not be duplicated in any other station.

It was pleasant doing engineering work again. Of course I would like scientific work better, scientific work that might change things, but long ago I made my choices, choices between family and career, between ambition and life. I had made my choices and my expertise was in operations, in moving the switches, cranking the valves, racking the breakers. But I could still do engineering work; I could contribute there still, although I would have some catching up to do. And it was pleasant to be back at a desk and a computer and drawings and codes.

Redoing control systems means dealing with control technicians, and so it was no great surprise when a stocky yellow tee-shirted stomach stopped in my peripheral vision, and I looked up to see the once familiar, nearly unchanged beard of Jim Haskel.

"Hello, Jim," I said. "You know you don't look that much different than you did in the picture the FBI was showing me."

"Really. I was in a picture. And what did you tell them about me?" he asked, his eyebrows rising and his expression jovial, as if he were the Santa Claus of control technicians.

"Oh, they didn't ask about you. I don't think they knew you were in the picture. I was in the picture and so was Ken Seagraves. They wanted to know if I knew him, which of course I did, and whether I'd talked to him recently, which I haven't."

"Oh, so you and I and Ken were in a picture together and they just asked about Ken," he said.

"There were lots of people we know in the picture, Jim. It was a good picture. It was from the May Day parade."

"Oh yes, the May Day parade. I think I know the picture. It was a good picture. It was a good day."

"I suppose you were interviewed, weren't you Jim?"

"Yes, I was interviewed. They asked me whether I knew you, and I just told them about how I know you here at Kankakee. They didn't ask me if I'd known you before, and I didn't tell them."

"That could be risky if they found out," I said.

"Risky, no way. It would be totally far-fetched for me to have put the contamination there. I hadn't been past the turnstiles much at all the whole week, and there's no way I have any access to the strange compounds that contaminated our people. I never worked at Kensington labs like you did."

"Maybe the tritium had been in there for a week. Maybe it had been there for a month, or a year. It was only because I had Kerwin's pocket tritium detector that we discovered it. And you were a chemist, Jim. You might have been able to do it if you've kept up on your original expertise."

"Well I haven't kept up, and I wouldn't have done anything so stupid even if I did know how to do it. And if you're telling the truth and you didn't do it, then I couldn't have done it either because I wasn't anywhere near the tech section that night when your mysterious message from Dennis Banks came through."

"Well, if it wasn't you, and it wasn't Ken Seagraves since there's no way he could have got into the plant, even if he wanted to, then who did plant the tritiated organics?"

Jim didn't hesitate, "Why you did, Henry. Of course it was you. It couldn't be any other way. You were there, you have the knowledge, and you have access to the crazy compounds at Kensington labs. I have to admire you Henry, or should I call you by your old nickname—Devil. You remember that—Devil. And you were a Devil, too. Devil, I thought you'd become a complete sellout and dead-to-the-world and here you go on a wild attempt to destroy nuclear power or stop bomb production or something by this bizarre tritium contamination."

I had never put the case against myself in quite so clear a form. I looked him in the eye. He was smiling. He was enjoying himself. I could trust him, he wasn't out to destroy me, but he saw so clearly the reason why I would always be under suspicion. "I didn't do it, Jim. Don't admire me; I'm not a crusader anymore. I just try to make it through the day, just like most people."

"Okay, Devil. Let's suppose that you didn't do it. I'll put your question back to you. Who did then?"

"I've no idea. Lucy did trace a message my computer received back to Trung's computer. Lord knows Trung would know how to make my computer send me a message, but I just can't believe he'd do that. He and I are friends. We've never had any big problems. There's nothing he should dislike me for."

"Unless it was the war, of course."

"The war was a long time ago."

"Yes, but wars are best for producing lasting anger, festering passions for revenge, for justice. Why I even sometimes remember and get mad about the war, and I wasn't even in it. Think how much more someone like Trung must feel."

"I still just don't believe he would do something like that. But someone did it; I know that. To tell you the truth there's been so much going on I haven't even really thought that much about who might have planted the tritium in the recirc room."

"I think you should think about it. Because unless they discover who did it, there's always going to be a lot of people who will think it was you."

Haskel had more. He had a real reason to come see me.

"Henry, keeping on the subject of the recirc valve room event, did you not find it strange that the control room didn't pick up the tritium alarm from the west fueling machine bay? For that matter, some detector should have signaled the control room about the recirculation room contamination."

"Yes, that was the first strange thing that happened that night. I picked up the alarm on the tactile interface, but the control room alarm annunciator didn't light up. That's an action item on the event follow-up agenda. Of course are lots and lots of action items. Kankakee will probably be decommissioned before we sign-off all the actions."

"Well, we can sign-off on why the control room didn't pick up the alarm. It's right here in this engineering change package."

Jim flopped the folder on my desk. He pulled out a control logic diagram that he had marked up in red ink.

"The old minus one error," he said. "Kerwin's instrument and controls whiz-kids put in the exact opposite of what was needed. You'll note Trung and Pete Kerwin himself signed as having reviewed the package. It was when Trung was working full-time for Anthem Electronics. Before he came back here. And Laura's signature appears as Central Nuclear's reviewer."

Jim had found an error in the control logic diagrams. The I&C branch of Pete Kerwin's company had been given a small contract to improve the plant access control systems. Two minus-one programming errors, inputting exactly the opposite of what the designer had intended, had cancelled each other and foiled the logic error detection programs. Haskel had found what the error-detection routines hadn't.

"You do good work, Jim," I said.

"Try to. Now would I have tried to contaminate this place if I care enough about it to get that close to the circuit level?"

"Actually I don't think you'd ever do anything that would hurt someone else physically," I said. "You always were something of a softy that way."

"I wouldn't hurt anyone physically, you say. You mean I might hurt them mentally."

"Sure, mentally. Spiritually. Don't feel bad about it. We all do it."

"You seem to have adopted a very pessimistic philosophy, Henry."

"Life has a way of doing that, you know. I'm sorry. I know I shouldn't think this way. We can act. We can make a difference. I try to think that, I really do."

"Careful Henry. Say things like that and they'll convict you of the tritium contamination without thinking twice about it. You'll get the logic error fixed?"

"Sure, but don't you want to do the paperwork. It's you who found it after all."

"No Henry. I hate paperwork. If you put it in they'll know you can still do your job, that you're not a full-time saboteur."

"I'm not going to thank you for having me do your paperwork," I said.

"I don't need thanks. Life is adventure enough," he said and turned to go back to the land of programmable controllers, relays, pressure transmitters, and all the signals that kept Kankakee alive, its nervous system. But about twenty-feet away he turned and said loudly so that most of the technical area could hear him. "I'm going to be sure to tell Pete Kerwin he should hire some competent engineers for a change. And I'm going to tell Trung that he should give up on reviewing logic diagrams he doesn't understand."

A voice deep in the maze of cubicles retorted as Jim left: "And we should hire some quiet control technicians!"

Haskel's visit reminded me that I was still the number one suspect for the FBI and the NRC and everyone else, and that I ought to do something about it and not indulge so much in the solace of engineering work. I hadn't looked at the diskette Lucy Watkins had given me, and for someone in my position that was unforgivable negligence.

The data on the diskette was good. Although there was no record of who might have gone into the technical section via the administration building, there was the key-card door data for those entering from the plant side. And on the evening of the recirc room event, Laura Brault, Trung, and Haskel had all gone into the tech section via the key-card door. And they had all done it before I received the e-mail signed Dennis Banks.

My computer had sent me a message because of a command sent from Trung's machine. And Trung had been in the tech section around the time the message was sent. Trung and Laura were there. And Jim Haskel had been there, too, even though he had just told me he hadn't been anywhere near the tech section that night.

I had the idea in my sleep. I had been particularly strong at my exercise session that day. There was a black muscleman leading the aerobics dancing, and the women had flocked there to go through the workout. The muscleman had the best music, he was the best dancer, and he had the best body. I pumped my exercise bike in rhythm to the music until my heart had been racing for ten minutes. Then I dismounted and began the weight lifting. I always do my best lifting right after climbing off the bike, and with the driving soul music I was putting up more weight and doing it more times than I ever had before.

It happened that night after work as I lay in my basement bed. I was in the deep sleep induced by the exercise when I had the idea. When a man and a woman love each other they get married. Sheri didn't love me, but maybe she would if we got married. Of course we were married, but maybe if we got married again it would put things right.

I should have done it sober. But saying something that shows my need so clearly always causes me trouble, I hate to do it even though I know I have to. I went to work in the morning and waited till the evening, till after the girls were in bed and Sheri had started her usual hour or two of work before going to bed. I used vodka and then whiskey before going to Sheri's office. She was sitting alert before her computer. The external modem's red lights were blinking. Sheri did a lot of e-mail; she had associates and partners all over.

"Putting together another deal?" I asked.

"I hope so. Pete and I are bidding on some work in Indonesia."

"I didn't know human factors was one of Pete's many areas of expertise," I said.

"Oh it's not. But he's done so many things, and he's had so much experience bidding on contracts that having his name on the bid is bound to help."

"He can't have more experience with contracts than you."

"Well, no, but then that makes the two of us near unbeatable. We'll blow away the competition, I'm sure."

I had to say what I'd come to say: "You know Sheri. I've been thinking about what could make it better between us, and if you'll take me back, if you'll love me again, we can get married again. We can get married, and it'll be like a new marriage. We'll be starting all over again with everything new, and we'll forget everything that went before and just try to make life wonderful for you and me and Tracy and Laurie."

She looked at me. Her face looked tense. She had her fierce look in her gray eyes as if her head would explode.

"Will you marry me again Sheri?"

"Oh I don't know." And she looked down with a flutter of eyelids, softness replacing the tension. "I don't know, but it's the nicest thing I've heard for ever so long."

She stepped close to me and she kissed me, a quick kiss and she broke it off, but the nicest kiss I'd had for ever so long.

She turned away from me, "I must think about it," she said. She sat back before the computer. "I have to work. Please let me think about it."

And so I left and went upstairs. Events sometimes come in quick succession and this was one of those times. The telephone rang. My mother. She had finally done it. She had bought a condo in Florida to be close to my grandfather and the other uncles and aunts who had moved south to escape what snow and cold there is in southern Indiana.

"So Henry, if you want some of the furniture, anything you can take away would be a great help to me," she said.

"Oh, Mother, this will be such a big job getting you moved."

"Yes, but it will have to be done. So many of the people I've known are now in Florida, so I'll just have to adjust to living in a smaller place. It'll make me feel good knowing that you have some of the stuff from when you were growing up."

"It will be important for me, too, Mother," I said. I hadn't told her about me and Sheri. I didn't want to. And Sheri had just given me a kiss. Maybe things would get better and mother would never have to know.

9

Going in on the Thursday after my mother's call, I arranged to take the following Monday and Tuesday off so that I could go to Center City to help her with the move. I made her promise to stay with her friend Madge in Trevelac while I was in the house packing up things. I didn't want her to tire herself trying to help out, and I knew she would start working and lifting things too heavy for her if she were there in the house while I was working. I didn't feel happy about her leaving, because once she left I'd have nowhere to go to in the town where I'd grown up. I'd have to take a motel room if I wanted to visit my home town. And it's a nice town with the hills and the leaves in the fall. And it's a gritty town with the not-as-prosperous-as-before factory workers contrasting with the money and the hope of the new engineering and software enterprises. I will always like to visit my home town. I will always visit my mother, but now I will have to do it in Florida. And will I really visit my hometown when I have no relatives there, when I've been away so long that I won't recognize my friends. Yes, I'll visit it for high school reunions. That will give me an excuse to take a motel and walk around the old town that I knew as a child, that seemed so magic then, and that seems so different, smaller, and yet still magic now that I have made my way in the world. Or thought I had made my way until Sheri made her announcement.

And I realized that after my mother moved I would be no closer to anything resembling a family than I would have been if I'd stayed in Canada. At least no closer to a family older than me. My girls would still be my family, and I would have to look after them as best I could in whatever time I was allowed to have with them. But who would take care of me? Daddies don't need anyone to take care of them. And it was true. I had taken care of myself for a very long time. I didn't need anyone to take care of me. But who could I talk to as if I were talking to my family? In Canada I just had Sheri. And now I didn't have Sheri. And where would I go when I wanted to go home? After my mother's house was sold, it would be very hard for me to call any place on this earth home. Home would be more a memory, a feeling, not something I could walk into.

They didn't give me any argument about taking the time off; since giving you time off makes them feel better when you announce family problems. Yes, you have a problem and we want to help you in every way we can. Take some time off. They fairly rushed to approve my forms.

And although Sheri announced that evening that she and Pete Kerwin were going to spend Thursday and Friday morning in Chicago discussing the latest new-build projects, I felt some speck of hope. When I came in Pete was just leaving, and it was obvious they were having a disagreement. Sheri has a stiff, square-at-the-shoulders look when she wants her way, and she had that look as she was saying her goodbyes to Pete. And Pete was apologetic; he said, "I'm sure we can arrange for more of your people to share in the work. We can change the wording, I'm sure of it."

The hope came when Sheri gave me one of her best smiles; she has a beautiful soft smile when she's happy and she's greeting someone she likes. She gave me that smile, and she even touched me softly on the shoulder, and I wanted to take her in my arms, but I remembered the times I had done that, to show her how much I wanted her, and she had stood there so stiffly until I let go. I didn't want that stiffness again, so I contented myself with looking at her as lovingly as I could.

And our evening went well. Tracy sang a song she had learned in school, and for once Laurie was not jealous when we paid attention to her little sister. And Laurie had received the top grade on her math exam, and we all felt happy at the supper table. Sheri's eyes met mine and there was no friction, she did not look away.

And before she went to bed Sheri said, "I'm sorry I have to go away tomorrow. But I'll see you Friday."

Thursday morning was hot with puffy cumulus stretching out forever as I looked past my computer out the window wall of the tech section. Even the flatness of northern Illinois was beautiful, even the drooping arches of the steel reinforced power lines stretching away to the north were beautiful. Corn and soybeans and industry. Industry and energy, a cradle for Chicago, the foundation of the illusion that the city is real.

Even the control logic diagrams brought up on my screen were beautiful. Diagram upon diagram just for Kankakee. Once I would have had paper all over my desk and the trash bins would be full as the corrections and revisions were made. But the computer changed that or at least would have if so many of us did not feel compelled to print, to produce our own paper copy to hold in our hands and spread on our desks as if the paper were somehow real, more real than the image on our screen. But it was all plans, designs, preserved tracks of some engineer's thoughts.

My phone rang and the readout just showed "Unknown Number" when I picked it up.

"Henry, it's been a long time."

"Really, who is this?"

"This is Ken Seagraves, you remember me from Madison?"

"Of course, as a matter of fact your name has rather been in the news these days. But then you always had a knack for attracting cameras," I said.

"As a matter of fact, your name has come up in some discussions I've had recently. Discussions with the FBI."

"Yes, they asked me about you, too. Wondered whether I've been in contact with you. Wondered whether I'd spread tritium in the recirculation valve room to help you anti-nukes out."

"I can assure you, Henry, that the Energy Coalition would never consider contaminating workers as a protest. We need contacts in the plant, of course. We have some plant contacts, but we can always use more."

"Jim Haskel?" I asked.

"Who is Jim Haskel?" Seagraves said.

"You know very well. From Madison. When meetings started to become boring, he had his standard yell, 'Don't you want to win?'"

"Jim Haskel works at Kankakee?"

"Very good Ken. You do that very well pretending you don't know about Jim."

"Listen, Henry. I didn't know about Jim, but we do need more contacts; we need to know what really goes on in the plant. But if you have the idea of radioactive sabotage, we don't want any part of it."

"You would say that, wouldn't you? You always were clever Ken, so I suppose time and experience and your legal pleading have made you even cleverer."

"It's not cleverness, Henry. Nuclear power is dangerous, expensive, and we don't need it near Chicago."

"I'm sorry. You have it. You have it to the max. Take away Kankakee and you'll still have it. And you crazies even want to stop Hydra."

"It's just another high-tech, elitist project that we don't need. I know you Henry; I know you know I'm right. And I figure you want to do something about it, and I'm just saying that if you would pass us information, it could be a great aid to us. Information could help us more than if you were standing with us on the picket lines."

"Yes, I've read spy stories too, Ken. Who are your contacts in the plant?" I asked.

"Sorry, Henry. For spy work inside the plant the cell size is one. None of you will know who the others are."

I'm not proud of what I did then, but I was beginning to feel desperate. I said, "You know, Ken, I haven't told the FBI about Jim yet. I haven't told them that he knows you. I'll bet if I told them they'd run all kinds of checks to see whether you and he have been in contact."

"You could do that, Henry. But you were in it with Jim and me and the others, and if you told the FBI about any of us it would be a violation of the trust we forged then. And if it comes to squealing, I know some things about you and I've heard rumors of other things. Things about White Sands. You were there, weren't you Henry?"

"Okay," I said. "I won't tell the FBI anything about Jim. You're right. But just tell me whether he's one of your contacts. Tell me whether he's talked to you and what he said. I promise I won't tell."

"Okay, Henry, I shouldn't do this, but I know you're in trouble. Jim is sort of a contact, although he insists that he's not really one of us. But I do talk to him from time-to-time. He hasn't given us much yet. Mainly he's worried that Kankakee is an unsafe design, that another type of nuclear plant would be okay, but that Kankakee is too risky. So he's not one of us, because we believe that all the nuclear plants are dangerous, that they should all be shut down."

"Thanks for telling me, Ken. I knew that Jim would have to stay in touch with some type of movement. Maybe you're right about nuclear, but I don't think you really are. It's a battle that goes on and on, a battle you've nearly won except in Japan and Asia and the former East-bloc. No one builds more plants, but no one really shuts down the ones we have because we need the power. So I try to do the best I can, and if I found out about something I really thought was more dangerous than the things everyone already knows about, then I'd pass it on. I'd make a phone call to your Energy Coalition or something. But you usually don't know where the next accident is coming from. Your contacts probably will think some things are problems that aren't really problems, and we'll miss the real problem. Anyway, it's good to hear from you Ken. And thanks again for telling me about Jim."

"How's Sheri? Does she feel the same way you do about nuclear?"

I remembered that Ken had always been sweet on Sheri. But then that wasn't unusual. "Oh, you know she was always kind of a hard-line pro-nuclear build-more-machines Marxist. She's into control room design, travels all over telling them how to make the worker's job easier. Sometimes she tells them how to do without workers which I suppose is kind of problematic for her, but then we all have our problems."

"So Sheri's doing alright."

"Her career is going very well. She's strictly an independent consultant now, and she has to turn away work."

"You have children?"

"Two little girls. And are you and Karen still together?"

"No. We split up a long time ago. She's out in Oakland. You and Sheri are the unusual faithful lefty couple."

"Actually we're having bad problems. Sheri wants to leave me."

"Oh, I'm sorry Henry. I know that can be hard, very hard, especially with kids. If you ever want to talk or just go out for some beers for old time's sake, please give me a call."

"I may do that Ken. But then I really will have a lot of explaining to do."

"You always were good at explaining. Comes from all your thinking. And remember, Henry, I've trusted you, just like we trusted each other in the sixties. You're honor bound not to tell the FBI anything about Jim or anything else that I told you."

"All right. Relax. I won't tell them about Jim and you. But I want you to know, Jim is one of the people who were in the right place at the right time to stage the tritium accident. If I can prove he did that I'm turning him in, movement loyalty or not."

"I couldn't blame you, but even though Jim used to talk a militant line, I don't think he'd do anything that would hurt anyone."

"Neither do I, but someone did it, and I have to suspect everyone, no matter how long I've known them."

"I'm sorry it's like that. Take care of yourself, Henry," he said and hung up.

So first Jim Haskel and now Ken Seagraves had contacted me after I'd been taken off shift and put in the technical section. The tritium incident seemed to be attracting all sorts of people and forces from out of my past, and they all seemed strung together and connected by the investigation. We all knew each other and we all knew Howard Crowder. I supposed we should have a party.

I left work early so as to be with my girls more. The pickets were back at the Arsenal Road gate, but I still felt so cheerful with the puffy cumulus cotton balls brightening the sky that I smiled and even called out to them. I even caught myself thinking that the distillation towers at the refineries looked good.

I took the curvy road by the creek again. Horseweeds hugged the road and I wondered if I still remembered how to find the worms inside to use for fishing bait. I'd passed a lot of time as a kid fishing in small creeks and gravel pits. And then in Canada with the magnificent rivers and lakes I hadn't fished at all. All a matter of my priorities at the time, I suppose.

Tracy was running and turning cartwheels as I pulled in the drive. Both girls could do full cartwheels, something I had never been able to do even once. But that's something girls always seem to know how to do. I wondered if I should try to learn how at my age and promptly rejected the idea as placing too much stress on my head's blood vessels. Better to admire my girls and laugh with them.

Sheri gave us a call from Chicago after supper and wanted to speak to the girls. But then she spoke to me and said she was anxious to get back home.

"You've always liked to travel," I said.

"I know. But the girls will be young such a short time, and I don't want to miss any of it."

"I don't either," I said, and promptly regretted it because there was a silence and then she quickly said her goodbyes.

The phone woke me at eleven-thirty and I wasn't fully conscious as I answered. I wished I'd put in call display at home because I was greeted with an unknown, distorted voice: "Hello, Henry, so now you've stolen plutonium."

The words brought me fully awake, but I felt stunned by the change in mental states. "I don't steal," I said.

"So maybe you've just borrowed the plutonium like you borrowed the tritiated organics so you could burn out those poor mechanics. I'm telling on you. You won't get away with it Henry?"

"It's not me. Tell as much as you like, but it won't be true."

"You've always been able to get away with things, Henry. Get away with doing things your own way, program your own programs, test your own way, read the specs the way you want. But your party is over. Goodbye, Henry. Sleep well because it'll be the last good sleep you'll get."

My heart was pounding. I could feel the throb in my neck. I cursed myself for getting so upset over a crank call. But where in hell did plutonium come from? It made no sense. I drank myself to sleep with Old Crow whiskey and tossed in my sleep with dreams of Jim Haskel and Ken Seagraves chasing me in a polluted creek. And Sheri was there. She was holding hands with Judy Peterson.

The Moraine Herald-Journal's morning headline resolved part of the mystery. "Plutonium Theft from National Laboratory" it read.

Of course the amount stolen was small. Kensington labs only kept enough for research purposes. There was more at the Kankakee experimental reprocessing center, but the plutonium hadn't been taken from there. It had been taken from the Health Physics labs at Kensington.

And I had worked there on the research projects. I knew exactly where the plutonium had been kept, and I could have had access to it.

10

A re people really watching you when you think they are? The meeting of eyes, the looking away. Are they thinking what you're thinking? I knew I had been one of those with access to the plutonium and would be a suspect. But did they know? Did the secretary for the reactor cooling group know about it when she greeted me in the aisle and then turned away with her pile of folders for filing? She looked down as she turned, and she seemed to hurry. Did she know? Was she afraid of me?

You don't really know what other people are thinking. When you think you know, it can be just your thoughts, intense thoughts that you put into the other people's heads. You are feeling something so everyone must be feeling it. They know. They are laughing at you.

And of course sometimes they are laughing at you—or worse.

I kept waiting for the call, for the memo, for the e-mail message asking me to report somewhere. I knew I would be seeing Howard Crowder and Sheila Rowe again. And I knew that they would ask me many more questions this time.

I decided to offer to let them search my house. But then that would show forethought, a desire to exonerate myself. And the plutonium could be hidden anywhere. A tiny lead can, even a plastic bottle and no radiation would escape. Only with the plutonium in your hand would you feel the faint, strange warmth.

Noon came without a call. I passed through the plant cafeteria line and selected fatty food to make me feel calm. French fries and meat. Pie with ice cream. I didn't want to feel even the slightest need for calories or energy in any late afternoon interview. Fat counteracts caffeine and gives confidence.

There were lots of people I knew in the cafeteria. Dennis Banks was there with a delegation of Japanese. Judy Peterson and Blair McKenna were there. And operators and technicians. I found a table with only one chair and wolfed the fat down. I wished I had some papers to look at, to pretend that I was busy. I felt the pressure build inside me, the pressure of thinking that people were looking at me, talking about me and that I must steadfastly ignore them.

But then Trung came into the lunchroom, swaying with his tray like a long, wan reed. He saw me and his face hardened. He turned and found a seat alone at a table about as far away from mine as could be found.

Trung was someone I couldn't ignore. Not if I was to continue to pretend to be trying to help myself by figuring out who had been the real saboteur the night of the recirculation valve room event. I piled what remained of my lunch onto a tray and walked solemnly over to confront Trung.

When I got to within ten feet of him Trung noticed me out of his side vision. He turned his chair to face me, his knees spread out wide, his head pulled slightly inward, his chin toward his chest, but his eyes were pulled up so he could return my gaze.

"I did not trick your computer into sending you a message, Henry McClure," he said.

"Somebody did. Even though I can't prove what was in the message, Lucy can prove that your computer sent mine a command, and that command might have been to send that screwy message."

"For all I know it was you," said Trung. "You find out my password or you take over my computer from your own and make my computer look like it's making yours do something."

"Come on, Trung. You know me better than that. I'm not a hacker. I couldn't do that in a million years."

"Oh yes, Henry McClure. You always act dumb. I remember that from way back. You act dumb, but when you want to do something you know how to figure out how to do it, even if no one's ever done it before. You could have done it Henry. You would study a little and ask a few questions and then you could do it."

"So could lots of people," I said. "So could Laura Brault. She knew your password, didn't she?"

Trung just looked at me, his eyes narrowing. I got tired of waiting and staring back at him, so I said, "I'm not saying Laura did anything. I'm just trying to figure out who could have sent me that message from your machine."

Trung said, "Laura could have sent you a message, but she would not have. She is the last person to ever do anything as unprincipled as that," he said, and with his last words he pounded the table with his fist so that people began to stare at us.

"Okay, Trung. I'm not saying anyone did anything. I'm just trying to see if the computer record can help us figure out what happened that day."

"If someone had not poured water over my machine after wiping the hard disk clean, it could have. But now they can get nothing from my machine. We will never know what went out from my machine to yours."

I felt listless after the fruitless exchange with Trung. His fury and energy when I'd brought up Laura's knowing his password had sapped whatever energy I'd started off the day with. I managed to stay an hour and a half into the afternoon, but then I decided to use up more of my swing time to leave early again. I wanted to see Sheri. I needed to be somewhere where I felt safe, where people would know I wouldn't steal plutonium. Where people would know I wasn't crazy.

Sheri's Plymouth was in the driveway when I got home. But there was another car there, too, Pete Kerwin's BMW. But Pete had known me a long time and we had successfully finished projects together, so I thought he would know that it was not me who would play with plutonium. I was not known as one for games or pranks. At work I might pursue some of my own interests, but they were engineering interests, they had some connection to my work. I did not try to obtain people's passwords or play computer practical jokes.

Sheri and Pete were in the living room. Sheri had her legs curled up under her on the couch. Pete was in the rocking chair pulled up close to the coffee table on which was a nearly empty bottle of red wine. And I started to feel the jealousy. Of course there might be another man involved. Maybe it was Pete, but then I rejected the idea because I didn't see what Sheri could see in him. "I'm glad you're drinking," I said, "because I need a drink bad."

"You're home early, Henry," said Pete. "What did they do, shut Kankakee down?"

"No, I'm off shift." I hesitated because I didn't know whether Pete knew anything about Sheri and me. "I've had some personal problems and, considering the tritium incident and all that, they're giving me some desk time in the tech section."

I poured one beer and as much as I could get of another one into a brown stein. I wanted to spike it with vodka but didn't because I figured they might notice. Nuclear operators are not supposed to be as desperate for booze as I was. It was Friday, I had survived another week, my wife was home, and I started to feel fine.

"Have you seen the paper yet, Pete?"

"No, but I've known about the plutonium since Monday. We have been using it in some monkey experiments."

"Why would you want to use plutonium on monkeys?"

"Oh, we're looking for treatments. And maybe we can debunk some of the screwball claims about plutonium toxicity. You know, the giving everyone on earth cancer with a pound of it story."

"It's just too much. First the tritium and now this plutonium thing. And I could have taken both of them, although I didn't really know anything about the tritiated organics. I just happened to have worked in the same room with them. I knew about the plutonium, of course. That's the isotope everyone likes to talk about. It gives you some pride to work in a place which has plutonium. It means you're a real nuke, right up there with Fermi and Oppenheimer."

"Oh, I'm tired to death of everything nuclear," said Sheri. "Even though it gives me contracts and the control room design work is probably the most interesting work I do, I wish I didn't have to deal with it."

"I've told you, Sheri," I said. "You can go to law school. A few years and then your work life would be totally different."

"I'm too old to go to school. I don't want to go to school. I want to live," she said, her face sinking into a frown. She was shrinking from me, looking down, becoming smaller before my eyes.

"Well, I've been saving some news," said Pete. "I had wanted to save it for a special moment when you were feeling great and would agree to anything, but I guess I'll use it now to get you out of this old nuclear fission blues. They've just opened the bidding for a scoping task analysis for the Hydra fusion reactor operator job. It's nuclear of course, but...."

"Oh, that's great, Pete," Sheri said, straightening her back and bringing her long legs to the floor. Her smile was stretching her face and her eyes were shining as she said, "You've got to let me in on it with you. You've got to."

"Well, I'd rather hoped that you would let me in on it with you," said Pete. "It's more your specialty, not mine."

"Oh, of course. I can hardly wait to start preparing the bid. Oh can we start now, can we, can we?" she said.

I might as well not have been in the room. I would have no part in any of Sheri's contracts. Pete would. And I wondered what I had done wrong. When Pete and I first met, he and I did the same work. And I was better than him, or at least I had always thought so.

"Certainly we can start, but probably not today. I'd better get a copy of the spec. And it's Friday, and Henry probably has some detritiation drinking to do, and it would be a shame to make him do it alone. And I wanted to thank Henry. His unfortunate incident has given this baby a new lease on life." Pete reached to the inside vest pocket of his sports jacket and brought out the long metallic cylinder of his miniature tritium detector.

"You've really got orders in spite of that report that said it was unreliable and near-impossible to calibrate?" I said.

"Definitely. There's nothing like a real-life event in which this detector was the only thing which prevented even worse overexposures than what happened. I'm even getting orders from PWRs and BWRs. Everyone wants to be sure they're doing everything they can about tritium, even if they're unlikely to have much of it."

"I was probably the only one fool enough to believe the damn thing," I said. "Everyone says it goes off for no reason at all."

"Nonsense," said Pete. "I agree you may have to take a little more care with it than some of the instruments, but nuclear workers should be able to handle it gently enough to keep it in calibration. For example, I've been carrying this one around with me for two days. I'm going to turn it on and I'm willing to bet it's not going to give a false positive."

"I'm not going to bet that a detector's not going to do what it shouldn't do in the first place. That's not exactly a good selling point," I said.

"Nevertheless," said Pete. "Let us put to rest these calumnies on what will soon be the international standard for tritium monitoring." Pete slid the switch and smiled. Three seconds passed and then our ears were assaulted with the high shriek I had last heard in the recirculation valve room. But this time there was not the noise of the nuclear plant to compete with the shriek, there was only the deafening, painful shriek.

I started to laugh. I yelled as loud as I could, "Sure, Pete, no false positives," but Pete was not smiling. He rushed down the stairs to the front door and went out to the yard. The shriek was only a soft high-pitched whine from there, and I could feel my muscles relaxing from the clench caused by the alarm. Then the shriek stopped. I could see Pete through the picture window walking around the front yard and staring at the instrument. Then he marched fixedly toward the house. I could hear the front door and his steps on the stairs. I could just see his head emerging over the top of the banister when the alarm started again.

Pete swung around to face us, his feet squared and he turned the detector off. "Sheri! Henry! Get out of the house. This isn't a false positive, I'm sure of it. There's tritium in here, not a lot, but more than we want to be involved with."

"Oh for crying out loud," I started, but I was drowned out by Sheri's crying.

"Oh, I can't stand it, I can't stand it," she screamed and she was rubbing her hands over her arms and clothes as if she was rubbing something off. Pete dashed to her, put his arms around her and said, "Hush, hush, it's alright. It's not a lot, it's probably just a false alarm, but let's get out of here." He led her past me. I was stunned and just stood there. I let them pass. I watched them start down the stairs.

"Come on, Henry, you too," called back Pete.

There seemed nothing else to do but obey. We found ourselves out in the front yard in the sun and I regretted not having brought my drink. "Damn't Pete, I have enough trouble without this kind of game."

Pete glared me full-face, and it was not a friend I saw. "This is not at all a game, Henry. I'm calling the plant now to get someone out here with a tritium-in-air monitor and a bubbler."

I wanted to protest but I was revisited by my nuclear conscience, a sort of intense man in a lab coat who I could visualize saying to me "Believe your instruments."

I had believed Pete Kerwin's tritium detector once before and it had saved me and the valve maintenance crew from a lot of dose. There was no reason not to believe it again.

"I have to get new clothes," said Sheri. "These must be contaminated. And Tracy and Laurie. We've got to stop them before they get to this damned house."

Pete nodded to Sheri, but then he turned to me, placed his arm on my shoulder, and said, "Henry, if there is tritium contamination in this house, someone has put it here. Think who has been here who could have done it."

I started to think but then didn't have to. "Anyone could have done it, Pete. Our deck party. Everyone who was anyone in Kankakee nuclear was there."

"Oh my God, you're right," said Pete. "People were all over your house. Little Laurie was giving tours. But listen, whoever this creep is, he's bound to slip up somewhere. What about that e-mail you received, have you gotten anywhere with that?"

"Well, Lucy can't prove what was in the message, but she has been able to show that my machine was sent a command file from another machine a little before the false message was sent."

"That's great, Henry," Pete said.

"Not so great," I said. "It was Trung's machine which sent my machine the command, and Trung was irradiated—irradiated worse than me."

Pete's face wrinkled up as if he'd just resolved a mystery. "Maybe Trung doesn't care."

"Care about what?" I asked.

"Maybe he doesn't care about beta radiation. I've watched him at Kensington. He's very sloppy with weak beta emitters. I even chewed him out about how he was handling some iron-55."

I tried to imagine Trung being sloppy about anything. I couldn't.

Sheri pulled on Pete's arm. "We have to get Tracy and Laurie!"

I nodded when Pete asked if I would wait until the rad techs arrived. I didn't really realize until Pete's car had backed out onto the road that Sheri was with him, and that I didn't know when I'd see her or the girls again.

I thought about how there was no longer any need for me to offer to let my house be searched. It would be searched whether I offered or not. The radiation technicians would arrive with counters and detectors of all imaginable varieties. And somehow I knew that they would find tritium. They would find tritium because everything about my job was going wrong for me these days.

I thought about how I had to drive to Center City to help my mother move. And I wondered where I would put anything that I took from her house.

I realized that any tritium they found would do me no good; I went into the house, turned on the exhaust fan in the kitchen, and began opening windows. Then I realized that if the technicians arrived with all the windows open they would accuse me of interfering with their measurements. So I reclosed the windows. I didn't want to turn the exhaust fan off, but finally I did.

Tracy and Laurie didn't come home on the school bus, so I figured that Sheri had picked them up. I was wondering how to call Sheri when the van from Kankakee arrived.

I went into the house with Jack Barber, one of the keen young Kankakee workers. His blond hair was cut short; his face was sharp and his blue eyes piercing. He held up a portable tritium-in-air monitor as he mounted the stairs. Numbers flashed on the LED readout and they showed Pete Kerwin to have been right. There was tritium in the house—not a lot, but tritium does not wind up in houses on its own. We backed out of the house and the technicians went to the van for their respirators.

They found a hot spot in the basement work room. There was about a foot square section of my work bench that had a fair amount of adsorbed tritium coming off it. The technicians carefully cut away thin strips from the workbench's surface and put them in plastic bags. That was a nice thing about tritium; the beta radiation would be totally blocked by the plastic. I knew they'd use liquid scintillation counters and spectroscopy to determine the chemical composition of the tritium-releasing surface.

After the NRC and the state of Illinois radiation protection experts arrived, the technicians did what I had started to do, open all the windows and turn on the fan.

"You work at the Kankakee station, don't you Mr. McClure?" asked the nice young man from the NRC.

"Yes." "Have you been doing any experiments in your basement with material from the plant?"

"I would never do that. My wife is terrified of radiation and I would never bring anything into the house that would have a chance of contaminating my children."

"So you have no idea how tritium got into your house?"

"Absolutely none."

"Well, the levels we found here are not that serious. We'd have worse if one of those tritium powered exit signs broke open in a closed room. So I wouldn't worry about your house. We should be able to stay and certify it as safe even tonight. But I think you're going to have to answer a lot of questions about how the tritium got here." The NRC radiation man had a nice smile, and I knew the people who tracked down little radiation accidents in transportation and medicine and industrial radiography had seen all sorts of weird situations in their work. He'd probably seen lots of scientists and technicians who'd contaminated their homes, the old professors who painted their stair railings radioactive so they could find their way in the dark. And he'd be used to finding radiation in unexpected places.

"I'm sure I will have to answer lots of questions," I said. "But I haven't knowingly brought anything more radioactive than a smoke detector into my house. I have no idea how any tritium got here."

"It was somewhat strange," said the NRC man. It seemed to be coming off some substance adsorbed on a section of your work bench. Did you spill anything there which might have been contaminated?"

"No, I haven't done anything there much except glue some of my kids' toys back together with superglue and epoxy."

And of course then we went down and I dug out my glues and turned them all over to the NRC. I realized as I was talking that I was in an investigation and anything I said would be followed up on, but when you're talking to someone it's hard to keep that in mind, it's hard to keep things from just flowing naturally.

They took samples of cleansers and soaps. The tritium aired out of the house quickly, but they organized a plan to cover the house inch-by-inch with their instruments. They opened pill bottles and old peanut butter jars full of bolts. They opened the food in the refrigerator and pantry.

Night came. Myriads of cicadas serenaded the numberless stars. The inspectors left and I was alone in my house with no idea where my wife and children were.

Pete Kerwin's number was unlisted and I couldn't find it scrawled down on our variegated phone lists tacked hither and thither on our kitchen bulletin board. I started in on Sheri's friends, but no one was answering. Finally I remembered that Laurie had been planning to go for a birthday party at her friend Barb's. I knew Barb; she was a tall, thin little girl with blond pony-tails. I couldn't remember her parents' names, but I found what had to be her number on the list.

"Hello, this is Henry McClure, Laurie's father. Is Laurie there?"

The mother said that Laurie was there and I asked to speak with her.

"Hi, Daddy."

"Hi, Laurie. You know that there was an accident at the house, don't you?"

"Yes, Mommy said that they found some poison in the house and that we couldn't stay there anymore."

"Oh, the house is alright now. You'll be able to come back. But where did you go after school?"

"Oh, we went to Mr. Kerwin's house. Mommy said we would be staying there for a while."

"Pete Kerwin? Mr. Kerwin?"

"I think so Daddy, the man with the house on the lake. We went swimming. And you know what Daddy?"

"What?"

"He has two keyboards so Tracy and I can play at the same time."

"Oh, that's nice," I said. "Well, will you tell Mommy to call me when she picks you up? Tell her the house is okay. Tell her the house has been cleaned up, and I'll be staying there tonight."

"Okay Daddy."

"And you have fun at your birthday party."

"Oh, I will Daddy. They have three cakes."

I stayed up till midnight. Sheri didn't call. I found Pete Kerwin's number in her address book. I found his picture too. He had his arms around my kids.

II

I came into my mother's house as I had so many summer nights before. Jackson Street was now four lanes, and that gave even more of a rush and clamor to the cars streaming by—windows open, radios blaring, street rods with their rumble and sedate cars of the heartland moving from mall to mall. There was the smell and the moon of summer, and I was moving into my mother's empty house.

I almost sat down in the now walled-in porch to look out at the passing parade of cars. I'd always liked that, especially on hot summer nights. But I had a job to do, so I moved to force the old black key into the lock and go inside.

Mother hadn't been gone long enough for the house to turn stuffy, and since she'd left all the shades down, it was even refreshing compared to the sweltering heat outside. And then I noticed she'd left the window air conditioner on. She'd lived without one for so many years, and now that she had finally had the electrician tear out Dad's old do-it-yourself wiring and installed circuits so she could keep at least one room cool, now when I finally wouldn't worry about her in the heat—it was like her to pick such a time to move south. Well, she'd have an air conditioner there, too, so it wasn't so bad for her. But I wouldn't have any connection to the place where I'd been raised. I'd be a tourist in my own home.

What to take? What a question. My mother shopped for bargains, and I suppose she threw things away, but I didn't know what. It would be best if I started with the heavy stuff. The stuff that would be the most trouble for her when she had to move out.

I hadn't turned on a light yet, but now I did, the light next to the stairs. I turned on the overhead fan, too, although I knew it wouldn't help me where I was going. Before I got to the heavy stuff, there was something I had to see. It had to be there. I knew she had kept it, even though I'd told her to smash it, to burn it, to destroy it past recognition.

I started up the stairs and the stifling heat immediately hit. The stairway light hadn't worked since I was a kid so I had to feel my way up, sweating as I went. I cursed and pulled my tee shirt off and dropped it on the stairs. The air was dry, searing hot, and breathless.

My rifle used to hang between two hooks on a pegboard above my desk. It wouldn't be there now, of course, and when I turned the ancient rotary metal switch, I saw the pegboard wasn't there either. I could feel the heat wave spread from the unshaded overhead incandescent and suddenly felt dizzy. I moved straight across the room and tugged at the ancient window sash closest to what used to be my bed. It didn't want to go up, and I cursed and jerked at it and at last it began to budge. More jerks and it was up, but the mere whisper of outdoors air which reached my nostrils was not enough to revive me. I slumped to the floor, rested my back against the wall, and ran my hands over my sweat-drenched chest.

I knew there had to be a window fan. Sure enough, I found two of them under the other single bed. The beds were bunk beds. I used to sleep on top, my brother below. Now they were both on the floor for grown-up guests.

I fitted a fan into the open window and forced the sash down onto it. It started with a roar when I pressed the plug in; it was already on maximum. I stood directly in front of it for a full minute, watching the lightning bugs flash below in the back yard. I hadn't seen so many lightning bugs since I was a kid and had trapped hundreds of them in glass peanut butter jars with holes punched in the lids. I thought maybe they were going extinct with the pesticides and all, but they were back in force this year, the back yard dizzy with gentle yellow sparkles.

I stepped to the other window of the pair. I had mastered the jerking technique and I had the window up on my first series of thrusts. I remembered that this window wouldn't stay up on its own and found the weather-grayed stick of splintery lumber we used to prop it up.

It was hard to leave the relative coolness of the air blast from the fan, but I wouldn't find what I'd come upstairs to find by staying put. I even considered lying down in my old bed, but if I did that I might find myself still there the next morning. I looked at my old closet, but I knew the rifle would not be there. I always went in that closet when I visited mother, and I had a very clear idea of what was inside the riot of boxes within.

I passed under the glare and heat of the electric light again and switched it off as I went out to the upstairs hall. My mother's door was closed. There was another blast of heat when I opened it and stepped inside. At least the window fan was still in her window, and I crossed over to it in the dark, not wanting to bear another blast of heat from the electric bulbs.

I went immediately to her closet. It was a big closet, and as full of boxes as my own. The close air and heat was worse than any I had yet faced, but my body must have adjusted or I was sufficiently excited because I did not hesitate to reach up to the bulb hanging from its cord and switch it on. I wondered if you could bake eggs in the closet.

It's not easy to hide a rifle. It is long and metallic and its shape jumps out at you. It was behind her clothes, propped up in the corner. There were shells in a little cardboard box beside it.

I slipped the shells into my pocket, held the rifle barrel up in my left, and switched off the light. I left both window fans running and went downstairs. I was greasy with sweat again and needed a drink. I knew where there was whiskey, my Dad's old stock. He'd preferred vodka, so there were two quarts of Old Crow left under the sink when he killed himself.

I'd been working on that whiskey ever since, whenever I came for a visit, which hadn't been too often when Sheri and I had started our family in Canada. Even so, one of the bottles had been almost done for the last time I'd left. I had a sudden fear that maybe the booze would be gone, but no, the bottles were still there back behind the trap in the sink piping.

It was dark under the sink, but I still saw one of the big black Indiana cockroaches lurking behind a bottle of bleach. They weren't fast like the little ones. They probably weren't cockroaches at all, but, no matter, its shell gave a most satisfying crunch as I caught it underneath the whiskey bottle.

I couldn't find a small glass, so I poured a big one half full and plopped in two ice cubes. In the heat, the alcohol hit almost immediately, and I loved the harsh burn of the whiskey down my throat. I took another big hit; I wanted that feeling to stay. Poor Dad, I wonder why he hadn't drunk the whiskey? I think he thought the vodka was pure, that it wasn't so harmful. But the taste of whiskey, the earthiness of it, it had substance and you knew you had drunk something, not like the smooth tasteless slide of vodka.

I suppose that's why I knew I wouldn't kill myself, knew that Dr. Chambers and my wife and all their talk about depression and heredity, and my sleeplessness being so bad, and how I wasn't myself, how my behavior was different and unpredictable—I knew all that was rot because I liked whiskey and my Dad had left two bottles behind untouched. I'd loved my Dad, but he wasn't me. I wasn't like him, not that way anyway.

The rifle was lying across the kitchen table. I was in the room with my old rifle, the one my Dad had taught me to shoot, the one which I'd pointed the wrong way once on a squirrel hunt and he'd yelled at me to point it at the ground like he'd showed me. There used to be an old shotgun around the place, but for most of the years when I'd been growing up, my rifle was the only weapon in our house.

So when Dad wanted to kill himself it was only natural that he'd taken my rifle. It was the only one around. He probably had forgotten that it was mine, that he'd given it to me for Christmas. If he hadn't taken my rifle, he'd have had to go to a sporting goods store and buy one and maybe he'd even have had to wait for it with all the new rules and regulations, and who could wait when your spirit cried out to be done?

The whiskey glass was empty. I sucked at the ice and set it down. I had the whiskey daze, my brain wanting to spin, but I held it back, kept it in place behind my eyes. I took the rifle in both hands and went into the living room to sit at Dad's old seat at the end of the sofa.

It was so much like you couldn't fight what a shrink said to you. And you couldn't fight what a woman said to you, not when it was about sex or love or whatever it is men and women are always taking such trouble about. Dr. Chambers was a shrink and a woman to boot, and my wife was a woman and they'd both sat in that room and said I was going to kill myself, or maybe they didn't say that, but they were afraid I might kill myself, and since my Dad had done it that made it more likely. "But I'm not like my Dad," I'd said and they'd smile, and Dr. Chambers' voice was so soft, "Perhaps."

I could feel Dad in the room with me, feel his brown eyes and his walk, so forceful, so sure, so strong. I'd always thought of him as strong—stronger than me; I could never be that strong. And yet he'd been weak, weaker than me, I could never do that. But then it was hard to do it, so hard.

Why did I know how he'd done it? Of course I didn't know, not really. I'd just been told something, told by my Uncle. When I last saw Dad, the mortician had already done his work and there'd been no sign of a bullet, at least I hadn't seen a sign, but then I didn't look, not for that.

The rifle was lying across my lap. I picked it up and slid the stock between my legs so I could look down the barrel. It was a short-barreled twenty-two, no problem at all to reach down and pull the trigger. I thought of the human factors' charts of anatomical percentiles showing what fraction of people could reach so far in what direction from what position. You could design any kind of machine for people that way, and why not a killing machine, too. Of course that was what human factors was mainly for, killing machines, the best controls for the best bomber or tank, devices to keep the soldier operational in the most extreme environments.

Now my brain was spinning and I forced it back in place. I wondered if I could see the bullet if there was one in there. Maybe Mother had taken to keeping it loaded in case there was a burglar. It was just black inside the barrel. I could pull the trigger and find out, but maybe the safety was on. I could feel it, but which way did the damn safety work?

I swung the barrel around and pointed it at the wall. I could test it now, but then I might wind up with a hole in Mother's wall. I was having trouble figuring out what to do. What I needed was another drink.

The whiskey was the best I'd ever tasted, harsh and clarifying. I went back to Dad's seat and started again. I could look down the barrel and then I slid it up into my mouth, the cold steel almost breaking a tooth as it passed. Dad hadn't done it this way, I knew he hadn't. So I was different from Dad, he hadn't put the barrel in his mouth.

The trigger was there and the safety and I still couldn't figure it out. I took the barrel out of my mouth, pointed it at the floor, and pulled the trigger. Nothing happened. The trigger didn't click. The safety was on.

"God-damned piece of motherfucking engineer's iron," I shouted and threw the rifle at the wall. It bounced around and made a lot of clatter before finally coming to rest. I had the illusion of smelling gunpowder, as if I had fired. Maybe it was the surge of anger through the whiskey. I was violent, rage engulfed me and I was going to do what I'd wanted to do from the first.

I picked up the gun and went through the kitchen to the basement stairs. They were treacherous and dark and damp, and there was a trace of egg-water smell in the air. I reached the unpainted concrete basement floor. The air was cool on my bare back, but the humidity and smell were so stifling that I didn't want to stay there long. I feared I would be forced to stay there a long time; it would take a long time to do the job I intended. It's not so easy to destroy a rifle, to destroy it utterly, not just a single disabling wound.

I wanted the barrel broken most of all. That was where the bullet had come from. I slammed the vice home on the stock hard, and attacked the black steel with an old hacksaw. Steel is always so hard to cut, but the hacksaw did take hold and I was in a fury. I ground the blade back and forth until my arms ached. There was a smell of hot oil and then I could tell that part of the blade had entered the hollow. I pulled the hacksaw out and laid it down on the workbench. Beside the workbench, leaning against the white-washed concrete blocks of the basement wall, was the old sledge hammer that I'd used to smash rocks when I'd dug our driveway. Dad had bought it used. Its handle was grey and grained, and the head was rusty but still hard steel and heavy. I picked it up and realized that it was stupid to try to use a sledge hammer in the low-ceilinged basement, but I wasn't doing anything that made much sense so I hoisted the sledge as far above the rifle barrel as it would go and brought it down hard, straining with my shoulders and arms and bending forward at the waste. The blow tore the rifle from the vice, and the stock caught me on the forehead.

I caught my breath and cursed with the pain. The basement looked clearer, extremely real as if I were sober and alert with wonder or fear. The rifle lay before me, a quarter of its barrel cut through, but you couldn't see the cut unless you looked closely. Otherwise it looked as good as new. I brought the sledge down on the stock and the wood splintered. I hit it three more times, and then I could tear part of the stock away from the metal.

I wanted another drink, and I knew there were concrete blocks out behind the garage. I took the sledge and the rifle and went back up the stairs. The rifle knocked over a pile of empty coffee tins from a wall shelf and they clattered and glinted as they bounced and tumbled down the stairs and across the basement floor. I turned the light off on them.

I didn't bother with the glass and ice this time but took two quick hits from the bottle. Then I took another bigger, slower one. My mouth burned, and I almost didn't get it down. It went straight to my head and I staggered out the back door. The stars and the moon were brilliant, but mosquitoes immediately attacked my bare and sweaty back. I thought about going back for my shirt, but I wanted to get it over with so I continued toward the garage, giving the air an ineffectual slash with the rifle.

There were high weeds beside the garage, but I could see the old concrete blocks. There were even more mosquitoes in the weeds and maybe poison ivy too, but I reached in twice to get the blocks I needed. I set them about two feet apart, and took some care in aligning them so they looked square and neat. I laid the rifle down on top of them so the cut part of the barrel bridged the space between. It felt good to swing the sledge up to its maximum height and I grunted loud as I brought it down on the barrel.

There was a bend in the barrel, but it wasn't broken. I hit it again and again and it broke apart just when I was losing strength and thought I could not lift the sledge again. I took the two pieces, the long part with the trigger assembly and the short barrel segment, and threw them into the trash can. I wanted to burn it; I wanted to incinerate it, to send it to hell.

I had no matches. I went around to the front of the garage and opened the unlocked door. My mother had put wiring in the garage, and I flicked on the light. The garage, stuffy with stale hot air, was crowded with debris I remembered from my childhood. I took a big cardboard box and the greasy galvanized gas can for the mower and went back out and around to the garbage can. I stamped on the box and rammed it into the can. Then I opened the gas can and doused the box. I always liked the smell of gasoline, and I splashed some on my hand and held it to my nose. I reached into the can and brought the long part of the rifle up so it rested vertically, supported by the surrounding cardboard.

I don't remember going back for the matches, but the next morning I got up from the couch where I must have laid down without taking off my shoes and went outside to see the trash barrel. There were fresh ashes inside and the rifle barrel was blackened and left black on my hand when I touched it.

12

I awoke on the downstairs couch. I didn't remember much about the drive back from Center City, but there was mother's furniture jammed at odd angles around my work-room to prove I had made the trip. I looked closer at the room. It was different. Sheri had been back to the house. A lot of the girls' toys were gone.

There was a note on the kitchen counter:

Henry, I've taken some of the girls' and my things and the VCR. I think what happened Friday is the final straw. I won't have the girls growing up in a house that is radioactive. We're staying with Pete. I've never told you, but I suppose you may have suspected that he and I have become very close. I'm sorry things have worked out this way, but probably it's best to make a clean break and put us both out of our misery, Sheri

If I'd read such a note just a week before I'm sure I would have collapsed in tears and screams. On this bright Wednesday morning it seemed like just one more thing. One more blow at my psyche, one more thing for me to bull myself through. I remembered the old comic book hero, Sergeant Rock. I felt like Sergeant Rock and how could that be since I'd never been a tough guy? Maybe it was the only way I could exist and still hope to make sense of and survive what was happening to me.

I would only have flex-time to thank for not being late to work. I pulled on wrinkled tech section casuals, ate peanut butter and bread with instant coffee, and brought my minivan out onto the road. There was a chance I could get back on what might appear to others like a schedule.

The atmosphere in the administration building on the preceding Friday, when there was only the missing plutonium to add to my list of suspected wrongdoings, was positively relaxed compared to what I sensed as I made my way to my desk. Fred Blyth, the station chemistry specialist actually turned his head away from me in a jerk when he saw me. No one said hello. I sat, put paper in front of me, made some marks, got out my calculator, turned on my PC and pretended to be calculating something.

At ten-thirty the phone rang. It was Dennis Banks, the man whose name on the mysterious e-mail ordering me to the recirculation valve room had started me off on my continuing nightmare.

I should have known what he had to say. I should have known it was an official call, but we had known each other in Canada, we had worked together, we had always been friends, and I'd been glad for him when he'd become production manager at Kankakee. I should have known it would be official, and yet I still felt like talking small talk as friends.

"Henry, I'm sorry to have to tell you this, but given everything that's happened, especially this contamination incident at your house, we're going to have to remove you from control room duties indefinitely. I'm sorry, I know your license may lapse, but it's the only thing we can do while all these questions are unanswered."

I wanted to talk about some old story; I wanted to say something to show him that I was still myself, but instead I just said, "Sure Dennis. I understand. I know you have to do what you're doing."

I was thinking about how I could talk about how I was innocent, but I couldn't think of a way that wouldn't make me look as desperate as I felt, so the conversation ended there.

I don't usually take my official fifteen minute breaks, but I did this morning. I went straight to the door and out into the sun and the heat. There was a walking path lined with lilac bushes that led down to the shallow lake that had been dug to aid the cooling towers for the secondary side cooling. I headed down the path fast and then broke into a run. I wanted to run and run until I hit something. I wanted to hit something bigger than a lilac bush, but then I turned and ran full force into one and found that lilacs are either stronger or I am weaker than I had imagined. I was on my rear in the dirt; I had a cut on my face, and I was laughing. I was laughing at everything I'd ever dreamed, laughing at everything I'd done and strived for. I was also laughing at being so stupid as to run into trees in the middle of the day.

My desk was still there when I got back. Kankakee station was still there outside the picture window. The flat ground stretched wide past the abandoned buildings of the old ammunition plant and on out to the chemical works and oil refineries. Everything was as it had been. The world seemed to go on as normal in spite of the absence of any semblance of normality in what was happening to me.

I decided I had to find out Pete Kerwin's home phone number. I had to talk to Sheri. Pete's number hadn't been in the book the day before, but I tried anyway. Then I called personnel, but they wouldn't release home phone numbers. Then I called Dennis Banks. Dennis and Pete had always been friends back at Darlington. I was surprised when Dennis answered because production managers, and especially managers like Dennis Banks, are hard people to find.

"Dennis, I'm sorry to bother you, but I have to talk to Pete Kerwin, and I thought you might have his home phone number."

"Henry, I'm sorry to hear about you and Sheri breaking up. I know you're under an incredible amount of stress. I don't want you to do anything foolish. You're my friend, Sheri's my friend, Pete's my friend. I'm sure it's hard for you, but sometimes the best thing to do is just let go and not do anything. Let life take its course."

"You know about Sheri and Pete?" I fairly screamed.

"Yes, there was a note sent to Blair McKenna saying how Sheri had moved in with Pete and that losing her was what had driven you crazy, that you thought that by being in the news so much and by absorbing so much radiation without it hurting you that she would change her mind about leaving."

"That's crazy," I said. "Sheri hates radiation. And she probably thinks that if I get exposed then some leaks out of me and gets on her."

"It's not the first note that's been sent," said Dennis. "Ever since the recirculation valve room event there have been notes coming in saying you've gone crazy."

"Well whoever's been sending the notes is the one who's behind all this crazy shit that's been happening," I said.

"Maybe so, Henry. But still I don't know if it's a good idea for you to be calling Pete's house."

"Dennis, if I can't find Pete's phone number, I'm going to drive right out there and not leave until I talk to Sheri. And if I did that I might see Pete there and that would be a lot more dangerous than anything I might do over the phone."

"Okay," Dennis said. "I'll give it to you. Just don't do anything stupid. You know how you say things to her now could affect a lot how you'll get along with each other in the future."

"Thanks Dennis. I just want to talk to her. I have to talk to her. I want to know when I can see my kids. I want to know lots of things. I won't make you sorry you gave me the number, Dennis."

I punched in the number Dennis had given me. No answer. I kept hitting redial. I turned back to the desk and pretended to calculate. I set the timer on my watch and forced myself to not go to the phone for five minutes. No answer.

What did I expect? Sheri worked. The kids went to school.

Then I remembered Sheri's business. How would she get along without her modem and fax and her answering machine?

"That's what I'll find gone from the house next," I thought.

I was put out of my misery by a call from Blair McKenna asking me to come down to Human Factors for a chat with the NRC.

"No FBI?" I asked.

"No, just the NRC this time," said Blair.

I was relieved, even happy to begin to face those who were investigating me and who by this time must be convinced of my guilt. My morning had just been waiting for this to begin.

Blair seemed positively cheerful, but then he was a cheerful type with a fleshy round face. His brown suit was smooth and slick like his brown hair. He was brown and smooth and cheerful.

Blair showed me into one of personnel's interview rooms. Sheila Rowe was seated behind the table. Her severity contrasted with Blair's conviviality, and the adjustment to dealing with the two personalities made me even more alert and almost eager to begin. Ms. Rowe's curly brown hair stood out in all directions like a bristly mop, but the ringlets were tight and tiny and almost gleamed. "So how did the tritium get in your house, Mr. McClure?" she started.

It was a good question, and one that I realized I should think more about. I was acting as if things just happened by magic. "I don't know," I said. "I suppose I could have been contaminated at the plant, but I haven't been in any known radioactive zones since the recirculation valve room event, and they certainly checked me out thoroughly before letting me leave the plant on that one."

I was going to continue speculating on whether there could be some unknown contamination in the administration building or elsewhere on the plant grounds, but Ms. Rowe cut me off. "It couldn't have been plant contamination, Mr. McClure, because the source of the tritium in your house was the same mixture found in the recirculation valve room and such a mixture has to be prepared in a lab. It isn't created in the operation of a nuclear plant."

"Unless some of the organics are present in the plant and they come into contact with tritiated water and react by some mechanism we don't know about," I said.

"Let's leave out speculation about miracles and stick to something we know must have happened. Someone took the tritiated organics from Kensington labs where they're being used in animal studies of tritium behavior; then somehow these tritium compounds wound up in the recirculation valve room and in your house, and you happened to be present when both of these contaminations were discovered. Both of these contaminations were discovered by the same instrument, an instrument which is not in common use in nuclear plants. Would you agree that's the main story we have so far, Mr. McClure?"

"I didn't know the stuff at my house was the same as that at the plant, but—yes—that seems to be what's happened so far."

"You'll be relieved to learn, Mr. McClure, that the health physics instrumentation is so precise that they were able to determine that the tritium compounds wound up on your workbench only very recently, certainly after the contamination was placed in the recirculation valve room."

"Wow. Picking up those differences of days in a twelve year half-life. I knew I should have gone into electronics," I said.

"Yes, very impressive," she said. "But that still leaves us with you as the person most associated with all of these events."

"Oh, so I'm supposed to have placed the tritium in the recirculation valve room for some perverse reason, and then later have decided I wanted to test out my technique by contaminating my house? I can see playing with it in my house before putting it in the plant, but why do anything except get rid of it after?"

"Are you admitting placing the tritium in the recirculation valve room?"

I looked at her hard. She was stone-faced. I realized that she might be trying to make me mad. I said, "No, I'm not admitting anything. As far as I know I haven't ever handled any tritiated organics, and for that manner I haven't been around much tritium in any form for quite a while. I realize I always seem to be there when the tritium is found. I'm trying to think of any way I could accidentally have brought tritium back to my house, but I really can't think of any way, especially since you say it was the same tritiated organics that wouldn't be found normally in the power plant. I haven't even been to Kensington labs for a month, so I couldn't have accidentally brought it from there back to my house if it's just gotten in my house in the last week."

"I understand the search of your house was quite thorough," she said.

"Yes, you're welcome to come back and search anytime."

"We may do that. Unfortunately tritium and plutonium are so easy to hide that it would be quite likely that you've hidden them somewhere else."

"I don't have any tritium, and I don't have any plutonium, either."

"I find it odd that a man who had such strong leftist convictions as a graduate student would want to work in a plant which produces nuclear weapons material," she said.

"We haven't really produced that much weapons material. It's not really needed right now. But I admit that if weapons material is to be produced, it will be us who will produce most of it."

"Don't you find that to be a conflict with your personal convictions?"

"It's not something I'm particularly proud of. I'd rather just be producing energy. But if I weren't doing it, someone else would be. The United States will not choose to be without the type of capability that Kankakee represents."

"I assume you were quite opposed to the Vietnam war when you were a graduate student?"

"Yes."

"But you weren't opposed to it when you were a soldier?"

"No, I was very opposed to the war long before I was drafted."

"So why did you serve in the army?" she asked, as if it were a simple question, as if one could just explain.

"You don't have a choice when you're drafted," I said.

"But I understand most people who were opposed to the war found ways to avoid service. By joining the reserves or going to Canada or something like that."

"Listen, life isn't that simple, at least mine isn't. And I think there were thousands and thousands of draftees who served and who were opposed to the war. I was so young and stupidly principled that I thought it was immoral to avoid service by a trick, and I thought going to prison or Canada had just too many disadvantages and penalties for me. So I submitted and served, and I even went to Vietnam. I thought maybe I could organize within the army; I had lots of dreams."

"So you thought maybe you could stop the war by turning the soldiers against the war?"

"Yeah, of course when I got there everyone hated everything about the war already."

"Maybe you feel the same way about nuclear power. Maybe you think you can stop nuclear weapons by working in a weapons plant. There was a lot of sabotage in the army in Vietnam. Maybe you think you can stop the production of nuclear weapons by sabotage. Maybe you're just doing the same things you've always been doing."

"All I can say is that's not the way I am. I'm not complicated; I don't hide things inside and then seek revenge later. I usually act on what's on my mind when it comes to mind. So if I were a saboteur you'd find lots of evidence that I've been doing it all along. You won't find any evidence. And I didn't even do any sabotage in Vietnam. I could think that maybe fragging was justified when I was a student and the war was just what I saw on TV. But when you're there and dealing with real people, then you know that everyone of those people is a miracle. Yes, every person is a miracle, and you'd better have a very good reason, you'd better be very sure you're right before you kill a miracle."

"Who are your friends here at Kankakee?"

The question made me pause. I had been going back into my Vietnam thought loops and had been becoming more and more aroused. This question showed me that Ms. Rowe was playing me like a fish, probing all the areas where my plentiful supplies of self-doubt were stored.

"I don't really have very close friends that I see a lot socially here. I seem to always only mix socially with my wife's friends, so now that we're separated finding friends is something I'm worried about. Of course I know a lot of people, some of them for a long time because there's probably ten or fifteen of us who joined the Kankakee project from Canada. But they're mostly married. I think I have to re-learn how to be single again."

"Is Ken Seagraves one of your old friends?"

"I knew Seagraves from my student radical days. I've told you that. And I told you the truth before when I said I hadn't seen or talked to him since then. But, funny thing, right after I told you that he called me. I suppose you know that already."

"No, why would we know that?"

"Oh, phone taps and that. Of course you're NRC, not FBI. Maybe the NRC doesn't do that sort of thing."

"Of course we don't. Why did Mr. Seagraves call you?"

"He wanted to tell me that he couldn't condone radioactive sabotage. I told him neither could I."

"Is that all that he talked to you about?"

"No, he told me he had recently talked to the FBI about me. He asked me to tell him any safety problems at the plant that I knew about."

"And what did you say?"

"I told him I didn't know of any big safety problems."

"If you did, would you tell him?" She leaned forward as if genuinely interested in what I might answer, as if she thought I might tell the truth.

"No."

"Why wouldn't you? If there's a safety problem shouldn't people know about it?"

"There are proper channels and we have to tell the NRC about anything like that. And what we tell the NRC is public information. You're NRC, you should know about that. I don't need to tell the Energy Coalition. The station will take care of safety concerns, and if they don't then the NRC will make us take care of them."

"I'm glad you have such faith in the system," she said, and she was smiling a clever smile.

I forced myself to not say anything, and we sat looking at each other. I knew the FBI knew about the message from Trung's machine to mine, and I was hoping they were taking it as seriously as I did, so I said, "Have you found anything more about the command that was sent from Trung's computer to mine the day of the recirc event?"

"Not really," Ms. Rowe said. "We know there was some transmission from Mr. Trung's machine to yours, but we don't know the contents of the transmission. Mr. Trung says he knows nothing about such a transmission."

"Have you asked him if he knows anything about how tritium could wind up in my house?" I said, the corners of my lips starting to quiver as I remembered Sheri and my girls fleeing our house.

"Do you sometimes cook for Mr. Trung? Do you feed him?"

"Feed him. No. What kind of a question is that? He isn't my child or my boarder," I said, with little success in keeping my rage and frustration out of my voice.

"Did you give him special hamburgers at your party?"

"Oh. Now I see what you're getting at. The oregano burgers. I fixed Trung oregano burgers once when we were both doing field work in Florida. Since then, whenever he comes over I try to fix him an oregano burger, and he never turns them down."

"How often do you give him these hamburgers?" she asked.

"I don't know. Once, twice a month? Whatever is this about? As far as I'm concerned, in spite of his being my friend, Trung is the person who could have most easily made my computer send me the faked message from Dennis Banks. Have you asked him why he went into the tech section the evening of the recirc room event? Have you asked him how his computer so conveniently lost everything on its hard disk?"

"We have asked, but I've no intention of discussing this further with you, Mr. McClure. Especially with it now appearing that Mr. Trung is certainly one of the victims of this campaign of radioactive terrorism, rather than one of the perpetrators."

"What do you mean—a victim? Trung didn't take that much tritium."

"No, Mr. McClure. He did not take that much tritium. But in the process of monitoring him with some new, more sensitive equipment, we found that he has been contaminated severely with a very unusual isotope, an isotope even more difficult to detect than tritium."

"There's no such isotope," I said.

"There is iron-fifty-five. Do you know about iron fifty-five, Mr. McClure?"

I nodded. More of my useless knowledge. I knew about the speculation that iron fifty-five had caused a surprisingly large amount of human dose exposure while the atmospheric testing of nuclear weapons was going on. But you wouldn't get much iron fifty-five in a nuclear plant unless you got a lot other things with it.

"I have something to show you." Ms. Rowe opened her brief-case with a sharp click, and slowly pulled out a folded piece of paper. "We've found your fingerprint on a letter which was sent to the Region III NRC office in Lisle," she said.

"Really," I said. I don't remember sending any letters to the NRC. But then I have touched a lot of paper in my time."

Ms. Rowe slowly opened the paper and held it open at her right shoulder. I leaned forward to make out the words formed by the crazy quilt of letters cut out of magazines. It was in the same style as the letter Judy Peterson had showed me after I took her psycho-logical test. But the plot line was longer on this one. The letter said: *First I do Beta Burn. Then I do Alpha Annihilation. Nothing you Pigs can do about it.*

She kept holding it open and glaring at me. I felt sick at my stomach, but finally I said, "I didn't write that. If my fingerprints are on it, then whoever wrote it must have taken some paper that I've touched."

"We need to search your house and your office here at work," she said.

"Sure. I can see you need to do that."

"I'd like you to come with me to your house now," she said.

"Of course. Let me first just report to my supervisor."

"There is no need. Mr. McKenna has already informed your supervisor and everyone who needs to know that you'll be with me for the rest of the day."

I followed her out of the office. Two radiation technicians with tritium sniffers and alpha contamination meters were waiting for us outside. Ms. Rowe went into Blair McKenna's office, and I could see her making phone calls through the glass. She said something to Blair, and they were smiling and laughing. I supposed I was rather a funny case.

I rode with Ms. Rowe and the two rad techs in one of Central Nuclear's vans. I guided them on the most direct route, all straight roads with nothing but fields and power lines on every side, but the blue of the sky and the sun and the puffy white cumulus and the surging corn made the day beautiful, and I even felt cheerful in spite of the reason I was making the trip. I love to drive with endless fields passing by.

Frank Crowder and three uniformed police officers had already started the search when we arrived. The search was very thorough and once again left the house a total mess. They took samples of every piece of blank paper in the house that looked like it might have been used for the Alpha Annihilation note. They looked through the newspapers and magazines in our recycling pile to see if any of them had letters cut out of them. They took samples of my homemade wine and of some thawed hamburger from the refrigerator.

They didn't find any radioisotopes. But then both plutonium and iron-fifty-five would be easy to hide. For a while there was a stir when the alpha scintillation counters picked up some radon in the basement, but it didn't take them long to identify it as natural-source radiation. They even had a portable multi-channel analyzer to identify the exact nuclide causing any discovered radiations.

Crowder confronted me toward the end of the afternoon: "We've got word back from the lab, McClure. The last note was made on the same type of paper we discovered on the desk in your downstairs office."

"That's my wife's office," I said.

"I'm sure you had plenty of access, McClure. You're not accusing your wife of radioactive sabotage, are you?"

And, of course, I wasn't. I could think of nothing much to say after that, except twice I told them that I didn't write the note, that I didn't plant any tritium, and that I hadn't taken any plutonium.

Police walked the grounds of my property looking for any signs of digging. They excavated a place where Tracy had buried a goldfish.

At the end of the work day the two rad techs took me back to the plant so I could pick up my car. We didn't talk on the ride, but as I got out of the van, one of the guys said, "Don't let it get you down, Mr. McClure. We didn't find anything. No court's going to say that a shift supervisor did the things they say you did without some damn good proof."

"I hope you're right," I said. "I've always stayed away from courts. Lawyers go there."

The van pulled away and I was alone with my car. I tried to think about my situation, but it was too much. I had tried to throw suspicion on Trung, my friend, only to learn that he was the victim of yet another contamination. And Trung was no fool, even if Pete Kerwin said he'd been doing sloppy work. And I had the terrible feeling that when they put samples from my house through the fancy ultra-sensitive lab detectors they would find iron-55. Whenever anyone was contaminated there was a trail leading to me.

I was alone with my car. I could drive anywhere I wanted to, and going back to my ransacked house had no appeal.

13

Coming back to Moraine from Chicago at night is eerie, with the lights glaring from the towers and smokestacks of the heavy industrial zones. The booze heightened the effect, but the aura of devastation and unfriendly other-worldliness helped to keep me awake through the alcohol relaxation.

I had gone to three bars and had asked three women to dance, all in the last place, the loud rock bar Roxanne's. All three had refused, even though they were tapping their feet, rocking their bodies, and leaning forward, straining their heads toward the music. They had all been young, I suppose, but then I always have a hard time with age. For sure the prettiest one had been very young, too young for me, too young for an old nuke gone on a bender, so he wouldn't have to go back into his empty ransacked house.

She had been part Asian, her skin shown beige and bright against the gleaming blackness of her hair. She had giggled and whispered to her friends immediately after evading my line.

So I'd been foolish, but I was lonely and had to do something. I'd lost my woman and although my brain told me that I didn't have to have a woman and that I was unlikely to find another I would love so much as Sheri—another part of me wanted to try. Wanted to try and try to find a woman.

Old locker room stories. The key to success with women: keep trying, keep asking.

Or stop asking because what you get is not worth the trouble of all you go through to get it.

I took the Arsenal road exit and drove past the refineries and Kankakee's front gate and on and on, taking the small roads toward Monee. I cut off on the service road for the properties surrounding one of the lakes created when an open-pit coal mine had been exhausted. Peter Kerwin's big house was on a rise overlooking the lake, and there was a spit of land going out from his property which allowed him to have the most private and extensive beach on the lake. I stopped my car, turned it off and stared at the house, dark except for an upstairs room. Behind which of those windows were my little girls? Where was Tracy laying her head and which toy was she hugging?

I cursed and asked myself why the hell I hadn't asked Sheri when I could see the girls. It hadn't occurred to me until then that I would have to act, to bestir myself and insist on arrangements for me to continue to be my children's father.

But then the one room's light went off, and other lights flickered on. And then the front yard was lit and Pete emerged, buttoning his shirt. Sheri was behind him but then caught up with him and took his hand as they walked toward Pete's car in the driveway. Pete opened the door, but then turned and took Sheri around the waist with his left arm. She met his kiss. He turned her against the car and his hand found her breast. It shouldn't have hurt because Sheri had already told me, but I had to fight down the urge to scream and get out of the car. Rage and sadness. Rage at the sadness and sadness at the rage.

I slunk down in my seat. Would he never leave? Would I never hear the sound of his car starting? It did start, but the engine noise did not changed. I peeked up. Sheri was leaning down at the car window. She was smiling and laughing.

Finally headlights played across my window and Pete's car went by. I looked up and saw Sheri opening the door to go back into the house. I started the timer on my watch and waited two minutes before starting my car and driving straight past the house, the opposite direction from the one Pete had taken and the long way around to get back to the main county road toward Kankakee station. My heart was pounding and I told myself I was stupid to get so excited, just as I was stupid to ask girls to dance, just as I was stupid to have ever done anything I'd ever done. But at least they hadn't seen me. My spying visit on the mother of my children had gone unnoticed. And I had one more blazing item of bad news to place on my pile of personal disasters.

I was cold sober and my eyes were sore and bulging in their sockets as I made my way through the night to my house. I didn't lock the door behind me when I went in. I stumbled over the mess, shoved my mattress back over the springs, dropped my clothes where I stood, gathered up sheets from the floor, and I thrashed at them until all of me was covered; I went quickly into a sleep which refreshed my eyes and some of my muscles, but not my thoughts of how I would ever have my family again.

The house looked no better in the morning. I called in sick and tried to decide which room to set back into some semblance of order. I first thought of the bedroom in case I found someone to come home with me. But there was no use cleaning the bedroom unless I had cleaned the living rooms and bathrooms first. And the chances that I would find a woman who'd want to sleep with me were no chances at all.

So I set to work on the kitchen. I like to eat and I keep whiskey there. With will power I didn't touch it until ten-thirty.

My house was a disaster and had recently been radioactive. My wife and daughters were with another man who'd been my friend, and I didn't understand why. Why was Pete better than me? I was distrusted by my co-workers, and—if I was caught drinking the way I was—my days in the nuclear industry would be short indeed. I saw the danger clearly.

The danger was that I had nothing, foresaw getting nothing, and there wasn't much to contradict my being nothing, nothing at all.

When the stovetop and kitchen table were clear, I started in on the living room. Books were strewn every which way. Sheri and I had too many damn books. And the kids had plenty of books of their own, encyclopedias of animals, volume after volume of pigs who talked and cats who were firemen. Just putting the books away would make it possible to walk in the living room.

I couldn't be nothing. I couldn't let it happen to me. My children would not have a father who was nothing.

I know that when you have problems, you should try to think if there is any way anything good could come out of it. The only thing good I could think could happen out of losing my woman would be to get another woman. Another woman who was younger and sexier. Another woman who I couldn't keep my hands off.

I quit early on the living room and went out to my car to drive into Moraine and get some lunch and look at women. I went over the women who might be single at work—Judy Peterson and Laura Brault, and there was the cute young girl with the fantastic breasts who had started sitting behind the desk in the records department. She was too young for me, she had to be. And yet, what would be lost by trying?

A lot can be lost if you get too much of a reputation where you work. I didn't know what I was doing. I was just doing.

I could see through the windows of the Farmer's Table restaurant. It was a big place, and popular and there were lots of waitresses. I could see one of them in her uniform through the window.

There are things you can do to your posture to make you seem more open, more available. Relax and keep your arms to your sides, don't cross them. And speak. Talk to the women. If you don't talk they won't notice you. And try to smile.

I did all that. The waitress was really cute, and she wrote her name, Debbie, on the check. I gave her a big tip and smiled at her on the way out. I wouldn't have time to go there for lunch when I was working, but I could go there on all the free days I had from the twelve hour shifts. And maybe she worked there in the evenings. And maybe if she didn't like me, maybe there were other girls in there who would.

I thought back over how I'd been as a young man, and I couldn't recall ever being this desperate to find a woman to like me, to get a date, to make love to someone, and I wasn't that particular who, so many women looked good to me.

But it's all right to open your posture and speak and smile, it's all right as far as it goes, but I knew I was going to have to do more than that. I was going to have to think of things to ask women to do with me. And I was going to have to ask them. Women had made the first move with me before, but it hadn't happened in a long time, and it hadn't happened that often. Had it happened more than three times? Would I need more than the fingers of one hand to count the times? I wasn't sure, but I was sure it hadn't happened more than ten times. If I waited for that to happen, I would likely wait a long time.

So what could I ask Debbie to do? Well, I couldn't ask her to do anything till I knew her better. So I'd have to keep going in there and keep trying to be served by her and keep talking. And then?

I could ask her to go with me into Chicago. Or Champaign. We could see a rock group. But I was too old for rock groups. No I wasn't, but maybe she'd think I was.

You can ask a woman to eat with you. Lunch is a little thing. Dinner is special. But Debbie was a waitress and she'd probably be working. I'd have to ask her to have dinner with me on one of her days off, and I didn't know which days those were.

I had never dated a waitress.

And I realized the main thing that attracted me to waitresses was that a lot of them were young—young and pretty with smooth skin and laughing smiles. And that probably wasn't exactly what I needed or could get, and would they go out with someone who worked in a nuclear plant anyway?

I could have gone home to continue the clean-up, but I didn't. I drove to the Green Door bar to better ponder the question of the woman I wanted. And Paula should be there and maybe Paula was the one.

Paula was there in her high boots and short skirt, and her top was open and loose knit with glimpses of white around her breasts. Even early in the afternoon there were men at the bar, and I figured they were there, like me, to watch Paula.

Paula walked tough and foxy, but she had a soft, high voice. It had been two weeks since I'd been in there, so it wasn't that obvious.

"What would you like?" she asked in her little-girl voice.

I locked my eyes to hers and kept them there. I asked if she had Pabst on tap. She did, so that's what I had. Then I had another.

I wondered what I could ask Paula to do with me. I looked at her closely. She knew how to dress to show the sexiness of her lean, long, and lanky body to best effect. But I could see some lines in her face. She wasn't that young, but she sure looked young. She looked like a million dollars, and I was far from a millionaire.

There was another girl who worked there evenings, and she came in and sat at the bar and had a beer and was talking to Paula. She was straight where Paula was curved, so she was even longer and leaner than Paula, and she had long straight black hair hanging down most of her back and on her shoulders. She wore blue jeans and a sweatshirt which might have kept me from looking at her and thinking about her had it not been for that gleaming hair and the generous bulge in her sweatshirt when she turned or stretched.

"You work here in the evenings, don't you?" I asked before I knew I'd done it.

"Just Thursday, Friday, and Saturday," she said.

"You like it so much you come here when you're not working."

"Yeah, I like it. I wish I could work more, but Paula here's got the lock on this job."

"Well, Paula's real good at her work," I said, and I looked at Paula when I said it and she smiled back.

Nobody was saying anything, so I turned to the long-haired woman and said, "Of course you're real good, too. My name's Henry, Henry McClure. What's yours?"

"My name's Jenny. I don't think I've seen you in here before, so how can you really know I'm good at my work."

"Oh. I've been in here before. I was in here two weeks ago and I remember you."

"That's nice," she said. "Maybe you can come in again sometime and say hi."

She was looking at me and smiling. I was looking at her hair and thinking it was the most beautiful hair I'd ever seen. I got out of my seat and walked over to her. I leaned close to her and said, "I'll be impatient waiting for the weekend. Would you like to have dinner with me tonight? Say Italian or Chinese?"

Her smile disappeared and she began getting out of her seat so that I had to step back. "No. I'm busy tonight," she said. She was up and starting to go around on the other side of the bar. I was trying to think of something to say, but she had the next words. "And I'm busy every night this and next week." She turned her face away from me and walked over to Paula. They both turned away from me and were talking softly together.

I went back to my chair. There was only a swallow left in my glass and I swallowed it. If Paula had turned I would have ordered another, but she didn't turn. I wanted to act unconcerned. I didn't want to rush off and I tried to sit there. But I couldn't stand to see them so close to me talking together, so I put three dollars under my glass and walked out. There was silence as I left.

It had been a long time since I had approached women in bars. I wasn't much good at it then, and it didn't seem I was any better at it now. The world hadn't come to an end. I was perfectly healthy walking to my car, the girls who had been at Roxanne's had probably forgotten all about the stupid old guy who'd asked them to dance. Jenny and Paula were perhaps just now finishing giggling about how I'd walked out. The worst I had done was to pay them an unwanted compliment, and I guessed women didn't really mind too much receiving those. Maybe I'd even be able to come back—maybe in a month or so I could go back to Paula's and maybe Jenny would be there and I could start over with her. But then it's hard to see how you can start over with a woman who not only says no to your invitation but says she's busy all the time as well, so don't bother to ask her to do anything else.

I was in my car intending to leave Moraine when I saw a tall straw-blond woman in blue jeans and a tee-shirt carrying clothes into a laundromat. She had a little boy with her. I pulled into the laundromat's parking lot and watched them go in. I looked through the window and there were two other women in there. I pulled back out onto the street thinking of the laundry I had to do back at the house. It wouldn't take me that much more time to bring it to the laundromat rather than doing it in our machine at the house. Of course the blond woman with her boy would be gone by the time I got back, but maybe there'd be someone else by then. And I realized that I stood the danger of having worked my whole life to become an unwanted irritation to women trying to do their laundry.

I drove back to the restaurant where Debbie worked. She was talking to two young men drinking coffee at the counter. Her red-dish hair went well with her uniform and she was laughing. That goes well with anything. I would come back to see her, but today wasn't the right time. But then there would never be a right time. I would feel ridiculous coming in regularly to a restaurant to make time with a young waitress.

I would feel ridiculous going to a laundromat, ridiculous going up to women in bars, and ridiculous going to restaurants. And yet just going to work everyday—assuming I would be able to keep my job at Kankakee—would not be enough either. And my two little girls. When would I see them again?

I had a newspaper back at the house, but I didn't want to waste time going back there to look at the movie listings. It would be too close to quitting time for me to call Judy Peterson if I did that. If I hurried it would seem as if I was calling her about break time. I pulled up to a Walgreen's. They would have a newspaper and they would also have booze. I wanted both.

I came back to the car with the paper and a pint of cheap whis-key. I poured my car coffee cup full with the whiskey and began to sip and read the movie ads. Nothing really appealed to me, but there was one movie playing with Jessica Lange in it, and I decided that would be my best bet. I thought a chance to watch Jessica Lange was worth sitting through a bad movie, and I hoped Judy would think the same way.

I wished I could think of something more exciting and unusual to invite Judy to, but I also thought that it was safer to start off with something common and simple. I wondered if Judy even liked movies. What did I know about her really? That she was young, lively, and her red hair was fun to look at. That she worked in human factors, could run the personality assessment automated software, and that I made her laugh now and again.

I could see a pay phone inside a grocery store and my head was starting to feel dulled with the whiskey, but it wasn't enough yet, so I poured the cup full again and drank fast. I could feel the whiskey taking stronger hold, and I wondered how long I'd have to walk around before I'd be able to drive home.

I felt young and alive trying to walk straight from my car to the pay phone. I squared my shoulders and pulled myself up straight. I looked at people who were shorter than me, fatter than me, with grimmer faces than mine. Why wouldn't a pretty woman want to go out with me? I was still a man and still had the life in me to do what I was doing right now.

Her voice came through the speaker bright and clear like my dreams: "Human factors, Judy Peterson speaking."

"Hi, Judy, this is Henry McClure."

"Why hello Henry McClure. You don't have to worry. I don't have any tests or interviews for you today. Of course I would have, but they told me you were off."

"There are advantages to not coming in," I said.

"What can I do for you Henry?"

I spoke slowly and as clearly as I could to convey the exact nature of my request: "I was wondering if you'd like to see the new Jessica Lange movie with me Thursday evening. It shows at seven and nine-fifteen."

There was only the slightest pause. "Well, thank you very much for asking Henry, but I'm afraid I already have plans for Thursday evening."

I should have had a graceful exit planned. All I could think of to say was "maybe some other time but I didn't want to say that because it would put too much pressure on her to be nice by lying.

Finally I managed to get out, "Well, have fun. I just thought that maybe you would like Jessica Lange."

"Oh, I do Henry. She's one of my favorites. Thank you again for asking."

"Well, would you like to see the film Friday instead?"

"Well, I'm afraid I have plans for Friday also Henry. You know Gerry Russell in the training department, don't you?"

I could picture Gerry. He was younger than me, but not much. He had one of those square fresh faces that some women seem to find sexy. But he was carrying some paunch and I wasn't. He'd been married once, but he didn't have kids.

"Yes."

"Well, I've been seeing him for some time now."

"Oh, I'm sorry. That's a very good reason for not wanting to go with me. I'm sorry. You can't blame a guy for trying."

"Good luck, Henry," she said.

I thought she had been very nice. She had turned me down just as definitively as Jenny at the bar, but somehow I felt better about it. Or at least I felt better about it for awhile until I started thinking about Gerry Russell and why he had to be the lucky one to go out with Judy. But then I thought it maybe showed there was hope for me since I didn't look that much older than him, and while he was a training department manager he didn't have that much higher a position than I did.

The whiskey was still taking hold stronger, and I thought I should use the high to make some moves on some more women before I lost my edge. The edge of being able to ask women to do things without their refusal penetrating too deeply. You almost didn't hear their "No," you were too busy thinking about who you were going to ask to do what next.

I couldn't think what to do. I thought of Debbie back at the restaurant, but then I'd already been there today. I felt so good from the whiskey that I might be up to trying to make time with Paula, but I'd been there already, too. I thought of Laura Brault, but she was my rival and I worked with her. But then I was in a mood to do things, so I went back to the phone. No answer and I figured I was lucky she hadn't been there.

I told myself I had done enough. I had fulfilled my weekly quota of trying to act normal by making advances to women. Two times a week. That should be enough. I'd asked for a date twice and come close to doing it a couple more times. That was enough for a guy whose wife had just moved out on him a week ago. I headed the car toward home.

I had stopped feeling drunker by the time I was on the final stretch of county road leading to my house. And then I was not drunk at all because I could see Sheri's car in the driveway. And there were kids moving in the yard and soon I was close enough to be sure it was Tracy and Laurie.

Without thinking about it I had pressed down on the accelerator so I was really flying toward my house with a towering flare of road dust kicked up behind me. But then I caught myself and slowed so that by the time I was within fifty feet of the driveway I was at an entirely respectable and legal speed.

Sheri came running out the front door, her hair blowing in the wind. She had a pile of papers in her hand and dumped them in the car. And then she was yelling frantically to the girls to come to her quickly because it was time to go. And then she hurried around the cars, put her arms around the girls, and urged them to move more quickly.

"Hi Tracy, hi Laurie," I said as I stepped out of the car.

Tracy's eyes went down but the corners of her mouth curled up in a smile and she said, "Hi Daddy." Laurie raised her hand in a wave.

"Come girls, I told you we couldn't stay here after your father came," said Sheri.

"Sheri, don't hurry off. We have to talk and I haven't seen the girls in so long. I want to give them a hug," I said.

"You should have done that before you brought tritium into our house," she said.

"I didn't do any such thing," I said. "You know I wouldn't do anything like that."

"Who else could have done it?" she asked, and I had no answer.

"If I did do it, it was an accident. I did it unknowingly."

"I'm not going to stay with a man who unknowingly contaminates his children!" Sheri had her hands behind the girls' backs, and she guided them into the car. Both the girls looked scared, but Laurie also looked as if she had tears in her eyes, as if she was about to cry.

"A father has a right to see his kids," I said.

"Not if he's a danger to them and to everybody else," she said.

"You can't do this," I said. "It's not right."

"I'll let you see them this weekend," she said, "but either Pete or I will have to be there while you're with the girls."

"Either you or Pete? Pete Kerwin is not their father. I am."

"Pete is very good with the girls and he cares about them a lot. He feels sorry he's never had kids of his own."

"Well, he's had plenty of chances. If he doesn't have his own kids it's not because there weren't any women who wanted to give him some. And speaking of women, what about Marie Anne. You know, his wife."

"Marie Anne is not that upset about the turn of events. She and Pete have drifted apart. She's back in France. She never wanted children."

"Well I don't blame her considering the creep she married."

Sheri was behind the wheel and she had started the engine. Her window was down. She turned her face up to me and said, "And if I'm not too old I'm going to be the one who finally does give that wonderful, talented man a child."

I stepped back from fear of how fast she backed out of the drive. The car went down on its springs as she braked, and then I was coughing from the dust kicked up as she and my girls sped away.

I waved and waved and I thought I could see Tracy wave back. I waved until I could no longer see the car's dust plume. Then I looked at the corn field across the road. I turned slowly and looked at my yard, my house. I had been raised in the Midwest but in a city, not out in the country and the deserted surroundings seemed strange to me, as if I did not really belong in my own house. Sheri would be going back to Pete I supposed. Who would I go to? No one came to mind. I supposed I must have some relatives somewhere in the Midwest. But the main relatives I remembered from my childhood had moved to Florida or died. I hadn't been at Kankakee that long, and since my arrival there I'd always behaved as a family man. I worked hard, was friendly but didn't make close friends with my colleagues, and I went straight home from work to baby-sit or one of the other myriad tasks involved in keeping a family together.

But of course my family was no longer together.

I supposed Jim Haskel and Ken Seagraves were the people I knew best in the vicinity. And I hadn't had a long talk or done anything with them for years. They would only know me from the way things used to be, from the time when we organized a strike and demonstrations and kept the university administrators on their toes. But of course we thought we were doing something to bring the Revolution that much closer. Or at least we'd say we thought that. I didn't remember ever conducting my life as if I were sure that there would be a revolution and all property relations would change.

Now, of course, I could conduct my life according to any ridiculous standards I saw fit. Except for my girls. I would have to keep myself looking decent for the sake of my girls.

I went inside to the kitchen. There were still cans and boxes on the floor. My cleanup efforts had obviously been sloppy, or maybe Sheri had made some new mess. I saw peanut butter and bread so I made myself a sandwich. I put a little water in a pot, turned the burner up to maximum under it, took some half-used broccoli out of the refrigerator and cut some sprigs off so they fell into the pot. Then I put two hotdogs in with the broccoli. The girls had always liked hot dogs, but they wouldn't be around to eat those.

I knew I should have some starch, especially since I was sure I would be drinking, but I didn't feel like doing the work to cook anymore. So I ate another slice of bread. Then I had a beer which might have lasted me a minute before I started on another.

I went to the bedroom to look for clothes that would make me look good in a bar. Not that I had any fancy clothes, but even I thought I looked better in some clothes than others. I found most of them in the dirty-clothes hamper, and I decided that doing the laundry was something I could do while drunk. I didn't bother finding a laundry basket but just opened my arms wide to carry as many of the dirty clothes as I could in my arms. Underpants and socks fell to the floor as I moved toward the stairs, but I decided that with as many troubles as I had I could delay washing anything that didn't make it to the washing machine.

There were three fishing poles lying in a tumble beside the furnace. One of them was my old spincast pole. The other two had been my Dad's spinning outfits. One of them was an ultra-light. Fishing was the thing I'd done most with my Dad. He did it first to humor me when I got old enough to do it, but then he'd become enthusiastic about it himself and would go fishing even without me. He'd go with friends, and he'd go alone. But I went with him a lot too. He had shown me how to find worms inside of horseweeds, he'd taken me night crawler catching, he'd taken me out before dawn, and we'd fished late into the night in a boat by moonlight. I'd envied him his poles when I was a kid. He could cast further than me, and the ultra-light made catching any fish more fun, since even a little fish could make the pole bend sharply, and the give of the pole kept you from forcing the fish in.

But Dad had been dead a long time, and now his poles were mine and I didn't fish. I had taken the girls twice, but they hadn't liked it that much. They wanted to let all the fish go. So now I had Dad's poles and didn't use them. I wondered if I would if I had a son.

I loved my father and he killed himself. I loved my wife and she left me. I loved my kids but didn't know when I would see them. I lived in this house in the country, and I didn't know why in the world I was there. Why in the world had I wound up in the nuclear industry in Illinois?

I started the washer and stirred the detergent into a pan of hot water. Then I lifted the washer lid and poured the dissolved detergent in. I headed for the stairs and another beer. I thought of the poles and could see my Dad casting in the moonlight with them and I was crying. I was crying for having nobody and crying for not wanting that much to have anybody.

I got a plastic bag out of a cupboard and filled it up with beers. Then I went back downstairs for the poles and rummaged around to find Dad's old tackle box. I took it all out to the van and tossed them inside. I would go to the river or the conservation area or one of the ponds left when the open-pit coal mines closed. Some of them were supposed to have fish, and I supposed I was going there for more than fishing. I had never been as intense about fishing as Dad. I always got distracted and stared at the clouds or daydreamed about girls and didn't see the first dart of the line when I had a bite.

I went back in for my supper. The pot with the broccoli and hotdogs was boiling over mightily. I turned the burners off and put all the food out on my plate. I ate it fast with beer, but then I felt lightheaded and lay down in front of the TV and turned it on with the remote.

I woke up and it was near dusk. I pulled my shoes on quickly. I would miss most of that best time for fishing, the time when the light is just disappearing. But I had other things on my mind, other plans than just fishing. I had never been able to concentrate just on the fishing. I went to the bedroom and pulled my swimming trunks out of where they were balled up with tee shirts in a drawer.

I drank vodka straight from the bottle in the kitchen and then went out to the car. Dusk had brought some coolness; there weren't many clouds, so the earth was actually cooling some, not like the overcast, muggy summer Midwestern nights which stay hot all night. The coolness made the dusk magical, and my van sped down the county roads towards Wells' pit.

Wells' pit, like many of the lakes around Kankakee and Moraine had once been an open pit coal mine. This one had been a lake for a very long time, and it seemed entirely natural. A later excavation had created a shallow area for swimming and recreation, and it was to this large shallow bay of water that I headed.

I pulled off to the side of the road and dimmed the lights and turned off the van. I drank a beer in the darkness and listened to the deafening drone of the cicadas. There had been a lot of cicadas the year Dad died, too. The trees were covered with the sticky, creepy, brown shells.

I slid open the van's side door and reached for the poles and tackle box, but realized I didn't really want to fish. I didn't really want to tie black jitterbug baits to the ends of lines, cast out, and tickle the baits in, waiting for the explosion that signaled a black bass hitting a top-water lure. I didn't want to pull hooks out of fish and find a stringer or fish keeper to preserve my catch for taking home and cleaning later. I didn't want to cut off fish heads and try to remember the right way to clean them out.

I let the poles drop and just reached over the front passenger seat for my swim trunks. There were trees and overgrown brush between me and the lake, and it took me a while to find the path worn down by other fishermen. It hadn't been used much recently because I had to force my way through branches and weeds. I thought I should have brought soap to wash myself in case there was poison ivy, but then I thought that poison ivy wasn't really much of a concern for me given everything else.

I emerged from the bushes and there was a volley of splashes from frogs making their escape. My face was stinging from the last branch I'd fought through, and myriads of stars speckled the sky above the lake. I had found myself a black place on this light-polluted planet and could see the stars as I'd remembered seeing them when I was a kid.

The waves were lapping, and the air had a moist smell with the coolness. My pants fell down around my shoes and I used my feet to pry off the shoes and step out of the pants. I pulled off my tee shirt and boxer shorts and I was naked at the side of Wells' pit with the frogs and the stars bearing witness to me. I wanted to just step into the water, but then, since I had brought them, I slipped my swimming trunks on.

The water struck cold in the sweltering night, and I could hear the frogs plonk in panic at my splash. Stars are not the brightest in summer, but they were bright enough, hazy in the milk and twinkling weirdly through my myopia. I felt I could swim forever and I'd never thought that way before. There aren't that many long water stretches in the rural Midwest.

The questioners, the interviewers, the enforcement agents, Sheri, and my Dad spun through my head like the stars on each roll for breath.

Give up, give up, end it here, my own way, not like my Dad. I could spit at Dr. Chambers from the grave.

I swallowed wrong and was choking and rolled to see the stars full-face. They were all so far away from root cause, the NRC, the FBI, and the united shrinks of "We know how to help you."

They were just specks on my brain's computer screen, but they'd always be there. No matter how far I moved I could always see them.

But I'd have to fix myself to keep them, and to do that I'd have to know why it all was happening. Who had sent the computer message sending me to the recirculation valve station and why?

Why was simple. They must have wanted to blame me.

But why, why? Who was down on me and could have known enough to make it work?

I rolled over and swam like the frogs. The stars were huge and complex and gleaming, but they were simple. They were far, just specks.

Larger than specks were the two faces I saw clearly in the sky - Laura Brault and Jim Haskel. And then there was Trung, but he was irradiated—a victim.

And then behind them, fuzzier, but just a chance—Pete Kerwin, brilliant Pete Kerwin, my friend from way back. I used to have as much as he did. But now he was my wife's lover and he had it all. Inherited money, a prestigious job, and my wife and children in his house. And Marie Anne had been his wife, pretty French Marie Anne. And I wished I could talk to Marie Anne. I wondered whether she had known about Pete and Sheri before I did.

Then my thought switched to another track. It had to be Laura. Laura had worked with Trung. She knew his password, or at least she had known it. And even if it wasn't her, I wanted to see her. There was water all around me; I'd never been out so far. If Dr. Chambers were right, I'd just dive and never come up. And even if Dr. Chambers wasn't right, I wasn't sure I was strong enough to swim all the way back.

I picked out where I thought I'd come in and started in with the crawl. I wanted to see Laura Brault and settle things with her—I didn't care anymore whether she got the fusion-plant job. My arms and shoulders felt all-powerful, plunging into the coolness and then out into the night air. I felt the sliminess of a weed on my next stroke, and then the water in front of me exploded. My heart raced in fear on top of the exertion as I stopped and stared at the roiling water, and then there was an eruption not ten feet from my right, and I could see the bass as it flopped back hard with an even louder splash.

So after swimming out half-intending to sink forever, I was now terrified by spawning fish. My laugh was like a loon's, and my stomach began to hurt as I didn't know how to stop. But then I was on my way again, slow, but with lots of noise towards the fish, and I was relieved that they stopped their fearsome mating and scattered to let me pass.

The lake was alive. One of the long, black water snakes crossed my path in front of me, and I didn't even slow down. The animals would just have to make way. My next stroke hit the muddy bottom, and I rose, panting and happy from my swim. I splashed the mud and algae off me as best I could. Frogs made their escape on either side of me as I made the shore, and I could see a furry shape that looked most like a giant African anteater scurry into the woods. It might as well have been a lion, there was nothing going to scare me feeling the way I did. So my wife had left me and I wouldn't live with my girls and I'd never invent fusion power and I'd never go to the Olympics. But maybe I could find out who was behind the things that were happening to me.

My shirt and pants clung to my moist skin as I started the van. I'd seen Laura at the Jukebox bar before. I had seen her when I'd begun to go out after the trouble between me and Sheri started. And I'd heard Laura and her friends—she had a lot of friends—talk about the stunts they'd done there. I was going to go there. If she wasn't there, then I'd stay and drink and ponder my next move. Ponder why I could go from swimming out in hopelessness to focusing alive and sharp on untangling the web of personal disaster and circumstantial evidence which had reduced me to nothing—no family and likely no job.

There were railroad tracks on the other side of the county road which led to the Jukebox. Rumbles of passing trains could be heard above the bar's loud music like a slow throbbing in your bones. There was flat white gravel all around the bar, and people could park the way they wanted, usually following the lead of the early-arrivals. And although the emptiness of the parking lot and the flatness of the surrounding corn and soybean fields suggested a country dive, the Jukebox was not a dive; it had a cheerful style and it was always spiffy and clean, inside and out.

I realized it was Thursday as I straightened out my face with the rear view mirror. Thursday had always been my lucky day. I had liked to go to dance bars on Thursdays. I'd done that long, long ago before marrying and getting a real job and then the kids. I'd gone there on Fridays too, and Saturdays and other days, but Thursdays were my lucky day.

I pushed through the door and into the bright part of the bar and saw that my luck had held. Directly in front of me, staring straight at me as I entered was Jim Haskel. And across the room at a big table near the dance floor stood Laura Brault, her hand on the shoulder of Pete Kerwin, the only man in the place wearing a suit. It was a blue suit and he looked good in it, and I was wondering why I'd be thinking that Pete Kerwin looked good in a suit as I made my way to Haskel. And I wondered whether it would be smart for me to tell Sheri where I'd seen Pete and who he was with. Probably not. Sheri had always said she liked considerable freedom within a marriage, and it had always been me with what she called limited attitudes.

"I didn't know you liked bars that much Jim," I said as I took the stool beside him.

"Not as much as you did," he said. "But it's grown on me, especially with the shift work, especially with nuclear."

"Nuclear workers are a clean-cut bunch," I said.

"There are exceptions."

"Speaking of exceptions, is Laura here often and are she and Pete an item?"

"I didn't think you liked Laura," Jim said.

"She and I have had our differences, but then who hasn't. Speaking of differences, who's the bigger phony, you or me?"

Some guys, especially old sixties lefties, will get upset if you say something like that to them, but Jim didn't even blink.

"Neither of us is necessarily a phony, but if one of us is, or if both of us are, and the question is about who is the bigger phony, then it has to be you because I am not a phony at all."

"You work at a nuclear power plant," I said.

"Leftist convictions and advocating nuclear power are not necessarily inconsistent."

"What if the radiation escapes?"

"The radiation's not going to escape, and even if it did, it wouldn't cause that much problem. Haven't you heard about radiation hormesis, that radiation's good for you?"

"You don't really believe in radiation hormesis."

"I don't know what I believe. There's as much proof one way as the other."

"So you've decided you like nuclear power now that you're getting a paycheck from it?" I said.

"Not at all. I'm still somewhat anti-nuke I think there are probably better power sources. But you must admit the issue seems somewhat less pressing since nuclear power is not exactly a growth industry. I've only been here a few years. I'm not a career nuke like you. And everyone has a right to earn a living, as long as what you're working at is not clearly immoral, and I don't feel that what I do is clearly immoral."

"You don't find producing weapons material immoral?" I asked.

"Well, that does bother me. But we're not producing any right now, so I will have the chance to quit if we do start to produce tritium or plutonium. And I grant lefties the right to infiltrate and spy on their enemies, of course?"

"And is that what you're doing? Spying?"

"No. I would have thought that might be what you are doing. But of course you're not spying, you're committing sabotage."

"It wasn't me," I said.

"If not you, then who?"

"I don't know. Maybe someone in this room," I said and looked at Laura. "Maybe someone I'm going to talk to right now. Keep the faith, brother."

Laura saw me coming toward her right away. She looked down and to the left, brought up her beer mug to her mouth, faced me squarely and looked at me over the glass. Her left arm crossed over to hold her right elbow so that she seemed closed up and protected behind the diversion of the beer. I looked around the room to see if I could see where Pete had gone, but I didn't see him.

"What a surprise Henry McClure. We don't see much of you in bars," she said.

"Well, I heard you were a totally different woman on the dance floor than you are in the control room, so I had to come see for myself. Have you heard anything about the fusion plant job?"

"No, have you?"

"No, and I don't imagine I will now that I'm suspected of every crime that's ever happened."

"Oh, Henry. Nobody really thinks you did it. You're not a mean person, just a little wrong-headed at times. Well, most of the time."

"Nice of you to say it, but I don't remember myself ever being wrong-headed. Of course there's a certain mysterious, glamorous woman operator I know who occasionally can be somewhat stubborn."

Her stance had opened, and she had shifted so she was standing on her locked left leg while her right was at an angle and just barely touched the floor. She was smiling at an angle too, and there was a dimple in her cheek, and her long black hair made me think she could never do anything really bad. And then I remembered how vicious and insistent she could be when she didn't get her way.

A country western song about fast women and fast cars ended and a new song didn't come on right away as it had earlier. A man in a black cowboy hat and a neck-mounted microphone stood at the end of the dance floor and invited people up for Texas two-step lessons. When he said the words "two-step" I had memories of cowboy bars at night in New Mexico, of violins and western music that I and my young soldier friends had wanted to end so that we could do our rock-and-roll.

"Laura, I lived New Mexico for six months. I learned the two-step there, but I haven't done it in years. Would you take the lesson with me?"

"Well, I know the two-step fairly well. I come mainly for the other dances."

"Oh please, Laura. Think of it as refresher training. You can never get too much practice, you know."

"Okay, I'll do some of the lesson with you, but I may want to take a break soon."

"Okay, that's fine. I really want to see if I can still do this dance, and this is my best chance so far."

And so the lesson began, and I was dancing forward with Laura who held herself well away from me in good two-step style. And she did know the dance very well, because when I followed the instructions for having her make a turn she would turn two or three times while the other women turned once, and her turns looked better with her hair and skirt flaring out from her long, thin, energetic body.

"You used to do some radiochemistry, didn't you?" I asked.

"Please, I come here to escape technology. But yes, I did spend quite some time at Argonne in a radiochemistry section."

"You wouldn't have done any work with tritiated organics, would you?"

"Absolutely none. And I'd barely heard of tritiated organics before your famous incident. You're fun to dance with Henry, and I know you're having a bad time with being a suspect and everything, but I can't help you. I'm sorry."

I looked into her blue eyes the entire time she spoke, and I had to believe her. Her face and shoulders squinched up the right way to show sympathy, and her skin was so white and her eyes so shiny that I had to believe her. I believed her even though I knew she had done everything she could to get ahead of me in the competition for the fusion reactor control room job.

I paid more attention to my dancing. She was a wonderful partner, and her smile flashed as she did something the instructor called the woman's underarm duck turn. I wanted to dance with her as long as I could, and I wanted to dance with her again as soon and as often as I could.

A new song started, and I couldn't get the beat. I looked at her feet and tried to follow, and I kept looking because I could see how narrow her waist was above her swelling hips. Her waist was so narrow that even though she was tall and thin, her breasts and hips flared out boldly in the vase shape men love so much. I didn't think she had the beat, either, but I kept trying to follow her. It became painful to continue the dance since we were both so lost.

When the tune came to an end, Laura said, "Well, I think it's time for my break now."

"Sure. Sorry I had trouble on that last song."

"Oh, it was a tricky one. Just keep practicing," and she walked back to her table. Pete Kerwin was there again, and Laura went right up to him and sat down beside him with a smile. I swallowed my rage and fear of behaving stupidly and strode toward them, my eyes fixed on Kerwin, and my thoughts trying frantically to find some rule to deal with the scene which was about to happen. When he finally realized who was walking toward him, his head went back and his eyes widened and shot back and forth.

"My wife not enough for you that you have to come out to the bars for fun Kerwin?" I said.

He turned his head away from me and stared fixedly at nothing. He sat there.

"Don't act as if it's me doing something wrong," I said. "It's you who's got my wife and kids at his house. It's you who's stolen my family."

He turned toward me with one of those beatific smiles. "I'm sorry Henry, I've known you a long time, and I'd still like to be your friend, but Sheri's an old friend too, and, you're right, she has become more than just a friend. I'm sorry it has to be like this, but you know—you've been around enough to know that these things happen. It's nobody's fault."

Laura had backed her chair away from Pete when the part about Sheri being more than a friend came up.

"How long has it been going on between you and Sheri?" I asked. "Were you lovers on those business trips you made together?" I felt glad when I saw that Laura had actually begun to frown at my words.

"I don't have to answer questions like that," he said. "You were Sheri's husband, but now you're not. Something between you didn't match. There was something which didn't make her happy. Don't blame yourself, Henry."

"I sure as hell don't blame myself!" I spoke coldly, restraining the scream that wanted to come out.

"I'm leaving," he said. "Sheri was going to join me here later, but I don't think you're in the mood to allow us to enjoy our evening. So we'll do something else. Try to be mature about it, Henry."

I wanted to hit him, but I didn't. My eyes followed him out, and I saw that Jim Haskel actually did follow him out, and I didn't believe Jim had just accidentally followed Pete out the door. But I couldn't imagine two people less likely to like each other than Haskel and Kerwin. Kerwin had always had ambition—ambition unfortunately not linked to extraordinary talent, or at least not talent as I understood it. And Haskel was talent without any goal, except perhaps the transcendent revolution to end all human misery which we had pursued in the sixties. Maybe Haskel still believed in it.

I liked being in the bar and I liked the music and I was happy Laura was still there. But I remembered what I had come there for, and I remembered all the trouble I was in that could only be put right if the mystery of the tritium sabotage could be solved. I had come into the bar following my vision at the lake that it had to be Laura. It had been Laura who had set me up in the valve recirculation room so that the way would be clear for her to take the fusion reactor control room job. And now I wasn't thinking anything about Laura except how white her skin was and how shiny her eyes. And her hair.

Pretty women can do mean things. Maybe pretty women are especially good at doing mean things. But Laura had me sold. She might slander my age and my abilities, but she wouldn't contaminate innocent people just to make me look bad.

So that left me with Jim or Pete. Or maybe it could be Ken Seagraves. But that was crazy; Seagraves didn't even work in the plant so how could he pull off a sophisticated job like the one that had been pulled on me. Maybe Haskel and Seagraves were in it together. Or maybe Pete Kerwin disliked me more than I thought he did. We had often been rivals, and I had gotten ahead of him more than once. I had that inner attitude, that inner certainty that when it came to anything technical and difficult, I could always find the solution faster, and my solution would be better than anything Pete Kerwin could come up with, even if he was rich and the president of his own successful company.

I headed toward the door. I should go outside and confront them. Get it out of them. Or hide in the shadows and follow them. Follow them and see what they did.

I did neither. I turned around and walked straight toward Laura. She was seated at a table and she saw me coming right away and she kept looking at me and I kept looking at her except I managed a smile and hoped my walk was nonchalant.

"Have you recovered enough to try dancing with me again?" I asked, and her blue eyes met mine and helped me keep my smile.

"Okay, I'll dance. I think I'm making a mistake, but I came to dance and I'll dance even with someone as crazy as you."

My two-step started coming back to me. I didn't make the mistake of trying to follow her but made her follow me. We got off the beat at the start, but I stopped, moved her arm and pressed her shoulder with the beat and we were off, and this time we were in form. She could do all the turns I remembered, and I was remembering more as we went along.

"I never took you for a cowboy, Henry," she said. "And I've never seen you dancing before. Do you have a secret life somewhere?"

"A long time ago I did this, back when it wasn't as popular as it is now. I even did it in El Paso where I fell in love with the girl with long black hair. But then there was that wild cowboy."

Lines formed on her forehead as she tried to figure out what I had meant by that, and since I had no idea what I'd meant I tried to erase it with more vigorous dancing and pivoted close to her to go into the whip turn. We touched full-body for just a second in a delicious softness, and I wondered what I had seen in Sheri all those years as Laura spun effortlessly through the two and a half turns to come out beside me in promenade position.

Her smile could have lit up Texas and she said, "That was fun."

"I'm afraid I've gone through about my entire repertoire."

"Come out here more often and we'll teach you some new things," she said.

"I think that's exactly what I'll do, as long as they haven't put me in jail."

I looked around the dance floor. There were couples of all ages, and I noted approvingly the couples with the man looking older than the woman. And although there were beautiful young Illinois women there, I was convinced I was dancing with the prettiest woman in the place, and I still could recall perfectly the thrill of touching her going into the whip turn.

The song ended, and I remembered that I was supposed to be trying to solve the mystery that had destroyed my life.

"How well do you know Jim Haskel?" I asked.

"Not well. Of course he reports to the control room sometimes when I'm on duty, and he always seems very competent."

"Is he particularly cynical about his job, or does he do anything strange?"

"No, with me he's always been about the perfect control technician. His reports are accurate and concise, and when I need something fixed, he fixes it. Of course, I've noticed he acts different with some of the guys. Like with you, for example." She gave my upper arm a tap as she finished speaking and I felt that things were going better than they had ever gone for me before.

"Yes, I've known Jim for a long time. I knew him when I was a student," I said.

"When was that?" she asked.

I didn't want to answer because that would tell her how old I was, but there was no way to escape it. I decided just to tell her about graduate school after the army, although I had known Jim Haskel before then, too. "Oh, early seventies. Seventy, seventy-one or so."

"Oh, I had been hoping you were one of those sixties student revolutionaries, but I guess you were too young."

"Well, you know the sixties just didn't end so fast. There was still quite a lot going on when I knew Jim. Vietnam wasn't over yet."

"I was just going to junior high then," she said.

I didn't like the implications of that, and I didn't want her to spend much more time figuring out the difference in our ages. The only diversion I could think of was to say, "I'd really like to dance with you again, shall we?'

"It would be fun, Henry. You don't dance too badly for a nuke, but I just saw my regular partner come in, so I think I'd better dance with him now."

"Sure. Thanks for the dance, and I hope I get another chance sometime."

I watched her walk away from me and up to a thin, tanned, angular man in cowboy boots, jeans, and a jean jacket. He had short brown hair and a thin face so tight and tanned that his cheeks were rounded hollow under his high cheek bones. His thin face was tanned brown which made him look old, maybe older than me, but then I looked closer and it was his muscularity and the tanning which made him look older. He looked the perfect cowboy, and he was smaller than me, more nearly a match for Laura.

I watched them dance and he was an expert. He knew the swing steps perfectly, and he and Laura began to attract a crowd as they swung in and out and round about on a fast one. I wondered how many years it would take me to dance as well as he. Sheri and I had not been much for dancing, especially not after the kids. But now maybe I would have the time, and maybe I would make the time to learn to dance swing and bop and jive—the dances you can do in a club and look good doing it.

I wanted to get another drink. I wanted to look around the bar and find another woman and dance. I wanted to have fun. But the only person in the bar who might know something about my tritium mystery was Laura, and she was occupied. Both Jim Haskel and Pete Kerwin had left; they would know something and I should talk to them. And although I wouldn't find them if I left the bar, I certainly wouldn't find them if I stayed, and so I left, but not before catching Laura's eyes and smiling. She looked away.

14

At least it wasn't hot as I walked across the gravel to my van. As drunk and tired as I was, if it had been hot I might have not even started the car; I would have flopped down in the back in a curled-up tumble and slept there. But there was a wind kicking up, as if a thunderstorm was coming, and I started to wake up and even felt good proceeding with caution down the country roads. My Dad would have wanted to go fast; he would have wanted to see how fast the car would go, but I was different from my Dad. I drove slowly because I knew I was feeling the alcohol. And I drove slowly at night anyway because not being able to see scared me. As I kept telling the shrinks, my Dad and I just weren't the same.

So Laura didn't like me and Sheri didn't like me. Sheri liked Pete and maybe Laura did too. Maybe Pete was man enough to have three women going at once—his wife, my wife, and Laura. I pictured Laura's hair and remembered how she'd felt when we danced. Of course I had kids and was older and was a suspected saboteur. And she wanted the job I did. No, even I couldn't see any reason for Laura to like me.

And I could see Jim Haskel and Ken Seagraves and Sheri and me and so many young and beautiful others sitting in meetings and arguing about what to do next, and factions would form and even be given names although it was more just how someone with a strong personality happened to see things at the time. And I laughed as I remembered that Sheri had usually been in a different faction than mine. But then of course I didn't have a faction, I'd never joined anything as far as I could remember. And I congratulated myself for having put together so many marches and picket lines and never having joined anything at all. Sheri was still receiving mailings from parties she had belonged to. And Jim Haskel. He had been People's Power. Maybe he still was if they existed. And groups like that tended to hold on as a little shell, a little office somewhere with a mimeograph. Maybe Jim was still a member.

We had sat in little rooms and argued and voted, and Jim had always said quite calmly that we had to act. That we weren't anything unless we did something that would be noticed. That all our talk and philosophy were worth nothing in comparison to an act that could cause even the slightest disruption in the capitalist system before it regrouped and rolled right over us with its money and resiliency.

The tritium incident had disrupted Kankakee station. And it looked like it could disrupt the rest of my life. And if I were disrupted, who could tell what I'd do. When it came to it, I usually surprised myself by how much action I could carry off.

There was a car in my driveway as I approached. I turned off my lights but thought better of it and turned them back on again. I drove past the house. It was Haskel's car. I drove on for another hundred yards to the next curve where I pulled far off to the side and stopped.

I pushed the van door closed as quietly as I could. Maybe my thoughts had brought Haskel out in the open. I remembered how he'd always been sweet on Sheri. Of course most of us lefty guys had been. And I remembered Jim turning brusquely and walking away when Sheri had asked me out for a beer, and we hadn't wanted company.

And then he'd always spoken out for action. Maybe he was acting. Maybe I was too. Of course I had told him to his face that he just made speeches about acting; he didn't really act more than anyone else.

I walked around the front of the van and went into the high grass which bordered the road. I walked right up to the corn and turned to follow the line of the field toward my house. And I almost laughed as I remembered the army instruction on night infiltration. I even stopped and did one of those ultra-slow moves, raising my knees up high with the arms out and stepping ever-so-slowly forward. I could remember doing it in training with everyone in army green in the dark. But if I kept doing it the army way, I'd never get to my house, or Haskel would be gone before I did, and so I started to walk briskly, hoping I didn't turn my ankle by stepping in a hole.

Haskel was sitting on a bench built into the sidewalk leading to our front door. There wasn't much left in the pint bottle he was drinking from, and he took another hit. I didn't remember Jim being much of a drinker, but then the years can give you a taste for booze.

Haskel was sitting in the light from the lamp post which illuminated our drive and sidewalk at night. I was still in the blackness, and I put my feet down toe first as I stepped across the grass toward him. When I was twenty feet from him I said, "Hello Jim."

He didn't jump. He just turned his body around slow, and then put his arm down straight to support his twisted torso. His eyes were shining beneath the dull red of his hair and above the duller red of his beard, and he was grinning as he looked up at me. "Hello, Henry. You've got one hell of a nice front yard here."

"I didn't know you were such a connoisseur of yards."

"No Henry, I must admit I have never had a yard. Even here in rural Illinois, where it's so hard to avoid it, I still haven't had a yard to call my own and take care of. I tell myself I'm staying close to the people."

"In Illinois the people have yards," I said.

His chest heaved up and then his shoulders sagged as he snorted out a laugh. He smiled angelically as he held the bottle out to me. "Have some?" he said.

I took a hit of the whiskey, but a little one, and held the bottle back out to him. "I don't remember you indulging in the hard stuff," I said.

"Well, the people in my apartment building drink it and, like I said, I try to stay in touch with the people."

"I think you may be going *lumpen* on us," I said.

"Oh no, that was more your style. All that emotion about the people and the working class. That was more you. Me, I have a brain. I think. I see. I've lived and I think; I don't just feel like you."

"And what have you thought lately? Anything about smashing nuclear power by concocting weird events?"

"No, I more just think and leave it at that. You remember, you always denounced me for no action. No, you're more the one to act. Feelings and action, the rot goes together."

"I think I'm flattered. Imagine having feelings and acting on them and managing to work in nuclear at the same time. No, I don't think I feel bad about that at all."

"There you go feeling again. For someone who feels as much as you, I'd think you'd have more of a line on the emotional configuration around certain recent events."

"My wife leaves me for Kerwin, who I'll never be able to see is any better than me, except he has more money. My wife leaves me and takes my kids, and every other day it looks like I've tried to over-expose more of my friends, and I'm going crazy out of my mind, and you don't think I feel enough about the emotional configuration?"

"You don't think those tritiated organics got into a secondary side room on their own, do you?"

"No. That's crazy. They couldn't get anywhere in the whole damn plant on their own, let alone the light water side."

"Oh yes. Your technological optimism. That's another thing I could never stomach about you. Think you know everything about everything, even about something as exotic as tritiated organics."

"You think there's something special about our reactor, so that it can start churning out isotopes that have never contaminated any reactor anywhere?" I said.

"I'm just not so quick to say things are impossible. But then I'm a thinker and see a lot more than you. On the other hand, there's not a chance in hell that the tritium contamination got in the recirculation valve room any other way than by someone putting it there. And as I said that person could only be you. Only you or...."

"Or what?"

"Only you or someone who wanted to pin it on you. Only you or someone who hated you. But then the hate might be only part of the motive. Maybe the motive could be very complicated. Maybe it could be a very complicated person we are dealing with. That is, if it's not you, and you just had some infantile middle-aged delusion that you could make up for your useless life by a descent into juvenile terrorism."

"I never knew you hated me," I said.

For a moment he looked surprised and his head wobbled, and I realized he was drunk enough to actually have trouble maintaining a seated position on my perfectly solid bench. But then he straightened and regained his smile. "On no, Henry, it just doesn't work. Even if I hated you, which I don't because you're much too unimportant and then you've always been kind of nice in a stupid Midwestern sort of way. No, it's illogical because I haven't done research at Kensington labs; I've never taken the slightest interest in radioisotopes except for the stuff you have to know to work in nuclear; I had been on supernumerary until two days before the incident, and my crews will truthfully swear we never went near the recirculation valve room. And I was hurrying to attend a class at the community college when you received the fake message sending you to the recirc room. Now I know I'm brilliant, but even I couldn't pull off anything like that."

"You went near the recirc room the day before the event," I said.

"No I didn't. How can you say that?"

"Lucy Watkins gave me the plant access records. You were in the recirc room sector about the same time Laura was. For that matter, you were in the tech section that afternoon. You could have been responsible for the time-delay message."

Jim at first stared at me blankly; then he looked worried. He shrugged his shoulders up and then let them sag. "Oh yes. I did go to the recirc room briefly."

"Why?"

He glared at me, "Because I wanted to talk to Laura. And before you ask me why, I wanted to talk to Laura because I like talking to her, okay."

I laughed. "Okay Jim. That's a justifiable human reason for wanting to do something if ever I heard one. I don't mind talking to Laura myself."

"No. I didn't plant any tritium there, and I didn't see Laura carrying anything suspicious either; I never saw her rubbing anything onto the pipes. And she didn't have a respirator or anything to limit the dose she would pick up just putting the stuff there. No, if you didn't do it, it was someone who hated you. Someone who wanted to fix you up good."

"I'm not aware that anyone hates me," I said as I realized I'd only checked the key-card access records for the tech section. Any number of people could have gone into the tech section directly from administration. I hadn't even done a decent check on who could have been at my tech section desk to send me the false order from Dennis Banks. I wondered how many other mistakes I was making while devoting myself to drink and chasing women.

"The guy you should hate hates you," he said.

I looked at him and he stared straight back at me. "Well, I hate Pete Kerwin now because he has Sheri. For that matter he and I have always been a little at odds even though we were friends."

"Oh. A little at odds you think. You think you're a little at odds and he thinks you're everything that's bad about Americans. He can be quite eloquent about it."

"You mean you've heard him badmouthing me?"

"It is not uncommon. Of course, he probably has cause. You are an arrogant son-of-a-bitch. And what was your interest in tritiated organics at Kensington lab anyway?"

The erratic wanderings of drunkenness had disappeared from Jim's face, and he was again looking me straight in the eyes with a tenseness spreading to all his body as if he were gathering strength to spring."

"I don't know what you're talking about. I never had any interest in tritiated organics at Kensington."

"Kerwin says you were quite interested in his samples and were always suggesting experiments that could be run with them. He said you wanted to be his partner on tritium retention studies."

"If Pete Kerwin told you anything like that he's either lying or hallucinating," I said.

"He also said you wanted in on his plutonium experiments. He said that you want in on his action because you realize he's on to something big with new treatments for purging plutonium from the body. He said that you've always tried to horn in on his ideas and take the credit for what he's developed."

"Sounds like you and Pete have been talking a lot," I said.

"Oh, he's taken an interest in me. He says he's fascinated by instrumentation and control, and he's especially interested in the access control system. And you know it was his company that programmed the error that caused the control room to miss the tritium alarm in the fuel bay."

"Doesn't he have enough access with all the experiments he's always running?" I asked.

"Nevertheless he has become quite informed about access control. He has become so expert that he even signed off as a reviewer on the logic diagram that had the error, the diagram I showed you there in the tech section. Did you know he was such a control expert, Henry?"

"No. Kerwin started out in thermalhydraulics, just like me. Then when he left WorldNet Simulations for Darlington he got into health physics."

"Well, maybe that's why he just signed one of the diagrams, the diagram that had the error. Kind of a coincidence, don't you think?"

"Yes," I said, and I could see that Henry had something to tell me that he was pleased as punch about knowing, and he was dragging it out.

"I thought it was a coincidence, too, so I called Roy Carlson, the engineer whose work Kerwin reviewed. When I told Carlson about the error, he was furious and denied making the mistake. He even claimed he had his original diagram on disk, and he could prove that the logic was perfect when he submitted it. Of course Kerwin said that Carlson was wrong when I asked him about it in the Jukebox parking lot tonight."

"If that's true, it's relevant to the recirculation valve room event investigation. Does the NRC know about Carlson's claim?"

"Not yet, but I think we'll have to tell them. But I haven't finished with Pete Kerwin and his interests. He has been especially interested in the ventilation system. He's always asking me questions about the ventilation instrumentation and controls. He says that the nightmare scenario put forward by the anti-nukes is putting plutonium in the ventilation system and giving everyone lung cancer. So he's quite interested in the access control for the ventilation system, not that there is much control."

"You say he has a new way of purging plutonium from the body?"

"Oh, he says it's mainly an old way, but he thinks he can document it and show that the plutonium is not nearly as dangerous as what people think, and then the way will be clear for reprocessing and breeders and putting uranium around the Hydra fusion reactor to breed plutonium in it from the fast fusion neutrons."

"And he said I was interested in tritiated organics?"

"Yes, according to him, you were absolutely fascinated by them. Always bugging him to let you use them. And you wanted in on the plutonium work, too. He said he hadn't told the FBI yet because of the effect on Sheri and the kids, but he said he may have to with the plutonium theft and with everything pointing to you being willing to irradiate your friends."

"It's all a lie," I said. "If he had any evidence, he would have told the FBI. I was usually busy when I went up to Kensington. I was always working with other people. Let them say that I was interested in tritium. Let them say that I've ever said a word about plutonium treatments."

Jim said, "You may be lying right to my face. You're capable of it if you think there's a cause. Or Kerwin could be lying. But I think this will have to come out. I think I'm ...."

There was a thud and Jim's chest showed red before the world exploded with the shot. Then I heard another one and I dove for the ground. Jim had slumped down off the bench and fallen to the cobblestone walk below. That had to be a safer place because it was protected by the berm of earth into which the bench had been built, so I did the fastest low crawl I could and went over the bench and tumbled down onto the walk beside Jim. I heard another shot, and as I cursed not having a weapon in the house I heard running, and I could see a figure come out of the weeds across the road. The figure leaned back as if to throw a javelin with both hands. Then what had to be a rifle went out in a high arc and thudded into the yard. Then the thin figure was off—someone in good shape, someone who could run, someone like Pete Kerwin. I crawled to Jim. The drunkenness had come back over him and he was even giggling. He said, "Damn Henry. This must be the revolution. I'm not sure I like it."

A car started and then there was the sound of gravel being thrown by spinning tires. I peered into the night but there were no lights. But then, after a minute, a car's lights came on just before the intersection with the state highway.

Jim said, "It has to be Kerwin. I've always thought there was something crazy in him."

And then Jim began to twitch and then thrash and he was stronger than I thought. Then he lay still. I pressed his wrists and then his neck. I pressed in hard trying to feel a pulse. I pressed my ear to his chest and heard nothing. I unbuttoned his shirt and crushed his red curling chest hair down with my ear.

I heard nothing and, though I reminded myself that I wasn't a doctor and couldn't find my own pulse half the time, I thought I could take a few moments away from Jim to see what had been thrown into my yard.

We had a larger floodlight mounted above the garage door. I used my key to activate the garage door opener, went inside to the switch box and flipped the floodlight on. The driveway was now bathed in bright light. I had always meant to install a basketball hoop so the girls could play basketball outdoors at night by the floodlight. Another one of my plans I had never carried out.

I walked quickly out into the driveway and realized, too late, that my night vision was now destroyed by the light. But I could see bent grass and an object that didn't belong there just at the edge of the floodlight's range. I hopped up on the berm and trotted to the object and as I got closer I knew what it had to be. It was Sheri's rifle, the one she had bought and learned to shoot with back in the seventies when she was in her Action Faction phase. The steel of the barrel stood out dull black against the gleaming brown of the stock. The rifle lay there brilliant in the light, a tangible sign of my enemy. Unlike the radiation I could see the black and brown, feel its solid coldness in my hands, and smell the lingering faint bitterness of the powder. And by knowing who had used the rifle, I knew who had unleashed the tritium plague.

15

My watch alarm beeped; I had actually slept in the back seat of my car. My body had demanded sleep. But I had slept without disposing of the rifle, Sheri's rifle, the rifle which had killed Jim Haskel. I had slept after dragging Jim to an emergency room and then running. Running to where?

I was running to find Pete Kerwin. And if I found him what would I do?

I could kill him. I could use the rifle. He had killed Jim, I could kill him.

And that would be killing myself.

I had to talk to Sheri. Maybe she would know where he was keeping the plutonium. Maybe she would know what he intended to do with it.

And maybe she was part of it. She had always admired Pete's business success, and maybe she was glad to help him roll up even more success. A treatment for plutonium contamination would be worth money now, and there would be big money later if fusion's first step would be to produce plutonium for use in conventional reactors or in non-conventional reactors like Kankakee.

It was still dark as I rubbed my eyes and went around to the driver's seat. I had picked up a beer from the trunk, and I drank it as I aimed my car toward Pete Kerwin's house.

I parked in the same spot from where I had spied on Sheri and him embracing. I hoped I wouldn't have to see something like that again. He had taken my wife, he fondled and loved her, he killed my friend, he had me suspended from my job, and he stood a good chance of being able to put me behind bars for a very long time

I supposed I must have underestimated him. He must have had talents that were not technical in nature. He must be very good at lying, very good at playing a part, and very good with charm. I suppose I found him charming myself.

Pete's and Sheri's cars were both parked in the driveway. I hadn't seen the car that had fled my house after the shooting, so I couldn't be sure it was Pete's. I didn't have my eyes or anything other than my reasoning and Jim's dying words to tell me that Pete was anything besides a hard-working engineer with a flair for the entrepreneurial.

And then the message that had started my whole nightmare came back to me. The message from Dennis Banks ordering me to the recirc room. I had copied and read that message so many times I had it memorized. But I had a crumpled copy of the message in the glove compartment under the passenger side seat, just as I had a copy in my desk in the tech section and inside a drawer in my bed table. I wanted to see it one more time, see the words on paper before me and not just my memory of them. I leaned over, fumbled with the catch, and pulled out the printout and stared at the signature—thankx, Dennis.

Thankx. Dennis Banks would have never written something cutesy like thankx. But Pete Kerwin—all his messages to me back at WorldNet Simulations came back to me. Thankx. He might as well have signed it himself; it was so much his trademark. And I had read and read that message and never seen the truth which was so clearly written there.

There was just the faintest pinkishness in the east. I set my watch to ring on the half hour, and I resolved to keep resetting it so I wouldn't fall asleep for long. Pete would be almost as tired as I was. He had been out at the Jukebox nearly as late as I, and he couldn't have gotten much sleep as he had planned how to come to my house to seek a more complete termination of my possible embarrassment of him. The man who steals the wife kills the husband. Or maybe he really had meant to kill Jim because of Jim's discovery of the control logic fault, reviewed and approved by Pete Kerwin.

I started to sleep in between my wristwatch alarms. It was definitely morning now, and I wondered how soon the police would find me sitting in my car close to Pete's house. That was more likely than that I would be able to accomplish anything by waiting till Pete left and then going to talk to Sheri. But I wanted to see her. I wanted to see her and the kids before the police found me. I wanted to tell my girls that I hadn't done anything wrong, no matter what they heard, and that I loved them.

I was slumped in my car, just barely able to look out over the dash. My eyes were open and so was the door to Pete's house. Pete's door was open and he was walking out of it. I had to give him credit.

He didn't look bad, he looked well-rested. He had a briefcase in one hand and in the other he had an environment-friendly cotton shopping bag.

Pete put the bag on top of his car while he fished out his keys to open the car door.

The soft-sided bag slipped down and revealed a silvery cylinder inside. Pete was carrying a radioisotope shielding canister.

You don't need shielding to carry plutonium. Anything will stop the alphas. So Pete was carrying something radioactive, but that was no crime for him, that was his job. It was his job to work with radioisotopes, but if there were radioisotopes inside the shielded transport canister, then Pete had brought the radioisotopes home, and that was the sin for which Sheri had taken my children from me.

Pete was all efficiency as he brought the bag back up around the canister and placed it on the passenger side of the front of the car; then he went around the back to get in on the driver's side. The car started immediately as he sat down, and I could see that he was already out onto the road before he started putting on his seat belt. I thought that was a little more aggressive than Pete's usual style. He was a hard worker, but it wasn't usual to see him in an obvious hurry.

I waited for his BMW to disappear around a curve before I started my van and made a U to follow him. I had to slow sharply once I rounded the curve because he wasn't that far ahead of me, and I couldn't let him realize I was following him, especially if it had really been he who had fired the shot that killed Jim Haskel.

I realized Sheri's rifle was still back at the house where I'd left it on the living room sofa. The police would find it once they searched my house, which they were sure to do since it was me who had taken him to hospital. And so I would likely be blamed for Jim's death as well.

I was seething and cursing all of the flatness of Illinois, as I was certain I would lose him because I had to stay so far back to avoid being recognized. But before five minutes were gone I could relax. Pete Kerwin was heading toward Kankakee station. There was no other explanation for his route.

So Pete Kerwin was heading toward Kankakee station with what looked to be radioisotopes in the front seat of his car. Taking radioisotopes to a nuclear power station is not usual since there is all the radiation one could possibly want there already. But Pete Kerwin was an expert, and no one would question his right to do so.

I wanted very much to know what was in the canister and why Pete Kerwin was taking it to Kankakee station. I couldn't tackle him in the parking lot. I would have to follow him into the station and confront him there. But how would I get into the station? Dennis Banks had suspended me from control room duties. There was no way I could even enter the control room without every licensed operator there setting off a security alarm.

But I didn't need to go to the control room. I just had to get into the plant. I had to hope that Dennis Banks hadn't bothered to pull my radiation badge and remove me from the plant access list. Dennis Banks was a friend of mine. He had taken me out of the control room because he had to, but there was nothing forcing him to take me off the plant access list, nothing except bureaucratic discipline. Of course bureaucratic discipline is not in short supply in the nuclear industry, but I had to hope that Dennis Banks had not gone to the trouble to ban me utterly from the station which I had helped to build.

Pete parked in a visitor spot close to the plant gate. He looked powerful, scientific and successful as he brought the transport canister out of its bag and walked briskly with it directly toward the plant entrance.

I parked my van close to his BMW as soon as he disappeared through the plant front door. If he managed to elude me inside the plant, I wanted him to know I had been there and close to him when he came out. I wanted him to know that it had not been me who had been shot in the middle of the night. It now seemed so long ago, even though ten hours had not yet passed from the time Jim Haskel slumped to the ground.

There was nothing to do except to try to go in, and I had no time to waste if Kerwin were not to get too far ahead of me. I tried to think of a plausible excuse of why I was trying to go into the plant, but I couldn't think of anything in the least reasonable as I went through the doors and was glad that I didn't recognize the guard in the security cage. Guard staff turnover was apparently not one of the station's performance indicators for determining plant security status.

It seemed an eternity waiting for the weapons scanner to clear me, and then I stepped away from the bomb sniffer too fast, and I had to go back and wait for the clear signal. The guard didn't seem disturbed. He'd seen it happen lots of times.

The guard turned to the rack after I'd said "five-fifty-nine" into the mike, and I was relieved when he reached out and pulled my photo ID and key card; they were mine and didn't seem to have any warning slips attached.

The guard held the ID to his chest and asked: "Your name?"

"Henry McClure," I said as if I were addressing a superior officer.

The guard smiled. "You guys seem to be getting more strack. Are they cracking down in there or something?"

"No. I just think you ought to show respect for security," I said and wondered where I had tapped this vein of duplicity.

The guard passed my ID and key card out through the flap, I picked them up and I was in, or at least I would be in if my key card let me through the turnstiles. There was just the chance that the computer knew I shouldn't be allowed in, even if the guards didn't.

The green light came on after I slid the key card into the slot, and I forced the wheel around and fairly bounded up the stairs to work-control.

I went through the ritual of registering my dosimeter into the computer and signing the book and getting my hard hat as fast as I could, and I was rewarded because when I exited through the key card door I could see Pete Kerwin about fifty yards down the west corridor. He still had the radioisotope transport canister.

I decided I might as well confront him immediately and almost broke into a trot as I followed him, but I could see him turn and go through the door leading to one of the west quadrant stairwells.

I broke into more than a trot then because if I didn't find out whether he was going up or down and to which level I might never find him.

I had to use the key card again to go through the door he had gone through. I immediately looked up and there was a door swinging closed up very high, the highest level in the plant at one-eighty-seven-five. My exercising to look better for Sheri had finally paid off as I bounded up the stairs two and three steps at a time. Pete had been moving fast to get such a big lead on me, but I knew I was making up ground fast on the stair climb.

I had just started to wonder what Pete would be doing at the top of the station when I went through the door I had seen closing. I even began to fear that I had gone the wrong way, that it had been someone else who had business up high and that Pete was now lost somewhere in the bowels of the plant where I would never find him until he came out through the full-body scanners. But then there was a movement up even higher on the platform near the station air dryers, and Pete came into full view. He was using a screw driver to open one of the access panels. The radioisotope transport canister was resting on the floor of the platform, and I realized that I was viewing the scenario of the worst-case radioactive terrorism attack—dispersal of plutonium particles into the atmosphere. And each inhaled particle a lung cancer.

I fought back the urge to call out to him and instead tried to move quietly toward the catwalk that led up to the air dryer platform. But Kerwin saw me and he turned and looked directly at me. His lips curled in disdain and hate, and I didn't look back at him any nicer, but I broke off the glaring match by breaking into a run toward the catwalk. Kerwin stooped down for the transport canister and then disappeared around the other side of the dryers.

"What you got in the canister Petey boy," I screamed out as I reached the platform and sprinted toward where he had disappeared. I grabbed the dryers with my right hand to help me turn the corner quicker, but when I came around Kerwin was directly in front of me and driving the screwdriver point toward my eyes. I dodged to my left and the screwdriver tore flesh out of the side of my neck. Kerwin tried to kick me but I blocked it with my right knee, and I think it hurt him more than it did me. Blood was poring from my neck, and I decided that I'd better try to kill him before I lost consciousness.

Kerwin swung the heavy lead-lined transport canister at me, but I blocked it with my left. I swung with my right, but it bounced off his shoulder as he started to force his way past me toward the catwalk. I grabbed his shirt, but he tore free and broke into a run off the platform and down the catwalk. I ran after him pressing the side of my neck with the flat of my right hand.

Kerwin was running away from the door through which we'd come onto the one-eighty-seven point five level and towards the east side of the reactor vessel. He was moving faster than me but I started to think that if I was still moving, then maybe the wound to my neck was not fatal. The noise of the steam and the pumps and the whirling machinery grew louder as we moved toward the center of the reactor building, and I even felt the view down onto containment was beautiful. But I cursed as I realized I was going to have to run faster if I were to catch Kerwin before he disposed of whatever it was in the transport canister.

I saw Kerwin stoop over to slip his key card into the reader guarding the stairwell leading past the reactivity control platform and down to the spent fuel bay. I ventured pulling my hand away from my neck and, while there were still some drops of blood flowing, I decided it was safe to run without applying pressure to my wound.

At least Kerwin wouldn't be able to lose me on this stairway because it only went down, and during reactor operation there was no way out which wasn't blocked by access control until you were down to the spent fuel holding pool level at eighteen-five. And after I got through the key card door I could look through the grates of the stairs and see Kerwin far below me racing down the stairs. And the transport canister was still with him.

I did not play it safe but instead charged the stairs taking four and five steps at a time. Kerwin was only three short flights below me when he slipped his card into the access port for the door leading into the spent fuel bay. He looked up toward me and I saw something on his face which I liked—fear.

We have plutonium at Kankakee station. We have a lot more than the amount which was stolen from Kensington labs, but the security on plutonium is so great that the amount stolen from Kensington would easily show up if it somehow found its way into the Kankakee plutonium holding room. Going for the plutonium was the only reason I could see that Kerwin might have for going into the spent fuel area.

Kerwin had left the door open so I did not even have to key-card my way into the long room holding our nuclear swimming pool, the pool for hot fuel rods. The water sparkled with a blue glow at the bottom from the Cherenkov radiation thrown off by the spent fuel rods, the rods clearly visible in geometrical arrays at the bottom of the pool. And the air was humid, the water of the pool overpowering the dry air from the plant. It was humid with light water, the kind we like and don't mind breathing.

To my amazement Kerwin was at the door to the plutonium holding room. And I remembered how Jim Haskel had said that Kerwin was always pestering him about access control. Perhaps Kerwin had a way of getting into the room.

My charge toward him cut him off, and he turned to face me. He let the transport canister drop to the floor, and he jumped out of the way just as I was upon him. I slammed into the door. A deafening alarm sounded and did not cease. I didn't cease either and I caught Kerwin with a clenched fist karate strike to his left forehead.

Kerwin closed with me and grappled and tried to knee me and we were struggling round and round against the waist high steel railing which surrounds the spent fuel pool. Then Kerwin caught me with a hard elbow to the face and broke free.

I sprinted in pursuit, but he had time to vault over the railing. I followed him over and we were both running on the metal grate which surrounds the pool and allows any water splashed out to drain down for treatment. I was faster than Kerwin, but he didn't realize it soon enough because I caught him while his back was turned to me. We crashed into the railing with him taking more of the blow than me. He struggled desperately and I was thrown off balance and we went tumbling together into the pool.

The spent fuel water was warm and pleasant. The water both cools the spent fuel rods and provides radiation shielding so that the room surrounding the pool is accessible. I realized that Pete and I had just lost some of that shielding, and we would lose more and more the deeper we went into the water. But there are forty feet of water in the Kankakee pool, and Pete and I would have to dive deep indeed to get into prompt radioactive trouble. Nevertheless, we were sinking since we were too busy fighting to bother with treading water in our heavy boots.

Pete reached for my eyes with finger claws. I turned away and let go. He used his arms and legs to surge up past me toward the surface. Then his foot was in my face and he kicked down with all his strength, so I was forced yet deeper into the pool and closer to the blue-glowing fuel rods below.

I managed not to breathe in any water, and I thrashed my way to the surface and gasped. Kerwin was already out of the pool; he seized one of the long hooked poles that the fuel handlers use as a backup should the fuel transport cranes be inoperable. I did not want to be in the water with Kerwin standing over me with one of those, so I clawed at the side of the pool.

I managed to haul myself out so that I lay stretched flat at the side of the pool. Kerwin was charging at me with the fuel handling pole out in front of him like a lance. I dug my boots into the grate and lunged up toward the pole, seized it, and stopped Kerwin's advance with a jolt. We stood pushing against opposite sides of the pole for a second, and then I forced him back hard so that he lost his balance and slammed into the controls for the fuel handling cranes and manipulators.

The sound of the alarms became higher and deeper at the same time, and now there were flashing red alarm lights on the fuel handling manual panel. A manipulator was rising from the special storage area and I remembered that we'd just pulled a big production run of cobalt 60 out of the core a week earlier. There was every chance that what was coming out of the pool was cobalt and, if so, nothing in the fuel bay could survive the intense gamma radiation once the cobalt cleared the water. And then, as if to confirm my fears, the sound of the alarms changed once more into an ear-splitting cacophony, and flashing high-radiation warnings erupted so that it seemed that the room was being barraged by photo-flashes of red and yellow.

I had a choice: either run for the exit or try to shield myself with the pool water. I didn't think I could make the door in time so I jumped in the pool, forced myself down, and began swimming under water as best I could toward the far end.

I came up for air and wasn't nearly far enough away from the gleaming rod of cobalt now hanging above the pool. And I saw that the crane was now pulling the cobalt through the air and toward the side of the pool where Kerwin was once again trying to go into the plutonium holding room. I went under once more and resumed my swim.

When I came up, Kerwin was coming out of the holding room. He smiled triumphantly and pointed the open radioisotope transport canister to me. It was empty.

"Do you feel a tingling sensation?" I shouted.

"Only thing I feel is happy as hell because you'll never be able to prove a thing, you Yankee bastard."

"Yes, but do you feel a tingling in your fingers, or toes, or anywhere?"

"As a matter of fact, I do," he yelled. "What of it."

"Oh I've always wondered whether people exposed to really massive radiation fields can feel it. Someone told me you might feel some tingling if you were exposed to hundreds of rads a minute or so."

Kerwin's face changed; he looked at the flashing radiation alarms and surprise and fear surged from his eyes.

"Kerwin, that's a rod of exposed cobalt hanging out of the pool there," I screamed and then I dove back under the relative safety of the water. But then curiosity got the better of me and I came back up. Kerwin was pressing buttons on the fuel handling panel and the cobalt rod was moving fast toward the opposite side of the pool. Then the crane stopped and the cobalt began to swing back and forth, a fearsomely radioactive pendulum.

Kerwin cursed and began to run toward the exit door. I could see that there were people outside the spent fuel bay, but they could not enter; the radiation alarms would have put security locks on the doors which could only be overridden by the shift supervisor at the control room panels. Kerwin would be able to go out, though. But then something seemed to go wrong with his coordination. He was weaving back and forth and then he fell.

I dove and managed to remove one of my shoes underwater and swam a bit more toward the end of the pool. When I came up I could see Kerwin opening the door and walking out. I wanted to scream, "Hey, I'm in here too, but then I realized that they knew where I was; they had seen me.

There was nothing for me to do but stay in the water and wait for them to figure out that the cobalt was out of the water and to put it back in from the control room. I didn't have to wait long. Even a glance through the observation ports showed the cobalt hanging above the pool, and re-immersion through the control room would be simple.

Lucky for me they moved the cobalt clear to the other end of the pool before setting it back into the water. I climbed out of the pool and didn't feel too bad doing it. I hadn't felt any tingling, but I might have missed it in the excitement.

The radiation alarms went silent as quickly as they had begun. I was at the door, but before I could open it, two men in plastics came through it and took my arm.

"You don't need plastics. There's no contamination," I said.

They didn't remove their hoods but just grabbed me by each hand and escorted me out of the bay. They kept their hoods on for quite a while before they finally removed them as we continued on our way towards the health physics laboratory. Pete Kerwin had already been taken away in an ambulance when I arrived for my radiation exposure tests.

16

I live with the hum now. The hum and the shimmering sunlight from the wind turbine blades. When I'm in the middle of the energy park, the turbines stretch in every direction and I cannot see the end of them.

I took ten years' dose limit in the spent fuel bay, so I can't work in a nuclear plant for a very long time, and I'm probably through with nuclear and radiation work for life. But they found this spot in the Prairie demonstration wind farm, so I'm still in electrical generation and still on a utility payroll.

I still work with transformers and electrical buses and switchgear; it's just that the voltages aren't so high, and the power produced not so immense.

Pete Kerwin died twenty-three days after his exposure. Central Nuclear did a plutonium inventory at Kankakee immediately after I told my story, and extra plutonium exactly matching the amount taken from Kensington labs was revealed. With my story, the control logic drawing errors discovered by Jim Haskel, and the photo record of our struggle in the fuel bay, the evidence against Kerwin became strong and he admitted the plutonium theft and the tritiated organic contamination a week before he died. He also admitted taking Sheri's rifle and killing Jim. He had done it for nuclear power. Nuclear power and his own profit. He was convinced that a treatment for plutonium contamination would be a strong blow against nuclear critics. How the tritium contamination would help nuclear power was less clear, but it did help him sell pocket tritium detectors, and it would let him discredit me and help him to win Sheri. And then when Jim confronted him with the evidence of the changed engineering drawings, Pete had become desperate and once more tried to throw the suspicion on me for the murder he saw no way to avoid.

He said that I had always tried to thwart him in our days at WorldNet Simulations and at Ontario Hydro's Darlington station. He said that he had vowed vengeance on my American arrogance long ago, and that he had finally found the way to take away everything I had.

After Pete confessed, I went to his house, to where Sheri and my girls were still staying. I told Sheri I wanted a reconciliation, that I was very angry with her, but that I still thought it would be better if we could get back together. She said that it was too late for that. Although Pete had deceived her and she had no one, she thought she had to take the chance to find someone who she really loved, someone who would love her and the girls.

I told Sheri to move back into our house and that I would find an apartment. She agreed to that, and I can go to my house now and find Tracy and Laurie playing in the yard. They run up to me with happy cries: "Daddy! Daddy!"

Sheri and I both have lawyers. It looks like we'll be able to come up with a separation agreement without going to court, but we now fight over the agreement even though we never fought when we were married.

Or at least we hardly ever fought. Sheri remembers a time that we fought and she puts more importance on our fight than I did.

I live in Dwight now. It's close to the wind park and it's such a small town that it's cheaper. I need to economize because my child support payments will be hefty. And I like the peace and quiet of the small town. I like to sit in one of my small rooms and do nothing.

It's a small town and the corn fields are close. But I know it is the illusion of rural life. We are in the orb of Chicago, and our farms are organized into the web of the city. Our parks are set aside, artificial—they would disappear in a flash if the law ceased to protect them.

It even makes me think I would like to be back in Canada, back to where, if I wanted to, I could really live where the wilderness has more substance. Of course, the Canadians live in cities, they are more urban than us, but if you want you can move far away from people. In spite of the taxes and the high prices and the cold, in spite of the jibes at Americans —in spite of all that, I might like to face the Arctic blasts with only the pines and the wolves for company.

But it is just a dream, at least for now. As long as Tracy and Laurie are here I must stay near them. So I will be an American and live with low prices and taxes and no universal health care. I will be an American with a gun in every house.

Later perhaps I can face the north, face open country where nothing has yet been built. Be a pioneer.

But of course that's my American side coming through.

I'm sitting in the office by the front gate now, looking out the window. It's almost quitting time. I'm alone. The other two guys on my shift are away at the maintenance building doing the parts inventory. We have to do a lot of work repairing turbines, keeping them turning and the blades intact. And we have to keep records of how many and what kinds of birds are killed by the blades. It's not so much different than nuclear work, just less of it and no plastic suits or radiation detectors. And I get out in the fresh air a lot more. I like the big sky and the big view across the flatlands.

For some reason, after my fight with Kerwin and my own overexposure, I've forgotten about dating and all the crazy things I was doing before. I go home, watch TV or read a book, and I've even started going to Wells pit and actually fishing. It started when I complained to Ned Banthien that I'd forgotten how to clean fish and didn't really want to do it. He'd looked up at me and said, "Well, Henry, you don't have to clean them. You can always let them go."

So that's what I do—I let the fish go. I let the other things go, too.

www.ingramcontent.com/pod-product-compliance
Lightning Source LLC
Chambersburg PA
CBHW070834120626
46556CB00002B/753